TO DIVORCE
A GHOST

R.R. MANGOLD

ISBN 979-8-9897340-5-4 (Paperback Edition)
ISBN 979-8-9897340-6-1 (Ebook Edition)

This book is a work of fiction. Names, characters, places, and incidents either are products of the author's imagination or are used fictitiously. Any resemblance to actual persons, living or dead, events, or locales is entirely coincidental.

Cover Art by Adam Mangold
IG @a_roth_mangold
Interior Design and Formatting by Talia Aden
TikTok @taliaaden

First Printing, 2025

TO DIVORCE A GHOST

R.R. MANGOLD

To the real life red-headed bachelor in D.C. that
inspired this story.
May true love sweep you off your feet.

1
Owen

Walnut wood stain seeped into my fingernails as I rubbed a banister with a rag. Blending into my dark skin. The baluster was missing when I moved into this Victorian house three years ago. I spent months hunting down a wood-shop that could craft an exact match to the remaining originals. Only I let it sit in the corner of my living room, forgotten and gathering dust for almost a year. But today, I refuse to let this house win. The to-do list is endless, growing like ivy creeping up the exterior walls, hiding more and more of the charm of the house from outside eyes.

Like the house, I have been hiding away more and more every day. My spirit decays like the aging wood. Although my body is strong, I have never felt so weak. A difficult day could break me like a twig. If only I could fix myself the way I am fixing this old house. Smother my grief with spackle. Nail my mouth in the shape of a smile.

I want to heal. Three years is a long time to be a shell of yourself. However, it's easy to ignore the pain I feel if I drown myself in projects.

Every time I turn the corner I find another project that needs to be done. This was supposed to be a fully remodeled bed and breakfast by now. Ready to wine and dine travelers. Or whatever you do at a bed and breakfast. I did not have the idea to buy and renovate this place. It was my husband Lucas's dream. The same husband who is currently sitting, well floating, and currently watching me from the top of the stairs.

"You're watching me. I can feel your eyes filled with judgement." I peak from the corner of my eye to look though the transparent form of my husband. Caught somewhere between his former self and an echo. A dull hue covers his brown hair that used to shine with highlights in the sun. His red sweater and jeans will never wrinkle or fade. And his chest will not rise with breath. Tears used to prick my eyes every time I saw him. Now it is as natural as breathing to see his face in this house. Comforting to hear his voice.

Three years ago, he died in this house. On the same floors I restored ten months ago.

The house is hollow without his bright smile and laughter. We are two glum spirits living in the same place trapped apart in different realms. I used to speak to his mahogany urn that sits on the fireplace mantle by our wedding photo. But now, I speak directly to him.

All the projects came to a standstill without having him as a guiding force. Then on a quiet morning, while

I was looking at tile samples for the primary shower. I heard a voice. His voice. First I thought I was going crazy. I made myself take a long brisk walk. I stopped drinking for a week. I avoided the tile samples in case they were cursed or that I was going crazy.

I was swapping out the light fixture for one I scored at an estate sale when I heard it again. The voice cut through the house, faint but unmistakable, like it was spoken right beside me. I had no doubts who the voice belonged to. The air turned icy, cold enough that I half-expected to see my breath fogging in front of me.

"That is art deco. It does not belong in a Victorian house on the historic registry."

The fixture cord slipped from my hand and sent it crashing to the floor. Green glass shattered into a hundred pieces beneath my ladder. I stood like a mannequin. Too stunned to move. My eyes darted around as I waited for Lucas to walk in from the next room. I knew it was him in my core. There was no mistaking his voice. Warm with a hint of know-it-all tone like always. I would recognize my dead husband anywhere.

Lucas did not walk through the doorway. Instead, a faint apparition of his form glided closer. Until he was near enough for me to reach out. My chest felt like it was about to cave in. It was my grief manifesting an apparition to torture me. A reminder of what I could no longer hold.

It no longer feels like torture.

Over the past three years his temporal form has become stronger and his voice much louder than the first whisper. As if my grief is still feeding him. If this were true, I would willingly grieve for eternity if it would make him solid enough to wrap my arms around once more..

I look up from my perfectly stained banister to where he hovers over the stairs. Light from a stained-glass window above the door shines colors through his transparent body. He grins at me. I want nothing more than to grab him, but we have tried. Trust me, we have tried. I smile back and tuck the dirty rag into the back pocket of my work pants. Adding to the stains left from many projects. Like a checklist of smears.

"You're watching me."

"I am always watching you." Lucas stretches his body to stand and comes down the stairs. He moves his feet to appear as if he is walking. A small gesture to make me feel at ease talking to a ghost.

Even if the ghost is familiar. *"What else am I supposed to do?"*

"Please don't say always. I love you but I need my privacy at times." Bending over I use a rubber mallet to put the lid back on the stain can. I feel the chill follow me to the back door. Lucas remains behind until I pass the threshold. I enter my workshop. A small outbuilding that was used by the previous owner for canning and candle making. Wax and berry-colored drops speckle the floor.

I trade out the wood stain with tools for my next project and head inside. I dart in and out of each room quickly out of habit. My need to know where Lucas is at all times has doubled since he died. Every day I fear he will leave me. For good this time. I've gotten used to his ghostly nature and I am selfishly hoping he never moves on. He becomes more visible as time goes on. I dream that he will just manifest himself alive like nothing happened. As if I wasn't handed an urn filled with his ashes.

At first, he was nothing but a whisper, a blur at the edge of sight. Now, I can make out the red of the sweater he died in. I can hear his voice as if he is standing next to me, alive. I cannot feel him other than the sting of cold he brings with his presence, but I see him testing his abilities with objects around the house. We dream he will be able to touch things soon. Touch me, hopefully. I need to cup his face in my hands and feel his lips on mine. That possibility is the only thing that keeps me getting out of bed every morning.

I undress outside the primary shower. The old one is gone. It was one of the first things Lucas wanted to tackle. He anxiously took the design lead, and I was happy to let him. It's just colors and shapes to me, but Lucas taught me about creating a mood that can be felt when entering a room. Together we would restore the house while adding bits of ourselves into the design. When we finish it would have become more than a house that was threatened to be torn down. It would become a home. First, you bring back love within the walls. Next, you add your signature.

We started with this shower. I replaced the old with white subway tiles and black grout, just the way Lucas wanted. Installing a European-style framed glass around it. I admit, he was right, it looks perfect in this space and allows the shower to be bathed in light from the singular small window in the bathroom.

Stepping under the hot stream, I turn slowly, letting the water wash away the first layer of sweat and grime.

When I open my eyes I am disappointed Lucas has

not joined me. We cannot touch each other, but he will occasionally whisper dirty things into my ear as I touch myself.

That is the extent of my intimacy these days. My own hand and his words.

To the outside world, I'm just a lonely hermit, a widower frozen in time, unable or unwilling to move on. But in my heart, I am still his now and forever, just as he is mine. Death may have taken him from my arms three years ago, but it will never take him from my heart.

2
Gabriel

A brown sugar latte warmed my hands through the paper sleeve wrapped around the cup. I am trying not to grip it so tight that the lid pops off. I sit stiffly on the opposite side of his desk. Every piece of furniture here was shipped from Holland. He insisted on owning the full collection from a cutting-edge furniture design company. The space feels both retro and futuristic. It's not my taste but fits his personality perfectly.

My boss, Carlton, greets me with a tight expression while rubbing the back of his neck. I try to recall if I made any mistakes on my recently finished project. Nothing comes to mind. I'm proud to always be the first one in the office in the morning. Even when it snows. And often am the last one to leave. You would think I am his perfect employee. Why would he be upset? I've never submitted site plans late. Not once. My last project had the clients glowing, and now it's up for an ASLA award, the American Society of Landscape Architects. That's a big deal. No one in this office has ever won. If it happens, I'll be the first. I poured everything I had into the Memphis River Walk. Every hour. Every bit of myself. And it worked.

I half expected a promotion but the air in his office confirms he has other plans for me.

My heart is pounding in my chest, the weight of expectations pressing down on me. I have to keep this level of excellence. Carlton will want nothing less going forward. Lucky for him I have no life outside of work to distract me.

"You're burning out, Gabriel," he says, reclining in his chair with a sigh. "You've got two weeks before we dive into the Turatello's Resort project. I want you completely out of the office. I'm disabling your email access. Don't even try to check in. Take the time to reset. I will need fresh ideas from a clear head. We cannot present them with regurgitated designs."

I swallowed hard, a sense of panic creeping in. Two weeks without work? It felt like being thrown overboard and told to float on a life raft until they return to collect me. I thought he was going to praise me or maybe give me a bonus. This is punishment. Before I can argue, Carlton levels me with a sharp look. "This is going to be our biggest contract to date, and I need you at your best. A break will give your mind the space it needs to be innovative. Creativity needs rest to grow. Work-life balance and all that bullshit from self-help books. Do you understand?"

I nod. But I don't agree. I am terrible when I am stagnant. I need to keep busy. The idea of being alone with my thoughts is terrifying. Is two weeks long enough to do a free-lance project? I need to calm down. It has been two minutes, and I am already spiraling. Carlton is raising his eyebrows at me. I can't let him see me freak out. I will never make partner at the firm if he thinks I cannot handle stress. Even if the thing stressing me out is stepping away for two weeks. That's not too long. I can handle two weeks.

"Sure, great idea. Nothing like the possibilities from a blank page and a pencil to force some brilliance out of me. Back to my artistic roots." I take a sip of my coffee and watch him over the lid.

"No." He interlocked his fingers in his lap. "I don't want you thinking about the Turatello project or any other client. I want you to rest, relax, and restore. The most successful people learn early on in their careers how to balance work with their personal life. Feed your soul and your mind will be strong. I read that in a book once."

This would be great advice if I had a personal life. And how does a person develop one without leaving their apartment? I guess I could become personally attached to some reality TV contestants.

"So, you want me to stay home for two weeks and feed my soul?"

"I never said you have to stay home." He motioned a picture on his desk. He was on a beach with his wife and three kids. "Get out of D.C. Go hiking in Maine. Book a room at a spa. The fancy ones that make you sit in minerals pools and cover your body with healing mud. I don't know what you like. See a football game."

I hold back cringing. Football. No thanks. I have no

problem watching men in tight pants get sweaty and slam into each other, but the oblong ball is just a distraction.

"What about the Willamette riverwalk addition? I was waiting on estimations for how many food trucks they want to fit before doing final adjustments to the picnic areas. I should probably do that before I take a break."

He waves a hand at me dismissively. "Candice has it covered. I already sent her all the project info and the current status."

"But I was going to add a rose garden feature near the welcome sign. Portland is the city of roses." I hold myself back from gripping my coffee hard enough to pop the lid off. Carlton pushes his keyboard to the side and clasps his hands in front of him. He gives me a firm expression that softens before he speaks.

"I appreciate your desire to work, but I want to create a healthy office. That includes mental health. I will email a list of books that have inspired me. Maybe you will understand why I am forcing you to take a break before we take on a critical project." He taps his temple. "Two weeks. Feed your soul and your mind will be strong."

"Yea. I will figure something out." I stood. "I see how this can help." I did not see. I am on a roll in my career. I should ride the momentum into the next project. Forcing me to take a break seems like a waste of time and my valuable talent. It would be no use to argue. Carlton is the type that reads so many self-help and success guidebooks that he is always toting ideas at the office. I have been able to dodge most of them until now.

A forced break, ugh, what a terrible idea.

I leave the office with my shoulders low, feeling like

I'd been fired rather than sent on vacation. Without my laptop, I felt naked, like a crucial part of me has been stripped away. I spent the entire train ride home in a daze, my mind balancing between frustration and a gnawing sense of emptiness.

All I wanted was to collapse onto my couch and let HGTV comfort me while I figure out how to survive the next two weeks. But the moment I walked into my apartment, my stomach dropped. A stranger was already occupying my couch. A man. Sprawled out and fast asleep, with a duffle bag on top of my Japanese coffee table.

Frowning, I turned toward Jackie's room and found her hunched over her laptop sitting on her bed, typing furiously. The same position I saw her in throughout college when I visited her dorm. There are papers and a mostly empty bag of nacho chips on her bed. I count four coffee mugs scattered around her room in various stages of rot. If I don't remind her, she will end up with the entire collection and I will find myself drinking coffee out of a jar again. A noble sacrifice to have a roommate that knows me well.

I knock with the back of my knuckle on the door frame. "Jackie?"

She didn't look up but held a single finger in the air. Her unruly curls were pulled into a large puff atop her head. Threatening to fall in her eyes. "Let me finish this sentence before you yell at me." I waited for a beat. The moment her eyes met mine I blurted out my grievances.

"Who the Hell is on our couch?" I huffed.

Jackie sighed and pushed her laptop to the side. "That would be my brother. Little brother."

I probably could have guessed by the resemblance. In

addition to the same warm brown skin, they have identical freckles that roll across the bridge of their noses to dust each cheek.

I groaned. "Doesn't he live in D.C? Why is he crashing with us?"

"He got kicked out of his frat and needs a place to stay for a bit." Jackie has the audacity to smile. She knows I hate people crashing on the couch. It disrupts the flow of the house. I can't walk out in a towel and make myself tea. I cannot lounge in my own living room after a long day.

"And that's *our* problem because?" I could have phrased that nicer. Or have not said it at all. But after being evicted from my job for the next two weeks, I am irritated to come home and find my sanctuary invaded. Sanctuary may be a stretch. This duplex has no charm. It lacks design and the landlord won't let me paint the walls or change the light fixtures. I begged him last year to let me put in peel-n-stick tile for the kitchen backsplash. He has denied many requests.

"Because I love him and he's my brother." she shot back, her expression challenging. "I would let your siblings stay here."

"Mine don't smell like a gym." This made her furl her brow at me. I was being a pain. No, she was being a pain. Maybe Carlton was right. I need to relax. I used to be easier going than this and now I am aggravated because of a slight inconvenience.

I scrubbed my face with my palms, exhaling sharply. "Jackie, our apartment is barely big enough for two people. I can't deal with a couch squatter. Turns out I won't be working for the next two weeks. My boss said I need to relax. Let my creativity recharge and other bullshit he read in a self-help book."

"Look, it's temporary," she said, standing up and placing a hand on my arm. Taking full advantage of her large brown doe eyes to make me melt. It's not fair. She looks like a Disney princess, and I look like the ginger sidekick in a Howard Hughes movie. "I promise. Just a few days, tops."

I grumbled, letting the discussion die as I exit the room. It wasn't like I have the energy to fight after the day I had. I just needed to make a new plan. And if there is one thing I excel at, it's making plans. I put my headphones on that hug my ears like clouds and let warm love songs calm my mood while I prepared food for myself. It was mostly working. I was barely thinking about work or the man snoring on my couch.

I held my plate of chicken alfredo in one hand and a glass of red wine in the other and looked from the dining table covered in a half-finished craft project to the couch with a sleeping man. With a sigh, I retreated to my room.

Balancing my plate on my lap, I pulled out my phone and started searching for cheap hotels. If Jackie's brother needed somewhere to stay, I figured I'd help by finding him a different place to crash. But as I scrolled through options, another idea bloomed.

If I was willing to spend money on lodging, shouldn't it be for me? After all, I was on vacation now, whether I wanted to be or not. The bonus I received from two projects ago has sat in my bank account. I considered spending it on many things, but in the end nothing felt right. This could be exactly what I need. A new location.

Somewhere on the water. To jump start my creativity as Carlton wants. I will come back in two weeks better than ever.

My search shifted to the site MisterBandB.com, a place dedicated for LGBTQ friendly short-term rentals. I narrowed the options to locations near the ocean within a driving distance of a few hours. Somewhere quiet, somewhere that would actually feel like a break. As I scrolled through the listings, one caught my eye immediately. A room in a charming Victorian house in Maryland. It had soaring ceilings, stained glass windows, and most importantly, no hosts living on-site. I clicked on the listing, taking in the cozy images. It had no reviews. Should I be worried? The listing was posted only hours ago. I could drive out there and be met with a trap. This could be the start of a horror movie. On the bottom of the listing it had the rainbow checkmark that promises the host passed a background check and the location has been verified. Something about the place called to me, a sense of warmth and escape that I couldn't ignore. So, I will be the first to book it. There is a first for every location. Why can't it be me? I would be a perfect guest. I am easy going, not messy, and intend to keep to myself. I guarantee I will not be inviting any houseguests while I'm there.

Screw it. If I have to take a vacation, I might as well make it worth it.

With a deep breath, I fill in the dates for the entire two weeks and hit "Reserve."

3
Lucas

My ghostly fingers creep over the keyboard. Itching to feel the cold plastic. The laptop hums quietly on the desk, the screen casting a glow against the dark wood. Owen left it open, cursor blinking over the listing that should have gone live months ago. Should have, but didn't, because he's still hesitating. He uses the excuse of all the many unfinished projects, but I am tired of him dragging his feet. Maybe he just needs a gentle nudge to make friends other than our neighbor who is a stay-at-home mom. We had a large queer community before we moved to Oxford. It was always our plan to post this house on MisterBandB and become amazing hosts.

I would have a cocktail hour for the guests or brunch. This house was supposed to be overflowing with life. Now it's just a husk for a sad man and his ghost. Me.

I get it. Change is hard. Moving on is harder. And grief has no deadline for when it should fade. But it's been three years, and I'm sick of watching him live half a life. It's like watching my own heart slowly forget how to beat.

I pass through the wall to the guest room on the other side. The bed is made and waiting for someone to dream. Moving back to the primary bedroom, I wish I could smell his cologne. Wish I could touch the spot where he lays his head. Nothing here is for me anymore. I am a shadow of the past. A glimmer of what could have been. But my place is not with the living anymore.

I float closer to Owen's desk, peering down at the laptop screen. This guest room is gorgeous. The other two are filled with furniture that was left behind. All in need of repair or restoration. They lay dormant covered in white sheets. Fitting for a haunted house. The house that I haunt.

We began fixing this room early on after moving in. It was meant to be a space for family and friends to visit. A test run before opening up to the public with all the rooms completed.

He followed my plan to finish the room and it's just as I imagined. Full of soft blues, intricate moldings, and an antique dresser he spent an entire weekend restoring. The space is warm, inviting. A perfect place for someone to rest after a long day. Someone who isn't Owen because he sure as Hell isn't resting. Maybe if he is happy again whatever has a hold on me will let go. This cannot be where I am supposed to spend my eternal days. Haunting my husband in the place I died.

There must be more for me.

There must be happiness waiting for him.

My fingers hover over the keyboard, but of course, they don't touch it. Can't touch it. Not in the way that matters. But my will, my desire? That's something else. The first months after I died I was desperate for Owen to hear me. I followed him around the house screaming his name. Until one day I nearly made him fall from a ladder. After that he has become able to see me. Most of me. He describes my form as a hologram. Translucent and stronger in low light. Nearly invisible in full sun. No one else has yet seen me.

I have been trying to touch objects. Move things and switch the TV on like ghosts in the movies can. Last week I managed to flip the light switch, but it took all my energy, and I couldn't talk to Owen for days. If I can just move the mouse…

I focus on my memory of what it feels like touching smooth plastic.

Imagine the click when I press the button down.

I narrow my eyes on the curve as my finger hovers over the mouse.

My ghostly hand trembles.

I can feel a tingle under my palm. Like my hand is waking up from sleep.

I add the slightest pressure.

The cursor jerks forward, clicking onto the "Activate Listing" button.

Done.

I sigh without breath.

The screen refreshes, with the listing officially live, open availability and all. Owen will probably freak out if he saw what I just did. I was always the impulsive one in our relationship. Buying same day event tickets or making an offer to buy a Victorian house that was falling apart after seeing a video on the internet of the mayor begging someone to Save-This-House.

I check the laptop frequently. It only takes a few hours for a soft chime to sound, and a message bubble pops up.

My nonexistent breath catches. That was quick. I expected it to take days not hours.

A profile picture appears. A redhead with a bright smile and blue eyes that sparkle. Name: Gabriel.

"Looking for a quiet two-week stay," his message reads. "The place looks lovely. Is it available?"

I don't hesitate. I force the cursor to click "Accept."

And just like that, the wheels are in motion.

I did it. I invited a stranger into our... Owen's house.

Owen would kill me.

If I weren't already dead.

4
Owen

It's a new day; I stand in my kitchen scanning the room over the rim of my coffee. Making a checklist of tasks in my mind. Half will be ignored or put off. It's a warm morning for April and the sun is peaking through the large window over the sink. I am leaning against the counter facing the middle of the room. Lucas has been blinking in and out all morning. His voice is barely more than a whisper. I am trying to prepare myself for him to just disappear. That is what I should logically want. For him to move on. To Heaven or wherever.

He deserves to be in a peaceful place filled with happiness. Not here watching my pathetic life. No longer able to do any of the things he loves. Watching me live must be torture. Especially since I am not doing much living.

Selfishly I want him to stay by my side forever. Rules of nature be damned, but that cannot be reality. He needs to move on, and I need to let him. Maybe even encourage him.

Not today. His anxiety is filling the room like heavy smoke. Following him from room to room. All I was to do is ease whatever he is feeling. Pull him into my arms and slide my lips along his neck. That always made his knees go weak and his mind clear. I loved how my touch would calm him. I was his anxiety cure. Vibrations radiate from him now even though he is not physically here. My own gut is twisting. I grip the handle of my mug in frustration. I cannot touch him. So, I remain against the counter as he attempts to communicate with me. His mouth is moving but his voice is muffled as if he is underwater.

Lucas paces, his eyes darting to the antique clock on the wall. He's restless in a way that makes my stomach tighten. Does he know this is his last day and he is afraid to tell me?

"What's going on with you?" I ask, looking up from my cup of coffee. "You're acting strange."

"When was the last time you dusted the guest room?" he blurts out. *"Do you know where the spare towels are?"*

"Lana dusts every room in the house on Wednesdays. You know this. You were the one to hire her remember. You said, our time is better spent restoring the house to its glory than cleaning toilets and washing windows." I mimic his optimistic voice from our first month here. I frown. "Why do you ask?"

Lucas hesitates, then sighs dramatically. *"I invited*

a stranger from the internet to the house. They are on their way now. Could arrive any minute. And they expect to stay for two weeks."

The mug nearly slips from my grip. "What? How?"

He shifts the way a person would on their feet except he is floating a few inches off the ground. He stops moving and links his fingers in a twisted grasp over his chest. A skill for those with hypermobile joints, as he does. I have body mass and no such flexibility. *"I may have… activated the MisterBandB listing."*

"You did what?" I practically yell, moving towards him so fast he instinctively backs into the wall. I follow him through the archway into the dining room. I have gotten used to him being a ghost, but I still blink twice when I see him standing in the middle of the table like it's normal. I take a deep breath and remind myself I am yelling at a ghost. Not just any ghost, but the man I love, and can't seem to let go of. "You can touch things now and the first thing you try is my computer? How long did you know you could do this? And why would you invite a stranger here?"

I force myself to take a steady breath. My emotions and layering over me like a weighted blanket. One of the reasons why we worked so well as a couple is due to my ability to stay calm. If he felt himself spiraling I could be the anchor holding him in place. Right now, I am tingling with confusion and fear. I want to discuss the fact that he touched something. My ghost husband touched an object. What could this mean? Unfortunately, my brain is stuck on the latter part of his confession.

Lucas crosses his arms. *"You need a friend, and I*

know you refuse to leave the house. I thought—what if—I could bring one to you. If it makes you feel better, he's gay."

I gape at him. He's wrong. I am not stuck in our house all the time. I visit my neighbor Adrienne's almost daily. Not to mention the owners of the hardware store and Mel's café know me by name. I even have regular visits to city council meetings. Not because I desire to be involved with local politics, but because Lucas purchased this house for next to nothing. It came with a contract with the city to restore it to its glory. The building is on the historical registry. Oxford received a state grant to supplement the project. Lucas wrote a letter that was dripping with charm along with his offer. I had no idea he even applied until the mayor called to approve us herself.

It took Lucas less than twenty minutes to get me on board buying the decrepit house and moving to a tiny seafront town. Lucas can be hard to resist. He is the smartest person I know, and I would trust him to lead me anywhere. He has a skillful tongue.

I am succumbing to his skills now. He uses the same pleading hazel eyes that are looking at me now. I cross my arms over my chest. Hoping my muscles will give the illusion that I am strong as a rock and a puddle at his mercy. A man about to give into whatever he asks. "You invited a single gay man to come live with me?"

"Not live with. It's only two weeks. And I never said he was single. Are you hoping he is single?" The corners of his mouth twitched. Fighting back a smile.

"Ugh," I groan, rubbing my temples. "I have to send him away. I'm not ready for guests."

"Why not? It's not like you have to entertain him. Just

rent a room. Be a ghost—like me." Lucas moved closer until he was hovering inches before me. I have a solid five inches on him in height, but he floats up until we are eye level. I raise my hand to grip his waist like I used to then lower it. Remembering I cannot touch him. This was not meant to be our life together in this house. We both know it.

"Like you?" I laugh a single note. "You just can't help yourself."

Lucas grins. The bricks of my walls fall at his floating feet. He has won. As usual. *"Better start preparing the finished guest room."* He gloats.

I mutter a string of curses under my breath as I turn towards the stairs.

5
Gabriel

The cityscape of D.C. faded into the background, towering buildings giving way to green stretches of trees. Blooming with pink and white flowers. The drive to Oxford, Maryland, was quicker than I expected, just a little over two hours. Or perhaps it went by fast because I wasn't waiting for my phone to ding with emails and design notes. I put on an audiobook and managed to not think of work the entire drive.

The route was beautiful, a winding road flanked by towering trees and glimpses of Chesapeake Bay shimmering in the midday sun. Despite my initial resistance to this forced vacation, I couldn't deny the tiniest hint of excitement creeping in. Maybe, just maybe, this won't be the worst thing in the world. I might even come out of it better off. With fresh ideas to drag into the Turatello resort project. Though according to Carlton that is not the purpose of this imposed vacation.

Then I pulled onto the final stretch, a long gravel driveway that groaned under the weight of my Jeep Renegade's tires. My poor Jeep rarely gets out of the city these days. The last adventure I took her on was up to Big Cork Winery outside DC last summer. My Jeep did not have the privilege to venture on trails like she was meant to. Her day was spent in a dusty parking lot while Jackie and I consumed a fair share of wine and flirted with a bartender to see which one he would be into. We could not tell. His eyes darted around both our bodies. Or it was the wine making us think he was interested. In the end we decided he was too complicated, and we had zero interest in trying for a threesome.

I've always wanted to travel more; take long road trips, see other countries, check places off my bucket list. But I am nearing thirty and the bucket keeps getting kicked further down the road. The truth is, traveling alone has never really appealed to me. I always pictured having someone by my side—someone I love. The kind of love that makes any place you visit feel like home.

Now, I've got two weeks with nowhere to be. No one waiting on me, except the office.

In the trunk, next to my suitcase, there's a box of books and a few bottles of wine. My survival essentials to get me through the next two weeks in an unfamiliar house. Nestled in an unfamiliar town.

I'm trying not to ignore how easy it is to vanish. How few things I wanted to take, how little I'm leaving behind. Just a boring room in an apartment that is now occupied by my roommate's brother. I left behind my overflowing bookshelf. The list of books I want to read far outweigh the free time I have. And on the floor of my closet are stacks of sketchbooks filled with ideas. That now sit covered in dust and forgotten.

I have a deep sense of fulfillment when I work hard and stay productive. To others, it might seem isolating or even a little bleak. Maybe there is some truth to that. But the whole truth is, I'm genuinely happy.

My breath comes out slow and controlled as I follow the final direction on my GPS. Turning onto a tree-lined street.

The rental house comes into view, and I swear, for a second, my heart skipped a beat. It is picturesque, fit for a ninety's movie about sisters with magic. To the average eye it's just a Victorian, and I find no issue calling it that. But my degree included classes on architecture history, which is why I know this house is a perfect example of American Gothic with elements of Queens Anne style. Featuring ornate accents that can either look whimsical or sinister depending on the color they are painted.

The wood siding has been painted burnt orange, and all the trim is black. Even the short metal railing on the Juliette balcony is black. I should hate it, but it looks like it belong in a Halloween themed snow globe.

Surely the original owners were witches, I am ready to put the lime in the coconut or whatever and dance around a firepit under a full moon. The listing failed to mention it has potential to summon a hot man. The magic oozing off this house could definitely draw in a soul mate if channeled correctly. At least that is how this would go if I were in a rom-com.

I park on the side of the house next to a large black

truck. Double checking the address on the listing because it said the owners do not live on site. I made sure to only look at listings on MisterBnB that were renting the entire property. I am here for peace and quiet.

Maybe the owners are here to hand off the key and leave me to my solitude. I push down my nerves and grab my suitcase from the back. There is an unsettling feeling like I am being watched. I look up and expect to see someone standing in the second-floor window, but the interior is dark. Except for a light on in the entry illuminating the beautiful stained-glass window above the door. I should sketch that window before I leave. It would be a great layout for a garden. The soddened lines could be the paths separated areas of flowers. Displaying an overview that forms a picture. Why have I never thought about planting flowers to make the colors look like stained glass from above? See, I am inspired already. Carlton may be onto something.

Am I am the wrong place? There is no lock box next to the door as stated in the listing. I set my suitcase down on the large front porch. With my phone in hand, I slowly walk up to the front door. After two knocks the door opens swiftly like the person was standing on the other side waiting. Although this person is not what I expected. He looks like a movie star playing the role of a blue-collar worker. A strong jaw covered in a dark beard. Warm brown skin and dark eyes. Did I shrink? Cause he is quite literally towering over me. Dear God, his muscles. He's built like he could throw me over his shoulder without breaking a sweat. And I would let him.

Obviously, I have been in the car alone for too long

because I should have said something. So should've he, but instead we are both staring at each other like animals caught in a motion sensor light.

"Uh," I hesitated, phone in my hands open to a picture of the house. "Hi. I'm Gabriel. I booked the..."

"My husband put up the listing." He cut me off. Ok so he is handsome but not friendly and married. Good, I don't have to worry about flirting awkwardly. The tension in my shoulders eased, but only slightly. He still does not look happy to see me.

"Judging by your scowl, I assume he didn't tell you I was coming." I try to smile and step back knocking into my suitcase. He lunges forward and catches the handle before it can topple down the stairs. He lifts it like it weighs nothing and moves into the doorway. Pausing to look at me over his shoulder.

"He created the listing before he died." The tension in his eyebrows dissipates, forcefully.

My stomach drops. "Oh. I'm...I'm sorry for your loss."

He made a noise that was nothing more than a grunt to acknowledge me, then stepped into the house, leaving the door open just wide enough for me to follow. "Come on in. I'll show you to your room. I'm Owen."

The inside of the house was warm, but not in the rustic, cozy way I had expected. It was stylish, modern with a gothic edge. It felt like a masterpiece a few brush strokes away from completion. Missing the finishing touches like art and other décor. I peeked from the entry into the living room and down the hall. I cannot believe I am going to have this whole place to myself for two weeks. It's kinds magical. Even with the dull paint and the lack of décor on the walls.

I turned only to find Owen waiting at the top of the stairs. My suitcase firm in his grasp. He must have grabbed it when I was gawking at the woodwork. I followed after watching him duck into a room on the left.

The room looked like something out of a hip boutique hotel. Curated for a gothic romance aesthetic. The first thing that draws my eye are the opulent blue curtains, heavy and lush, pooling slightly on the floor like sacred robes. The room is framed with intricate crown molding carved with floral swirls and leaf motifs. The walls have been painted calming blue gray. Like a storm but somehow inviting. The walls are missing art, making it feel like a set for a play. I choose to think of the empty space as room for my imagination to fill.

The plush bed is inviting me to collapse onto it and never leave. Teasing me to submit to its softness and warmth. The grey bedspread is actually silver. Shimmering in the sunlight peaking in as I move further into the room.

I'm already feeling at ease. The next two weeks could be good for me. I might actually enjoy this. Yes, this will be good.

I hear a throat clearing behind me and I turn to find Owen standing in the hallway. He is looking at the floor with a hand resting on his neck as if he was rubbing out stress. It took me a moment to remember this listing had no reviews yet and I could very much be his first customer.

"The room is perfect." I peered out the window expecting a beautiful yard to match the house but all I saw was partially decomposed piles of leaves that were probably raked last fall. As well as overgrown bushes. I cringed at the lack of landscaping. A masterpiece like this house deserves a plot that matches. "The town is adorable also. At least the half I drove through to get here."

"Yes, Oxford is great." He makes eye contact with me, and I marvel at his dark lashes. They give the illusion of wearing kohl liner. "I will be working on projects most of the day. So, you don't have to worry about me bothering you. Make yourself at home. You won't even notice me here, unless and issues come up, my phone number is on the fridge. And my room is at the end of the hall if you need something in the evening."

"Your room?" Now I am really confused.

He nods.

"The rental said there was no host on site." It suddenly felt very cold and the hairs on the back of my neck tingled. Owens eyes were moving around the room as if following small particles of dust floating in the air. He must think I'm worried the room isn't clean or up to par. But it's fine, really. What I didn't expect was being just down the hall from someone else. A stranger. I thought I'd have the whole house to myself. Two weeks of silence, rest, and recovery. After all, that's what I was sent away for.

"Did it?" Owen said through his teeth. He seems aggravated and I am strongly considering finding the nearest hotel or driving back to DC. I open my mouth to speak, but Owen cuts me off. "Lucas, my husband who passed created the listing. I did not check it very carefully and to be honest it went live by accident. You were promised one thing, and I can see this arrangement bothers you. I will find another place to stay, and you can have the house to yourself as you were promised."

He turned quickly and moved down the stairs before I

can respond. My nerves are begging me to sit on the bed and relax. My heart is racing in my throat. I almost feel pushed forward towards the open door. I followed the thumps of his loud boots meeting him back in the entry-way. He was ready to rush out the door when my arm grew a mind of its own and flung out. My hand grasp his forearm. My first thought was "fuck, he's all muscle" followed by "I am touching a stranger." I promptly let go.

"If you are comfortable staying, I don't mind. It looks like you are in the middle of projects, and I am the nuisance. You can refund me, and I will find somewhere else to stay. No big deal." He is not looking at me. His eyes are locked onto the top of the stairs.

I watch his shoulders drop and he turns to face me. The smile on his face feels forced. "I want you to stay."

Is this a trap? I am not buying it. His words are inviting but his body language is begging me to leave. My suitcase was left upstairs. I consider leaving it and jetting out to my Jeep. It can't get more awkward than this.

"Look. I can tell this was a mistake. You don't want a guest. Seriously I can find another place to stay." My eyes meet his and they soften. This time, when he smiles, small lines branch from the corner of his dark eyes. My cheeks warm and I fear my face is turning red with him just looking at me. When did we stand this close? I should back up. Oh God.

"Let me start over." He holds out his hand. "My name is Owen. I am the owner of Hammond House. A historic Victorian in Oxford Maryland. I would love it if you'd stay here for two weeks as my first guest. It would be very helpful to have honest feedback from someone trustworthy."

Is this real life or have I fallen into the Hallmark Channel? His voice is smokey and deep. I would pay big bucks for him to narrate my favorite romance books.

"What makes you think you can trust me?"

"Your face." He clears his throat again. "You have a very trustworthy face."

I look past him to my Jeep and then down to his hand. I grip it with my own and shake. "I'm Gabriel. Not Gabe. Gabriel. And I would love to be your first houseguest."

How long are you supposed to hold a handshake? This feels longer than usual. We both let go at the same time and move apart. The air behind me is cold and I shiver. The drafts in this house will require my most comfy hoodie.

"Perfect. Do you have anything else to bring in?" He say's pointing over his shoulder to the driveway.

"Just a box of wine and books."

"Wine and books?" He begins to walk down the porch stairs, and I follow, pulling my keys from my pocket.

"Well, I expected to be alone and the only plans I made were to read, draw, and drink wine." We reached the back of my Jeep, and I press the button on the fob to open the cargo space. In addition to the box, I have a handful of junk scattered in the trunk. Bartender supplies from my friends last cocktail party and an umbrella straight out of the Adam's Family. I'm thankful there is nothing too embarrassing in there. "Just the box." I point.

I tried really hard not to stare at his arms as he lifted the box. Veins, muscles, the whole rugged package straight out of a romance novel. I came here expecting solitude, not to end up sharing a house with someone who looks like he walked off a movie set. I walked next to him, trying to think of something clever to say. Anything. My mouth kept opening like I was going to speak, but... nothing. He brought the box all the way up to my room, placed it on the dresser like some casually perfect gentleman, and I was still trying to remember how to form words.

I breathed in my new space. My home for the next two weeks.

I set my keys on the nightstand and waited for him to leave. He did not. Owen remained in the doorway facing me. There was conflict on his face like his conscious was telling him to say something and he was fighting it.

"What do you draw?" He blurted out.

"Huh?" His question caught me so off guard I forgot to answer it. I just stared at him in aw that he was still talking to me.

He rubbed the back of his neck. "You said you had plans to draw."

I could tell the truth. Explain I'm not supposed to be drawing anything work related. But I know myself too well. The moment I pick up a pencil, I'll end up sketching outdoor gathering spaces designed around unique landmarks. It's the reason I was drawn to Washington DC. I always imagined redesigning the most famous memorials in our country. After years in the city, I find the more intimate projects become my favorite.

"Yeah. I am a landscape architect. So, I mostly draw garden plans and various forms of vegetation as seen from above. It can be simple like a strip between building on a college campus or a huge memorial garden built around a museum. My projects vary quite a bit." He nodded and didn't ask for details, thank God. I'm supposed to be taking a break from work, not mentally revising site plans in my head. Maybe I'll actually draw something that doesn't involve perfectly spaced hedges or benches meant for mourning. "Do you work? Outside of MisterBandB hosting."

Owen's smile caught me off guard. It was soft, almost shy. Like a secret he hadn't meant to share. And I couldn't help but feel like it meant something.

"I used to be a General Contractor outside Chicago. Helped develop a couple new neighborhoods. I was on the path to burn out. It was-" He paused and looked towards the window. "It was my husband's idea to start over in a small town. I like Oxford. So, I guess he was right. He was right most of the time. Not always." He cleared his throat. "Anyway. I will let you get settled. The house is yours to enjoy as you wish I will try not to bother you with my projects."

"I'm the intruder. I promise you will barely notice I am here."

"Hm." He entered the hallway but stopped to poke his head back in. "If there are nights you don't feel like eating in town or cooking for yourself, I always have enough. I eat dinner about 6:30."

Well, that's a turn. Did I just go from expecting a two weeklong solo vacation, to sharing a house with a stranger and possibly eating dinner with him? A handsome stranger that may not give off gay vibes but did post on MisterBnB, a queer vacation rental website. He had a husband. Had. It's just him and I in this large house.

My throat bobs as I gulp down my nerves.

"Thanks, Owen. That sounds lovely."

He left and I quietly shut the door behind him. Falling back on the bed I covered my face with my hands.

"Thank sounds lovely. Who the fuck talks like that? Why the fuck couldn't I be cool or normal? I have to go and make an awkward situation more awkward. Ugh."

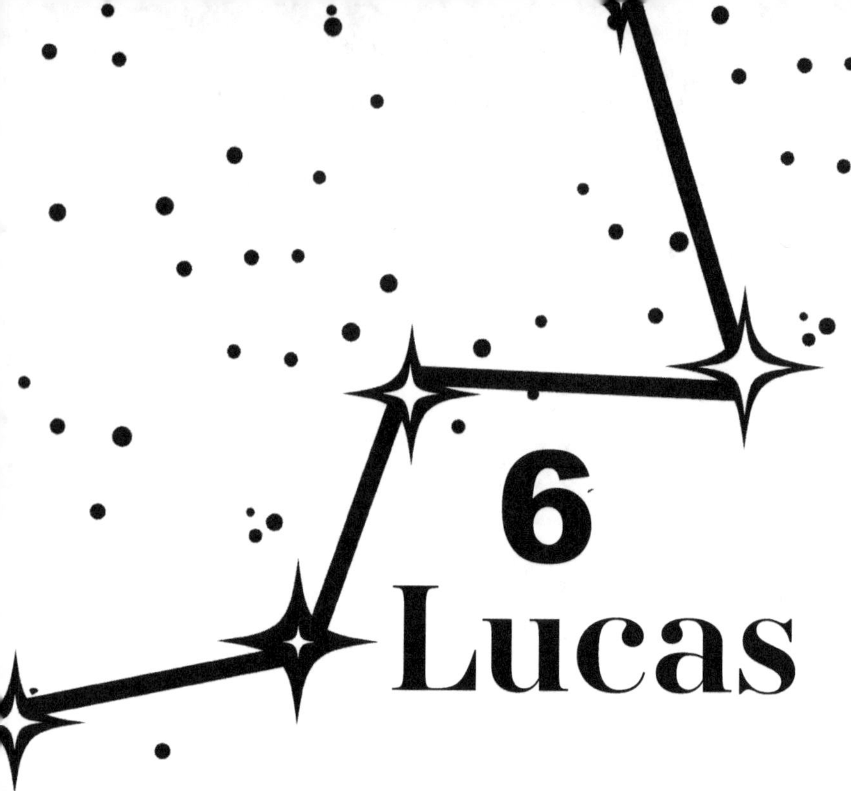

6
Lucas

I drifted in the shadows of the kitchen, watching Owen pull a casserole from the fridge. The vintage Pyrex dish clinked softly against the counter. His muscle memory took over as he peeled away the foil, setting it aside before sliding the dish into the pre-heated oven. Although the meal is homemade, I know it was not by his hands. Despite being a great cook, Owen has barely used the kitchen since I died. He makes himself breakfast in the morning. A plate of two eggs, two sausage links, and a hashbrown patty. Just like a customer ordering the same thing from a diner every morning.

This casserole was from a well-meaning neighbor.

Making sure he does not starve from grief. He would have been at risk of fading away for the past three years if it were not for the town's generosity.

"You should cook. I used to love your cooking." I sighed and listed off a few things I loved Owen to cook. *"Pasta carbonara. Chicken Marsala. Hot wings with-."*

Owen shot a pleading look at me. Right now, I feel like I crossed a line. I brought a stranger into his space, hoping for what, exactly? That a friendship would form? That something deeper might spark? For the past couple years, I wanted nothing more than for him to have something steady. A close circle of friends, maybe even a partner who truly sees him, values him, loves him.

I can only love him from the outside. I cannot offer an embrace when he needs it. I cannot walk hand in hand through a farmers' market with him. I cannot be anything more than a ghost.

But can I really handle watching this? Watch him flirt, kiss, and fall for someone else? Am I strong enough for this? My grasp on this world feels brittle as it is and my heart is frozen with pain.

I paced back and forth. Floating from one thought to another and landing on a moment I witnessed earlier back in the guest room. I saw Owen look at Gabriel with a hint of lust. He tried to smother him down, but I know him well enough to recognize the look of desire on his face.

The fact is. He is attracted to Gabriel. I just need to get Owen to rip the band aid off. Get that first kiss post my death out of the way. I have told him I was ready for him to move on. I even suggested it was the thing keeping me here. Stuck. Unable to move on. Yet he refused to download dating apps. Refused to go out to any gay bars. Barely left the house at all.

I stopped pacing and looked at Owen.

Doubting is useless. What's done is done. My husband is sad, lonely, and still handsome as Hell. And there is a single, intelligent, not to mention, fucking adorable red headed man staying in this house for the next two weeks.

Owen opened a bag of lettuce mix and poured the contents in a bowl. He walked into the lush dining room and placed it on the table. He didn't want to make it appear Gabriel's attendance was expected. That led him to set all six place settings. In the center were two brass candlesticks void of candles.

I walked through the wall. Then watched from the mid-century hutch that Owen converted into a bar.

"Why are you smiling?" Owen whispered.

I have no intention to share my match making plans with him. *"You set the table properly."*

"Yeah." He paused. Sucking on his bottom lip the same way he would when he was nervous. "Is it too much? I don't want to make it look like a date."

"Too much? You know I had big plans for this place. Fancy brunches and cocktail hours for the guests. I would have done so much more. So, no. I do not think empty candlesticks and a salad bowl are too much." It shatters me, this distance I can't close. Every time I reach for him, all I leave behind is a chill. A shiver from the cold that acts like an echo. A reminder that I am no longer alive.

Owen placed his hands on the back of a chair and

rolled his shoulders forward. The antique wood groaned under his weight. He let out a big sigh. "I don't know what I am doing."

I moved through the table. I have become far too comfortable without having a physical body. Moving through objects has become second nature. I stopped in front of him and put my hand below his chin. He moved his face even though I could not touch him. We locked our eyes.

"You are hosting a guest for the next two weeks." I nodded until he nodded with me. *"All he needs is a quiet place to relax. Ya know, a break from the city. Nothing more is expected of you."*

"I can do that."

"I know you can." I floated back. *"Don't be surprised if you see less of me the next two weeks. I don't want the guest catching you talking to yourself around the house."*

He laughed and I wanted to wrap my arms around his middle to feel the rumble. To bask in his warmth. Warmth I do not have. Owen was alive, but he wasn't living. And that thought weighed on me heavier than my own death.

It has been long enough. I don't want Owen to spend the rest of his days stuck in this fog, half-existing. A shadow of the man I fell in love with. The Owen I knew was vibrant, warm, always moving forward. Now, he is just numb. And I hated it.

And then there was Gabriel.

I'm not sure if Gabriel is the answer, but I can hope. If nothing else, he might be the one to shake Owen out of his funk, to remind him that he is allowed to feel again, to love again. Because Owen deserved love, even if it's not from me anymore. I cannot offer him a full version of the love I have anyway. My love is just words and memories. Both can fade. I will love him from a far if I ever ascend to a place beyond. Heaven or wherever.

As if summoned by my thoughts, Gabriel's soft footsteps sounded on the stairs, each one causing the old wood to creak in protest. He padded into the main hall off of the entry, glancing around. His gaze landed on the patchy walls, covered in different swatches of paint, each a testament to Owen's half-hearted attempts at design choices. I have been trying to let him make decisions. This place is no longer mine and I need him to understand that. It should feel like him and not a reminder of what he lost.

Owen popped his head out of the dining room before quickly retreated back as Gabriel walked by. I sick into the walls to make it less obvious while I eavesdrop.

"This place really whispers unfinished charm," Gabriel said, unaware Owen had stepped the hall in behind him. He brushed his fingers over a paint swatch. "Still narrowing it down, or did indecision win the battle?"

Owen huffed a laugh, startling Gabriel slightly. "I struggle deciding. It's been like that for two years I think. I don't want to have to repaint it because I screw up on the color choice. When I do decide to list this house, I want it to be perfect. The entry is the first thing people will judge when they walk in."

I watch as Gabriel tilted his head, studying Owen. He shifted his weight to one hip and studied the choices. His big blue eyes narrowed at the choices.

"I like the dark emerald green."

Gabriel gave Owen a soft smile. I hoped Owen noticed what I saw. The charming sparkle in his blue eyes.

A definite invitation to flirt. The slightly crooked smile. All the things that make Gabriel adorable. I know his type better than anyone. I can tell by the way Gabriel is holding eye contact, his heart is racing.

For a brief moment I think Owen is going to flirt back, but he makes his expression stoic and slides his hands in his pockets like he is bored with the conversation.

"Dark emerald green, eh." He looks at the swatches casually like he knows which green is the correct one."

I pop out of the wall and point at the same time Gabriel touches the same spot. Instinctively I pull my hand back fast. Scared to touch him even though he would not feel it. I back away until I am almost out the door. I give Owen an apologetic look.

"That could work." Owen tries hard to ignore me, but his eyes betray him by glancing over Gabriels's shoulder to where I float. "Any update I do has to keep with the style of the house. Do you think that will be too modern?"

"Hang art in brass frames. Maybe a map of the town and boom, an inviting entryway that is not boring."

They both moved into the dining room, and I took it as my cue to make myself scarce.

7
Gabriel

Dinner is awkward. Not bad awkward, just filled with silence that stretches too long, punctuated by the occasional clink of silverware against ceramic. I wondered if he was avoiding eye contact because he keeps glancing at the empty chair at the head of the table, like he expects someone to be there. As if he is wishing someone will appear and fill the silence. It's weird, but I don't say anything. Instead, I poke at my chicken and rice casserole and break the silence. "So, you didn't actually post the listing?"

Owen exhales sharply, shaking his head. "No. My husband set it up years ago. I was looking at it. Debating on deleting the account entirely." He cleared his throat. "I'm not sure how it went active."

I raise an eyebrow. "Guess it was good luck I was looking online at that precise moment. Unless you are a serial killer. I mean, luring someone in before you deactivate the listing would be a clever move for a serial killer. Then that would be bad luck."

Owen chuckles. "Fair point."

"You are supposed to say something to reassure me you are not a serial killer." The theater kid in me playing up the suspicion. Although, I'm not suspicious in the slight. Owen does not give off big scary vibes. I pride myself on my excellent judgement of character, and Owen may look like a big grumpy jock, but I can tell he is a teddy bear at heart. Stuffed with muscle and not fluff. His energy is like a warm blanket and his deep voice should be used to narrate nature documentaries. If the situation were different and I wasn't an uninvited guest imposing on his life I might have attempted to flirt the pants off of him if we met at a bar.

"How does one convince someone they are not a serial killer?" He dabbed the corners of his mouth with a napkin and leaned against the back of the chair. "Would you like to check my closets, or perhaps a tour of the basement."

"That right there," I pointed my fork at him. He responded with a wicked grin. "Is exactly what a serial killer would say."

A laugh barreled out of him. "Sorry, this is not polite conversation for a host and houseguest. Especially since we are strangers. I guess you will just have to take a chance and trust me."

"For now. But the second you are acting strange, or I hear visitors in this town tend to go missing, I am out of here." He nodded while gulping down his water. I could see him hold back a smile as he put the glass on the table. We lapse back into silence, but it's less uncomfortable now. I swirl my fork through the casserole, watching him before speaking again. "What made you want to restore this place?"

"Lucas, my husband, always wanted to design and run a bed and breakfast," he says, voice a bit distant. As if he was pulling it from a memory. "I was never fond of the idea of having a revolving door of strangers. No offense."

"None taken."

He exhales, shifting in his chair. "I was burned out from my general contractor job in Chicago. I used construction to fill the gap in my life when I stopped playing college football. The weather here sounded nice, and we had enough saved to tackle the project with little risk. Half of the renovations are funded with a grant from the Town Historical Society. We-" His pause cut like a knife. "I... I have six months to get the house including the historic Hammond pumpkin patch up and running. But I'll most likely sell after I finish the repairs on the main house."

"That's a lot of pressure. To do it alone."

He nods slowly. "It was easier when I had Lucas here to make the design decisions. I've been struggling with what shade of green to paint the entry for weeks. Thanks for the suggestion."

"No problem. The dark emerald will be perfect." I say without thinking.

Owen stills, "Lucas said the same thing."

I shrug. "He was right. It's inviting and also alluring. The whole house is actually. You're doing a great job."

His lips twitch keeping a smile at bay. "So, you like interior design as well as landscaping."

"Landscape Architect. And yes, I like many types of design." I say, smirking. "I watch too much HGTV when I can't fall asleep."

Am I flirting? Is he flirting?

No, that's not what this is. It's just been too long since I've had dinner one on one with a hot, single, gay man. It's just dinner. I need to remind myself this is very much not a date. It's not.

But the air between us has shifted. Not in an obvious way, the bumps have subtly smoothed. The quiet between the clinks of our silverware is no longer painful to my ears.

He starts telling me about his work on the house. Giving me a long list of projects that he hopes to accomplish. His shoulders drop as if accepting defeat against relaxing. I relate to the feeling well and try to push the stress from my own body to match.

Owen thought he would miss the chaos of city life, managing construction crews and juggling tight deadlines, but the slower rhythm of this town has grown on him. I learn he went to Illinois State University on a football scholarship. That explains the Redbirds hat I noticed hanging on a hook in the kitchen, next to the back door.

At some point in the conversation, we have become something different. I am amazed how fast he doesn't feel like a stranger. We are host and guest, but those titles don't feel entirely true.

Friends maybe? Or two people that enjoy each other's company and are on their way to being friends.

To people that like each other. Leaving a door open for many possibilities.

After dinner, I start gathering plates, but he waves me off. "You're a guest… go relax or something."

"Thank you for dinner." I nod once and realize it looked too much like a bow. Embarressment flushes my cheeks. My feet move quickly to the living room. Hopefully, he was too distracted by the dishes to notice. Perhaps my instinct is to bow because of his large frame and perfect face. He may as well be a prince—no, a king.

I try to relax, but it doesn't come easy. I flop onto the couch, pull out my phone, and attempt to log into my work email. I'm still locked out. I huff, tossing the device onto the cushion beside me.

Relaxing, it seems, is going to be a challenge.

8
Owen

I buy two gallons of dark emerald paint from the hardware store, the shade Gabriel and Lucas both picked. Gabriels has motivated me to work on the aesthetic of the house and not just the problems hidden in the walls. I admit, those items on the list have been ignored for some time.

As the shopkeeper rings me up, she gives me a curious look bursting with small town gossip.

"Heard a rumor someone's staying at your place," she says casually while pulling out wood paint stirs from under the counter.

I sigh. "Oxford is living up to small town stereotypes."

"Jason mentioned something. But didn't know the details."

How did Jason, a man I have met a handful of times

know I had a houseguest? The first suspect that comes to mind is Adrienne. My neighbor has not been subtle encouraging me to date for the past two years. She has tried to give me multiple books about moving on after loss and ways to deal with grief. I would skim the pages then hide them away. Moving on meant flaunting my happiness in front of my husband who still haunts me. Literally. And I am not convinced there is a proper way to deal with grief. A one-size-fits-all healing journey.

For all I know my love is the one thing keeping Lucas here. What would happen if I push my feelings aside? I shake my head at the thoughts.

"I am renting out a room for two weeks. He is a temporary tenant. Nothing more." I assure her. She nods like she understands but the expression on her face suggests she suspects it is more than that. Something tells me I will be squashing rumors for months after Gabriel leaves. This town has nothing better to do than worry about the love lives of their nonmarried citizens. I feel like I am stuck in a regency drama, and they expect me to display him on a walk on the promenade. I restrain from rolling my eyes while leaving.

Before heading home, I detour from my driveway to Adrienne's house, arms full of empty baking dishes that were sitting on my truck's passenger seat. She's kneading dough at the counter while her two youngest kids wreak havoc around her feet, crayons and toy cars scattered across the floor. She looks up with a knowing smile when I step inside.

"Did you tell everyone in town I have a house guest? Janis at the hardware store knew someone was staying at my place and it's been less than twenty-four hours."

"No, I told Carol, from the bank." she says, completely unapologetic while tucking a stray light brown strand of hair behind her ear. I have never met anyone that fits their life as perfect as Adrienne does. She never wears makeup but looks perfect. Natural blush on her sun kissed cheeks. An updo that looks effortlessly perfect. She even makes overalls look chic. "And I'm sure Carol told her daughter, who's dating the son of the owner of the hardware store. Jason, I think. I was just excited to see you not alone for once. An overnight guest."

She wiggles her eyebrows.

I shake my head. "It's not like that, Adrienne. He's just a guest. Booked a room for two weeks. I already took the listing down, so don't get too excited. Gabriel will be the first and last houseguest. I assure you."

"Gabriel is a nice name," she muses, shaping the dough.

"Bye, Adrienne." I place the empty casserole dishes on the counter. Tucked between them is an envelope of cash. She insisted on cooking for me after Lacas died. After months of eating her home cooked food I told her I would only accept them if it were a meal prep service that I paid for. Now it feels less like charity. Although I know she would continue to deliver them if I stopped paying.

"There's a lasagna in the fridge," she calls after me. "Cooking instructions are written on the foil."

Oxford is the kind of town where people don't lock their doors. Adrienne and I have fallen into a pattern. She slips into my house when I run errands or am deep in a project. Although I pay for the food now, finding meals in my fridge waiting has been a comforting surprise. On the days where I am missing Lucas hard, they can act as a reminder of how I am failing to take care of myself. The last step before moving on.

I wave in thanks and head towards my house, after I grab the paint cans from the truck. As I approach the house, I see Gabriel sitting on a bench facing the overgrown yard. The large yard threatening to swallow him up. It looks terrible. Pumpkin vines sprawling wildly, the old hot cocoa shack still battered from a windstorm one year ago, and a pile of firewood half-toppled next to the house.

Gabriel has a notepad on his lap. A journal or sketchpad, I cannot tell. I am drawn to go over and see what he is doing. I could offer a cup of tea or coffee. That's what Lucas would do.

My feet move towards him just to halt before he can notice me. I remember he is here to be alone and relax. This is not a man visiting an old friend. We are strangers, despite having one pleasant conversation over dinner last night. I am the short-term landlord that just needs to provide a safe place to sleep and leave him be. I pivot towards the front porch.

Lucas appears in front of me; arms crossed with a smirk on his face. He's floating a few inches above the grass.

"You should go talk to him." He whispers.

"No," I mutter. As I move past him my shoulder moves through him. My subconscious is hoping to be met with resistance. Testing if he has become more solid. He has not. I pass through him as if he is a figment of my imagination. Perhaps he is and I have been losing my mind for the last three years.

Heading into the house, I can feel him following by

the chill at the nape of my neck. Continuing into the butler's pantry, I set the paint cans down. This space was once used to prepare food and probably was used for many bougie parties back in the day. Now it held my supplies for drywall repair, wallpaper removal, and countless other tasks I have started in the past three years. I quite like it. It's like having a mini workshop inside my home. Every house should have one. I don't have to run out to the shed or a garage. Even the cabinets are filled with tools, screws, and various grains of sandpaper.

I begin to gather paint supplies like I am preparing a charcuterie board. A tray to hold paint, small rollers, and a drop cloth. Lucas hovers in the doorway. I expect to see a judgmental look on his face when I turn with an armful of supplies. But he looks somber. Like I broke his heart.

"What?" I keep my voice quiet in case Gabriel is back in the bouse. "You look like I just kicked your dog."

"One, did you forget I'm allergic to dogs." He put his hands on his hips dramatically and I could not help the smile grow my face. *"Two, I like Gabriel. He's nice and cute. I think you could be friends. And lord knows, you need gay friends. Maybe he will take you out to a bar in the city. You could live again."*

"Live?" I frown. "How can-"

"Don't finish that sentence. Life's not a song, Life isn't bliss, Life is just this, it's living. You have to go on living. So, one of us is living." Lucas floated away slowly with a triumphant grin on his face.

"Did you just quote Spike from the Buffy the Vampire Musical?"

I hurry after Lucas, my dirty boots echoing as I stomp

into the hallway. He floated away too quickly. Pleased with himself. I come to an abrupt stop when someone steps directly in my path.

Gabriel.

He appeared suddenly, coming in through the kitchen, back door creaking shut behind him. We collide when does not stop in time. Hard enough to make both of us drop supplies to the ground. Paint rollers clatter and bounce. One object catches my eye as it slaps on the hard wood. A sketchpad.

We both freeze, momentarily stunned, caught in the awkwardness of close proximity. I take a step back and whisper an apology, but Gabriel's already couching down, calmly gathering items.

The sketchpad lies open, and I glimpse an overhead view of what could be a hedge maze. Clean lines form spiraling paths, entirely whimsical. At the center, the shading suggests a round fountain. Gabriel notices me looking and he blushes before snatching the sketch-pad. He holds the drawing against his chest as if he is ashamed by his talent.

"I'm sorry." He says, although I am not angry at the excuse to talk to him again. Dinner was far more enjoyable than I expected, and I was waiting to be near him again. He continued. "You are probably not used to having someone in your house. Maybe I should wear a collar with a bell."

"Oh fun, a collar." Lucas whispered only for me to hear.

I stiffen.

"A collar?" My arms were once again filled with

painting supplies. I stood and looked down at him. We were standing close. Too close. I took a step back and tried to look anywhere but his deep blue eyes.

"I meant-" His cheeks were tinted pink. "Ya know, a bell. So, you can hear me coming. Forget I mentioned a collar. Is that the green paint for the entry?"

I turned my body and spoke over my shoulder while walking away. "And hallway, yes." I scanned the room to see where Lucas was, but he was nowhere to be seen.

"Let me put my stuff down and I will help." Gabriel walked up the stairs to his room.

My chest warms with excitement to work alongside him. He is easy to talk to, and I like the fact that he does most of the talking. Then I remember what brought him to my house in the first place.

"I can't have you help. You are a guest remember."

"Please let me help. I cannot be alone with my own thoughts any more today." He popped his head out of the guest room. "Unless you don't want me around and then I can wonder into town or something."

At the top of the stairs, Lucas stood nodding his head with enthusiasm. I tried to smile naturally and ignore the ghost of my dead husband hovering next to the man staying in my house. The single gay man. The adorable man who is effecting my body in ways I haven't felt in a long time. Fuck when did I start liking redheads. Has this always been a thing that I haven't explored, because every time I look at him it has rose higher on my list of things I am attracted to. Maybe it's not his hair. Maybe it's just him.

I am not sure when Lucas slipped away. He must have witnessed me staring at Gabriel too longingly. I have never been great at hiding emotions on my face. Lucas hinted that he wanted me to flirt with Gabriel. Maybe it was easier for him to want that before he saw me lean into it. Allowing myself to get swept up in conversation while staring at Gabriels soft lips and the loops of his read hair. Even now I am thinking of Lucas, and it somehow blended into Gabriel.

The last thing I ever want is to hurt Lucas. Or lead Gabriel on. Lucas is the love of my life. And always will be. Gabriel is only here for two weeks.

I mean to deny Gabriels's help, but when I look at him retreating up the stairs it appears my brain has different plans.

"I would love your help." I finally answer. He responds with a warm smile that thawed a bit of my heart. I rush to the hallway before I melt and begin to set up the paint.

9
Gabriel

Just like during dinner, there were long stretches of silence while we painted the entryway and hall, but this time they felt easier. Intentional and almost comforting. At one point, I snuck a glance at Owen as he reached up with a roller. The hem of his shirt lifted just enough to flash a glimpse of abs that could've been carved from obsidian.

I worried my lingering eyes were overstepping until I caught him with a similar expression as he watched me lay on the floor, carefully painting a clean edge along the baseboard. Before I could finish forming a smile he quickly turned away, he looked flustered, a bit shy. Lustful thoughts go unspoken. It pulled me back to those high school days building theater sets, when I used to flirt with the only openly gay boy in school.

He was also a jock. Maybe I have a type. Not like I am trying to get with Owen, my host, whom I am paying to stay at his house. I should aim for friendship. I should ignore the urge to flirt. Becoming comfortable with silence is a good start. And our silence feels oddly comforting.

It didn't take long to realize he's a man of few words. That suits me just fine. My mind goes a million miles a minute, so it is nice to be forced to slow down. Now, if I can only figure out how this break from work will improve my job performance. Perhaps this is a Karate Kid moment where the act of painting is a secret lesson. I will return to the office a new man. Better than ever. Focused.

I move around the narrow hallway and entry making sure not to bump into Owen. His wide shoulders are evidence of his football years in the past. I bet he could lift me up with one arm. And I would gladly let him. Maybe even beg for it.

Standing next to him, I feel like a hobbit trying to steal a ladder from a giant. I'm not exactly tall to begin with, but every time I reach for the ladder, Owen snatches it away or blocks it with his body. Unsure of his reasoning, I just stand there while he scales the rungs with the dark green paint in tow. He effortlessly reaches the highest parts of the walls, while I watch like a damsel from below.

At first I thought he was worried I will do a shitty job painting. Then I happened to look down at him the only time I made it to the top of the ladder before he could stop me. His features tightened. Worry etched itself into lines on his forehead. It hit me—I never asked how his husband died. For all I know, it could've been a fall from this exact ladder. No wonder he looked so tense. I'm usually more in tune with people's emotions. My mom raised me on empathy. She carries compassion like a torch into every room she enters. I let mine flicker and forgot I am in the presence of someone who still grieves.

I spent the rest of the time painting with my feet safely planted on the ground. He seemed to relax, his jaw no longer tight with tension. Which I took as a minor miracle and a very good sign. I get the impression he is about as good at relaxing as I am.

After nearly an hour of painting in mostly silence, my anxiety brain started buzzing from the stillness. I debated slipping on my headphones and escaping into an audiobook. But I knew that would come off rude. I want to at least keep myself open to conversation if Owen wants to talk. Although there is a steamy hockey romance waiting for me. Full of brooding rivals who fall hard for each other despite being on competing teams. I was remembering the locker room scene I listened to last night, causing a grin to fill my face just as Owen looked over at me. His eyes lingered a second too long. Thank God he can't read my thoughts, because I had just started picturing him in a hockey uniform, and not much else.

"You look like you are actually enjoying yourself." He said.

I set my roller down in the tray after adding the finishing touch on the entire wall under the stairs. I took a step back to admire my work. I have to admit it was the right color for this space. The light from the stained-glass window reflects beautifully off of it.

Arms folded proudly over my chest; I admire how we transformed the room into something new that still fits the aesthetic of the house.

"I am enjoying myself. It's been a while since I've done any real physical labor. Not that this is, like, hard or anything. I mean—I'm not out of shape. I'm definitely not built like you, but I can hold my own at the gym. You know... if rolling around on a giant pink yoga ball counts as a workout. Which it does, by the way. Core strength is very important. My job doesn't require me to have all that-" I gesture to his body, "Usually I'm walking through job sites judging other people's work from a safe distance. Not doing the construction myself."

Oh God. Talk about word salad. I bite my bottom lip to stop myself from talking.

Part of my job is pitching design plans in crowded boardrooms for multi-million-dollar projects. Yet I am struggling to have a simple conversation with Owen. I am fucked for the next thirteen days if I can't keep my damn mouth in check.

The sun is threatening to set below the horizon. The only light remaining is the tiffany style overhead light playing with the colors in the room. His dark eyes glint with flecks of gold in the low light as he looks down at me.

"Um, okay."

I mentally face palm. Great, my idiocy has stunned him into more silence. I open my mouth to speak and quickly shut it again. This vacation is punishment. An evil plan from my boss and all my exes. Working together to have me embarrass myself to death. I have been too successful. This is how I get knocked down a few pegs. I'm clearly an easy target. All karma had to do was lock me in a house with an overwhelming hot single man for a day and I unravel like yarn. Limp rainbow yarn that has been forgotten about after being stuffed down to the bottom of a basket.

I turned to accept defeat when Owen lightly grabbed my arm. It was only for a second, but my cheeks burned instantly. Damn ginger genetics.

"Thanks for your help." He motions to the walls. "I think you were right about the color. Now I just need some art."

"In brass frames." I rock back on my heels. "Maybe a mirror. Just don't put the mirror on that wall, it ruins the Feng Shui." Pointing to the wall directly across from the front door.

"I'll take your word on that." He moved like he was going to rub the back of his neck and realized there was a paint-soaked roller in his hand. "Why don't you rest. I'll clean this up and have dinner up in an hour."

"Okay." I step over the paint supplies to the stairs. "I will see you in an hour."

I hold my breath as I walk up to my room. Trying my hardest to keep more word-vomit from spewing out of my mouth. Why am I acting like he just asked me on a date? This is not a date. I am literally a paying guest in his house, and I am acting like the prom king just asked me to the movies.

My anxiety is working overtime as I take a quick shower. Then grab my sketch pad and take a seat in the cream wingback chair near the window. Letting my curls air dry despite the chill that passes through my room. Old houses like this are always drafty.

I gaze out the window looking for inspiration. In the distance I can see dark clouds rolling in. Promising rain. I keep my eyes on them as my pencil glides across the paper, sketching without look-ing down. It's something I used to do as a kid, back when the world felt too loud. Drawing quieted it all. Sitting here now, I realize it's been years since I sketched for myself. Everything I've created lately has been for someone else's vision. Not mine.

I draw abstract shapes on paper, forming the build-ings in the town. From here, I can see a church spire. A restaurant with a faded wood sign that still has a hint of what I'm guessing is a lobster. I lean closer to the glass until the house next door comes into view. It has beauti-ful carved gables on the front porch that match the dor-mer windows on the second floor. I absorb the patterns into my memory and flip to a fresh page. I sketch the curves and spindles of the wood as if they are a map. Looking down, I change the lines to look like paths and hedges. Imagining it's a giant rose garden fit for the white house.

I sank into the chair, sketching until multiple pages were full and my pencils too dull to hold a point. The trance only broke when I heard two soft knocks and Owen's voice calling me down for dinner. Every inch of my body felt relaxed. The first time in years. The Mr. Miagi method worked. Exhausted from painting and thoroughly embarrassing myself, I gave in to something I hadn't felt in years. The creative spark that first led me to art school, long before I shifted paths to landscape architecture. A part of me I've kept tucked away for far too long.

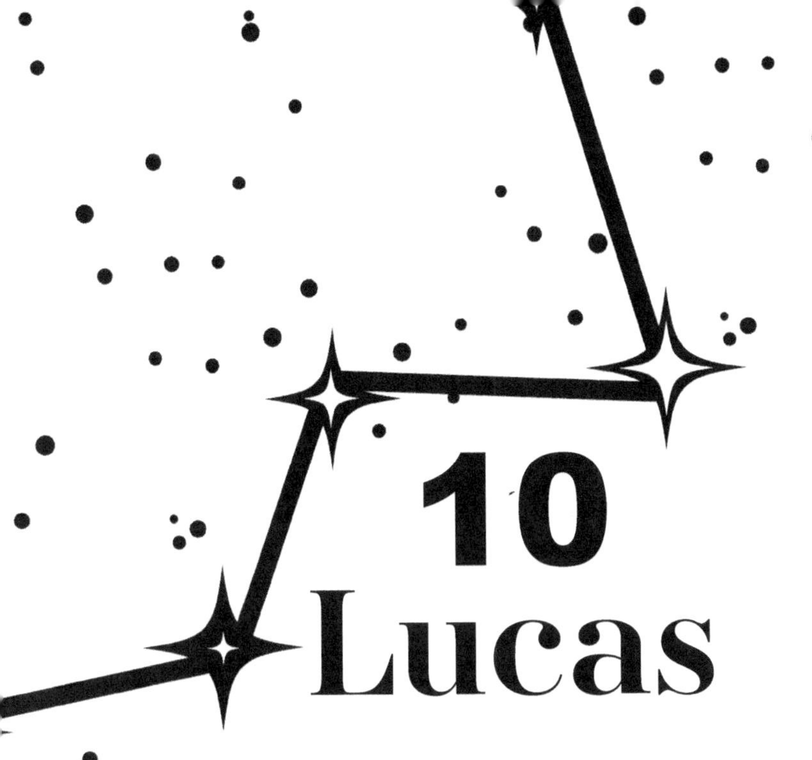

10
Lucas

I stand in the open field next to the house, beneath the midnight sky. The grass does not bend beneath my feet. The wind does not stir my hair. The cold does not bite my skin.

There's no rhythm, no pulse, yet my heart aches with a fullness I can't explain. just the echo of a body, flickering like a hologram.

My eyes drift up to Owen's window. Moments ago, his light went out, plunging the room into darkness. I remain here and wait. The same way I do every night. I wait for something or someone to come and claim my soul. Take me from here and let me move on. This can't be what waits for us when we die. Endless days of haunting the ones we love.

I don't know why I linger here after my death, trapped

between life and whatever comes after. I only know that I can't leave. Or maybe something won't let me leave. If I try to walk away I black out and find myself back at the house. Floating in the living room over the spot I took my last breath.

These thoughts are selfish. Owen is grieving. Because of me. Because I died, and in doing so, I took part of him with me. The part that was optimistic and spontaneous. We love—loved each other. Love is supposed to be eternal, but this… this is something cruel. A curse. A tortuous echo. My presence binds him to the past, keeps him from moving on, from finding something beyond grief.

I should go. I should let him go.

But the light never comes for me.

Isn't that how it's supposed to work? A bright glow, warm and welcoming, pulling you into whatever peace waits after death? If that's true, then maybe my parents were right the night I came out to them. Maybe I have no seat in Heaven.

Maybe this is all I get.

All I deserve.

11
Gabriel

The late morning air is crisp as I step out of Owen's Victorian home, inhaling deeply as if I can breathe in the charm of Oxford, Maryland. The town is picturesque, like something out of a holiday Hallmark movie with its historic homes, well-kept sidewalks, and a general air of slow, deliberate living. It's a stark contrast to the breakneck pace of Washington DC. Precisely why I'm here, forced into this so-called vacation to prevent burnout. Despite my initial resistance, I fear Carlton was right.

Minute by minute it is starting to feel less like a forced situation and something I will miss when it's over. The barely over two-hour drive from D.C. is not bad if I need future breaks. Owen might not put his place back on MisterBandB after dealing with me, but I'm sure I could find another spot in town to stay.

Watching Owen work on the Victorian has me reflecting more than I expected. Lately, I've realized how little intention I put into the spaces I call my own. Nearly every ounce of my creative energy goes into designing for other people. Usually for massive, faceless corporations that care more about profit than purpose. There's no soul in it. No connection. But seeing Owen meticulously think about every detail hits different. It makes me want to create something different. I want to create something that matters. Something with heart.

I navigate my way to the small coffee shop I spotted yesterday. The bell above the door chimes as I enter, and the scent of freshly brewed espresso and baked goods blanket me. The place is cozy, with rustic wooden tables, mismatched seats, and a few locals scattered about, chatting or working on laptops.

I order a vanilla latte to stay. The barista serves it in an oversized mug with a leaf design on top. I settle into a table by the window and pull my book out of my messenger bag. This is what determination looks like. I am determined not to think about work. Easier said than done. The first thing I notice are the empty plots of dirt that create the curb strip. Judging by the patches of grass it appears the town attempted to grown something at one point. Now they are neglected and barren.

I shake my head and refocus on the pages in front of me. Breathe. Just be. Enjoy the moment. Read about a knight that falls in love with a dragon shifter and enjoy your latte.

The time passes in a way it rarely does for me. Without the weight of responsibility pressing in. And not a single notification chime from my phone to interrupt me. I sip my coffee, lose myself in my book, and relish the quiet murmur of the cafe around me. When I get up to leave, I stop by the counter and purchase two pastries, just in case Owen wants one.

As I step outside, I reach for my keys, but before I can unlock my car, a man strides in my direction from across the street. A middle-aged man with a big smile on his face like we are old friends. I look around to make sure he is not looking at someone behind me.

He is wearing jeans and a tweed blazer. The look gives 'I am not like the other professors; I'm a cool professor' vibes.

"Hi?" I greet him with a questioning tone.

"Hello, hello! Gabriel, right?" He doesn't wait for confirmation before thrusting an envelope into my hands. "Could you pass this along to Owen?"

I blink at the envelope, then back at him. "Of course. How do you know my name and that I am staying with Owen?"

"Have you seen the size of this town?" He chuckles with a hand on his heart as if laughing too hard might kill him. "I am on the city council and the president of the Oxford historical society. The is just some council business. He'll know what it's about."

I slip the envelope into my bag. With my hand out, I formally introduce myself. "You already know I'm Gabriel."

"How rude of me. I am Thomas Garcia." He gripped my hand in his. "But everyone calls me Mr. Garcia, ya know, due to my importance in the town." He winks.

I nod. "It's a great town. Like a seaside Stars Hollow."

"Don't know what that means." He tugs on the lapels of his blazer and puffs out his chest. "But we are pretty magical. People seem to stumble into our town at the exact time in their life when they need us most. Makes me wonder what brought you here."

"My boss basically kicked me out of the office. I've been working nonstop, jumping from one project to the next. And with a major one coming up, he was worried I'd crash before we even got started." What is happening to me in this town? I wouldn't call myself anti-social, but rarely do I strike up conversations with strangers. I have been talking Owens' ear off and now I am spilling everything to a random city council member of a town I do not live in.

"Do you feel like you are gonna burn out?" Garcia asks.

I open my mouth to answer and pause. It is a question I have never asked myself. Do I feel like I am going to burn out? I like my work. I feel fulfilled when I work. I love seeing people walk around and enjoy my designs. I have accomplished quite a lot in my career, and I am not even thirty yet. Although I still live with a roommate even though I could afford to live alone. Jackie is my crutch that keeps me from feeling complete loneliness.

When I was in college, my internship was to design a veteran's memorial garden in a small town. Their budget was not much but the people in the town wanted a place to lay their loved ones to rest that would honor their service. I could not make it to the grand opening ceremony, but one of the locals mailed me a copy of the newspaper. Dozens of residents cheered as a red, white, and blue ribbon was cut. It was the moment I realized architecture was more than building or landscape planning. It was a chance to create something that would last decades, maybe even centuries. A gift for generations to come.

Now I mostly create spaces for the wealthy to lounge around at expensive resorts.

Mr. Garcia noticed I was taking a long time to answer and tilted his head at me.

"Maybe not burn out completely, but I do feel like I am running in circles a bit." I finally pushed out.

He checked his watch. "Being pushed off course is a great way to stop running in circles. Sounds like you stumbled to Oxford at the perfect time." He grinned. "What's that word, serendipity?"

"Great word. Also, a great movie."

"I will take your word on it. I don't watch many films." He took two steps back. "It was great meeting you, Gabriel. Don't forget to give the envelope to Owen."

Garcia tipped an invisible hat as he walked back across the street. The cars stopped for him and every driver waved. I opened my car door and headed back to the house.

When I walk in, Owen was perched on a ladder in the living room, carefully touching up the white paint on the crown molding after patching a hole. He's focused, precise, and I hesitate to interrupt him. I clear my throat to make my presence known. He looks down at me with his dark eyes and long lashes. My cheeks heat under his gaze. Pinned like my clothes disappeared.

When he smiles his face is warm and bright. Full of light. But his resting face is not bitchy. It's friendly in a seductive way and my heart can barely stand looking at him. It has been too long since I have been on a date. Put me in a house with a man and my body assumes it's go-time.

The ceiling light casts a starburst that creeps towards the edges of the room. When the light hits the walls you can see they are not plain cream colored. A pattern of vines and flowers are woven into the wallpaper.

"Welcome back. How was the town?"

"Really nice actually. This looks amazing," I say, shifting the messenger bag on my hip and opening the flap. "Oh, and Mr. Garcia gave me this for you."

"Mr. Garcia?" Owen balanced the paint brush on the edge of the can and stepped down the ladder. With both of us standing on the floor I still have to look up to him.

"He was very…um… welcoming." I pull the envelope out and hold it in his direction.

He wipes his hands quickly on a rag before taking it from me. I pause for a moment like I was going to hover while he read it before remembering my place and turning on a heel. I head toward the kitchen and place the bag of pastries on the counter.

The scent of damp earth lingers in the air, rich and grounding after last night's rain. An invitation I cannot ignore. I'm planning to park myself in the sun with my sketchbook and attempt creativity. I grab a pastry, nestle it on a napkin and I'm almost ready to head out to my new favorite bench.

I pass a shopping list on the counter. All items were already checked off. I pick up the pen and write on the brown paper bag with one pastry left inside. My hand hovers, not knowing how to address him. I settle with "for Owen" and leave the paper on the bag.

I head upstairs to grab my sketchbook and pencils but

pause when I catch sight of Owen. He's standing still, pinching the bridge of his nose, eyes burning through the letter. I look away. We're not friends. Not roommates. Whatever is written on that page has nothing to do with me and is none of my business.

12
Owen

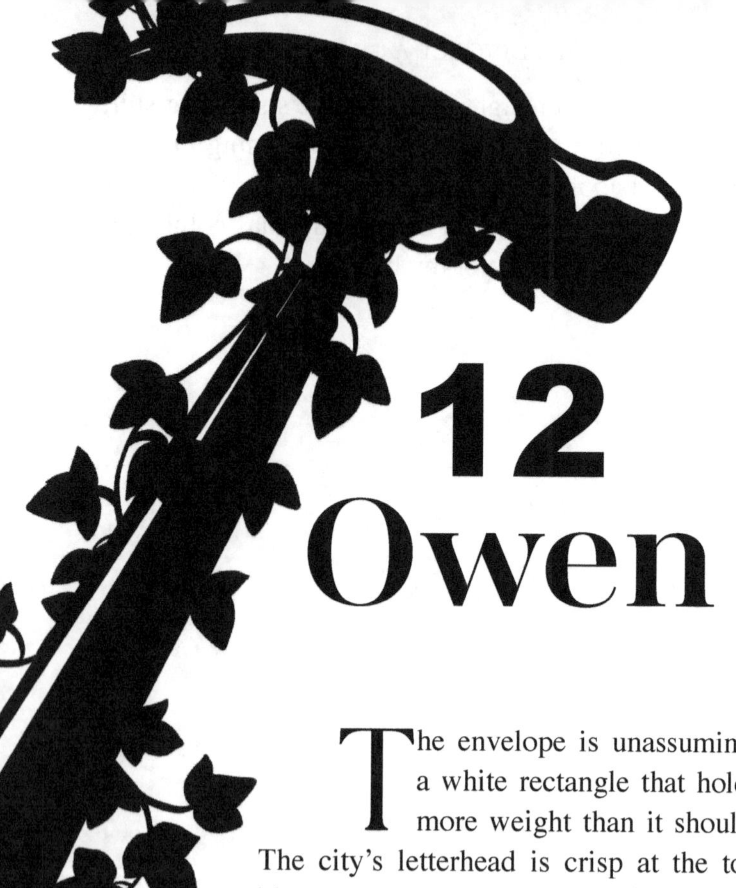

The envelope is unassuming, a white rectangle that holds more weight than it should. The city's letterhead is crisp at the top with my name written in a flowery script in the center. My stomach knots as I skim the first paragraph of the typed letter, my breath hitching when my eyes land on the date.

May 17th.

The air in the living room stills, thick and unmoving. Holding me in place. My fingers tighten around the paper, crumpling the edges like I could crush the date off the page. Three years. It's been three years since Lucas died. Since my life cracked down the middle. Splitting me in two. The anniversary stares up at me: May 17th. Of course it does. A day I would rather stay in my room and sulk and now I have to spend the day with a joyful mask on my face. The same day the city council has scheduled their walk through to see updates on my renovation.

Only three weeks away.

Lucas and I got this house for next to nothing, it was wrapped in a contract with big promises: restore the main house and revive the old pumpkin patch. It cannot be sold to investors of any kind. The owners must remain residents of Oxford. It was all part of Lucas's big dreams—breathe new life into something old with roots in a small town. He always kept an eye out for churches for sale or old fire station. But Hammond house spoke to him the moment he saw a picture. He made an offer before stepping foot on the tattered wood floor.

And now, I am standing here, holding a date that feels both like a deadline and a gift to a ghost. My chance to complete his legacy.

"Picture it," he told me once. "We grow old here. Everyone in town becomes our family." I'll admit the plan it sounded wonderful back then. A dream, even. But now? It feels like agony. My plan is simple: fix the house just enough to sell. I might not even finish restoring the pumpkin patch. That credit can go to the next owner. They would probably do a better job anyway.

I'll cut my losses, walk away. Maybe my father can find me work in Utah, now that I'm returning alone, no husband in tow. I have never wanted to move back, but that was mostly because I was in a same sex relationship. Utah is not known for their openness to queer people. If I can be a hermit here, why not be a hermit closer to family?

Someone else can buy this house, take on the legacy, and be the proud owner of a historic landmark. It doesn't have to be me anymore.

No one wants a sad widower to be the one greeting them when they pick out pumpkins or drink hot cider. Hammond House is meant for a loving couple. Hosts that make this place feel like home to everyone that visits and not a temporary space for the lost.

I exhale sharply and shove the letter into my back pocket just as the back door swings open. Gabriel steps inside, and I meet him in the kitchen.

There's a lightness to his walk, something I envy. The tension in his shoulders seems to melt away more with every hour he spends here. I wonder if he has ever thought about owning a Victorian house. He fits better than I do.

"Hey." he says, beaming, running a hand through his copper curls.

"Hey."

He leans against the counter, eyes flicking toward me. "Need help with any projects today?"

Next to him I spy a bag with my name written on a scrap of paper lay atop it. I tilt my head. "Is that for me?"

"Yes. The barista said you often get a cheese Danish with your coffee."

"I do." There's a pause before I add, "Thank you."

It's not that I'm unfamiliar with food as a gift. Adrienne drop off meals to me like it is her part time job, at least until I insisted on paying her and making it a real job. She never argued. I think she enjoys the extra money to spend on herself and the kids. I am grateful to have something to eat on the nights when the idea of cooking feels too heavy. When my sadness hinders my ability to function as an adult.

But this pastry feels different. Knowing Gabriel walked into a coffee shop and thought of me—asked the barista about my usual order—this warms my chest. Maybe Lucas is onto something when he decided to pull strings to bring him here. Summon someone into this house whose equal parts comforting and intriguing.

"Nope to your question about needing help on projects."

This made him frown. I clarify, "You are the guest remember. It is not your job to tackle my to-to list."

"Yeah, yeah whatever." Gabriel sets his sketchbook on the table. He whines "No one will let me work."

His exaggerated huff pulls a smile from me before I can stop it.

"I'm about to make a sandwich. You want one?"

"Yes please." His face lights up. "But I am helping. Being idle is going to kill me."

We move around the kitchen in tandem, an easy rhythm of passing ingredients and brushing shoulders. Gabriel hums softly as he slices a tomato, then a pickle, then cheese. I find myself staring at his hands. They're steady, sure... the kind of hands that make you wonder what else they're good at.

"Am I doing something wrong?" He interrupts my thoughts, and I realize that I am hovering the spicy brown mustard over a slice of bread. Frozen like a stature.

"No. Not at all. I am good at construction but when it comes to knife skills I have always been a bit of an amateur. I blame my big hands." I immediately regret this conversation. What type of asshole talks about his own big hands. I add "and the tiny handle."

"My mother always said I had artists hands. Good for holding a pencil or paintbrush." He slides the cutting board in my direction. The lettuce, tomato, pickle, and cheese are lined in perfect rows. He grabs the mustard and butter knife from my hands. "I am the middle son. My brothers were athletes. Competed in every sport. I tried. But in the end I was drawn to more creative hobbies. Theater and art mostly."

"This is the extent of my creativity." I hold up my sandwich. Worthy of an advertisement. Gabriel holds up a nearly matching sandwich.

"Joey Tribbiani would be drooling if he saw that sandwich. You are an artist. Look what your hands can do."

I have no idea who that is, but I kept that to myself. I don't need Gabriel thinking I am an uncultured jock brute with a hammer.

"They can do a lot more than make a sandwich." I carry the plate with my sandwich to the table. I look up to find Gabriel bright red and standing in the middle of the kitchen. The inuendo dawns on me. I consider letting him think my intention was to have him think about my hands on his body. I enjoy knowing the idea has caused him to flush all the way up to his ears. Then I decide to smile and remove the inuendo from his mind. It was not my intention in the first place—at least not subconsciously. "I meant building and renovation stuff."

"Right. Renovation stuff." He says quietly and takes up the chair across from me.

The flirtation voice inside my head wins. I cannot

help but bring it back. The disappointment on his face was clear. He wanted me to flirt with him. He enjoyed it. That makes two of us.

"Not to say I don't know other things to do with my hands. It is just not appropriate for me to suggest things to my paying house guest. Not professional." Someone stop me from continuing this conversation. He is going to file a complaint with MisterBandB claiming sexual harassment.

"Maybe I should ask for a refund."

"What?"

Gabriel takes a bite of his sandwich. I wait for him to chew and swallow. It takes painfully long.

"I am just kidding." He finally says. "It just seems like you have been hung up alone in this house for a long time and maybe you need a friend. If me being in a position of paying to stay here is keeping you from speaking freely, maybe I should get a refund and stay as a friend."

I let his words roll around in my head. Just as Lucas floats in and hovers in the corner of the kitchen behind Gabriel. I try not to make it obvious that I am looking at something behind him. The flirty tone of this conversation is stronger than I am comfortable having in front of my husband. Ex-husband. That feels weird to say, even in my head.

I bite into my sandwich to keep from saying something stupid. "I should refund you. My house isn't really ready for guests. I had nothing planned to qualify as a Bed and Breakfast." I gulp down water. "And if I am completely honest. I think you are right. I would rather have a friend than a tenant. Right now, at least."

"Any friend? Or-" It's cute, the way he fidgets slightly, his fingers tapping against the table. Behind him, Lucas chuckles only for me to hear. *"Both of you are adorable, beating around the bush because you don't want to admit that you like each other's company."* he murmurs. *"I know you; this is your poor attempt of testing if he is interested in more than just friendship. But your flirting may be too subtle. Lay it on thick,. Don't friend zone him just yet."*

I hold back any reaction to Lucas's words. My husband is encouraging me to flirt with someone else. This life is strange. I was slowly chewing. Lost in thought when I realized Gabriel is still waiting for a response.

"I'm going to refund you. I would love to have you stay the next eleven days as a friend if you accept." And there it is. I am laying a small piece of my heart on the table before him. It only took two days in his company for me to need more. Want more. More of his fast-talking pop culture references. More of the way he speaks about design. And most of all, there is part of me that wonders what those hands would feel like on my body. It's been so long, and the desire grows with every minute near him. I will keep that last thought to myself. Lucas is happy to see me making friends and attempt to flirt. That does not mean he wants to see me jump into bed with another man.

"I'll earn my stay by helping you with a few projects." He covers his mouth with his hand as he speaks but I can tell by the sparkle in his eye that a smile is hiding beneath.

Lucas chimes in. *"It's good to see you being yourself again."*

I swallow hard, glancing at him above Gabriels's

shoulder. He looks content, arms crossed as he mimics a lean against the far wall, watching with an expression that almost resembles peace.

Gabriel shifts in his seat, drawing my attention back. "Hey, I was wondering if you have any restaurant rec-ommendations in town, I'd love to check something out. I love home cooking, but I'm trying to force myself to get out more."

Lucas's voice is immediate, teasing. *"Take him out."*

I clear my throat. "I could take you somewhere. My treat."

Gabriel blinks, surprised. Then, his lips curve into a slow smile. "Yeah? That sounds nice."

As we finish eating lunch, I lean back in my chair, tapping my finger on my empty water glass.

"I think I owe you dessert with dinner."

"Dessert?"

"Yea. Cause you helped me paint yesterday." I grab his empty plate and stack it atop my own. He places his hands in his lap.

Gabriel smiles, warm and rich. "Dinner and dessert sounds wonderful."

Lucas smirks from the corner, hazel eyes twinkling. *"Now we're talking."*

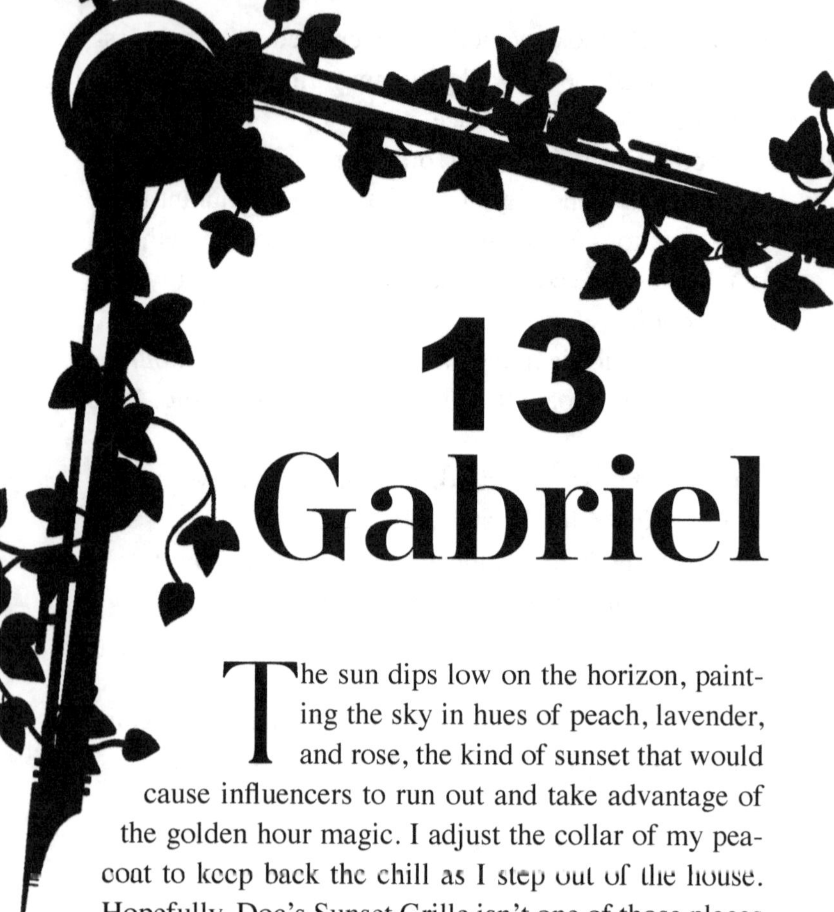

13
Gabriel

The sun dips low on the horizon, painting the sky in hues of peach, lavender, and rose, the kind of sunset that would cause influencers to run out and take advantage of the golden hour magic. I adjust the collar of my peacoat to keep back the chill as I step out of the house. Hopefully, Doc's Sunset Grille isn't one of those places with white tablecloths and candlelight. I am more in the mood for something casual. Not to mention, I did not bring any date clothes. Not like this is a date. We are just two individuals that have agreed to be friends. A friend date.

The weird progression is not lost on me. I began as an unwanted tenant and have slipped my way into something more within days.

Owen is already waiting by his truck; arms crossed over his broad chest. The thick cable-knit sweater he's wearing clings in a way that should be illegal, and his jeans, with not a single smudge of paint or grease, feel like a minor miracle. I realize I have only seen him in handyman attire up until this point. And although he looks good in a sweaty shirt under a flannel, he looks like a movie star in that sweater. His aura feels like he is wearing a tux. I cannot keep the smile off my face as I walk towards him.

He opens the door for me. I hesitate, just for a second. It's been a long time since someone held a door open for me, at least without expecting a tip afterward. My nervousness must be obvious because Owen drops his hand immediately.

"Oh. Sorry," he says, rubbing the back of his neck. "That was weird of me. This isn't a date. I should've let you get your own door. I just- I'm not around people much these days. Especially not..." His jaw tightens. I chuckle. He sounds like me. Tripping on words.

I raise one eyebrow. "Especially not what?" I prompt.

"Nothing. Forget it." He shakes his head; gaze fixed on the front porch behind me. "You're here for vacation. Rest and relaxation, right? I'm just making you uncomfortable."

I slide into the truck and mumble, more to myself than him, "I am very comfortable. Maybe too comfortable."

The drive is quick. Oxford is not a large town. Not even a medium-sized town. If I'd thought to check the population before booking, I would've learned it barely tops a thousand. There are only a handful of restaurants, and I'll probably cycle through all of them more than once while I'm here.

I didn't really need to ask Owen for a recommendation. I think, deep down, I was hoping he'd offer to come with me.

I swear, I'm not trying to charm my way into his heart… not *intentionally,* anyway. It is very clear that he is still grieving. Relationships are all about timing. And me showing up in his life like a stray firework? That's rarely the beginning of something good.

We both steal a quick glance at each other while he drives. The sunset catching his eyes and turning them a glowing chestnut under his dark lashes. We're so different, but something about him pulls me in. Maybe this is the start of a lasting friendship, something steady. Maybe he's the breath of fresh air I need when the city gets too loud. And maybe, in some quiet way, I can give that back to him too.

Doc's Sunset Grille is casual. Thankfully. Nestled right on the water, it has an easy, lived-in charm, the kind of place that doesn't care if your shoes are designer or if they are dyed with mud. The ceiling is high, showcasing polished wood beams, while an entire wall of windows faces the shore. Soft, golden light fills the space, and the sound of waves crashing against the pier drifts in whenever someone opens the door. It's the kind of atmosphere that makes my shoulders unclench, the kind of place that feels like it belongs in a Nicholas Sparks movie.

I exhale slowly. This is nice. Exactly what I was hoping for. The kind of place where two friends hang out and definitely aren't on a date.

Not that I'd mind if it *were* a date.

Owen blends right in with the rustic charm, like he

was made for it. Of course he'd bring someone here. He would bring a date here. Everyone in the town will think this is a date.

Now my thoughts are spiraling. Thank God he can't hear them.

Owen leads us to a table by the window, and we sit. I notice there are menus clipped into a large crab claw. I immediately grab one and search for the strongest fruitiest cocktail. I settle on a Seabreeze and look around for the waiter. I notice Owen staring out the window. The ocean is beautiful, sparkling under the moonlight that has taken over the sky. His posture is not one of a man reliving happy memory. He appears to be lost in something almost painful.

The hostess drops off two glasses of water before quickly moving on to a couple waiting at the podium. We both take a sip in silence. He finishes half the glass in two gulps.

"Are you alright?" I ask, even though I already know the answer. He must have come here many times before with his husband. I wonder if this is his first time returning since his death. This must be torture. How insensitive of me to even suggest going out to dinner in his small town. I'm sure every inch of it is painted with memories.

"Yes." His voice came out quiet and raspy like he hasn't spoken in days.

I attempt to keep my tone cheerful. Hoping I can make this dinner less painful for him. My mother was one of those people that became more cheerful when surrounded by grumpy people. She was always cheerful around my father. "Not a big talker, are you?"

"Not really."

I hum, scanning the dinner menu. He grabbed a menu and did the same. "Not many places to eat in Oxford. I assume you've been here before."

"Yes."

I glance up at him. "With your husband?"

Owen's grip tightens on his menu as he turns his head towards the window. He stares back out at the water, his expression unreadable, as if the answers he wants are floating somewhere just out of reach. Or his husband is watching us from a buoy. The silence stretches, thick enough to choke on. I shift in my seat, my own anxiety prickling at the edge of my hairline. I restrain myself from reaching up and twirling a finger through a curl. It's a nervous habit that I try not to do because it makes me look like a bashful schoolgirl.

The silence is killing me, and I consider canceling dinner and offering to leave.

"Sorry," Owen says suddenly. "I'm terrible company."

I pause my hand waving at the waiter.

"Everything still reminds me of him. Lucas was the best part of me," he admits, and there's a rawness to his voice that makes my chest ache.

"I understand." I put my menu down. "Perhaps if you tell me about him, it will relieve pressure from your chest. No one says you need to forget him and push down all your memories of him."

Owen blinks at me like I've just suggested we go sky-diving. "You want me to talk about my dead husband at dinner? With you?"

"I really do." I rest my chin on my hand. "How did you meet?"

Owen huffs a short, humorless laugh. "It's not very romantic. And everything sounds depressing now."

"Try. I am a huge fan of love stories." I smile, tipping my glass toward him. "I want to hear it."

For the first time since we sat down, something shifts in his expression. The ghost of a smile. A flicker of joy in his eyes. He exhales, like he's about to say something, then stops himself.

I let the silence cover the table like a blanket. This time I treat it like an aisle runner preparing for his words to stroll down.

There is a twinkle in his eyes before he starts speaking.

14
Owen

The nerdy tutor rolled his eyes before I even sat down. I didn't know his name yet, but he clearly knew mine. I was required to be there. My football scholarship was on the line after I missed the history final. It was not my fault it was the day after the big Alpha Kappa Alpha sorority party. Okay, it was my fault. I knew of the test and chose to go to the party. I was not in a good head space and was hoping to find someone to occupy my time long enough to make me forget the pain in my shoulder from last week's game. I should be fully healed by now, but a twinge of pain lingers under my muscle.

I had missed the test, was covering up an injury, and

had been assigned a tutor who reported straight to my coach. On top of that, I had to rewrite my entire history paper and agree to make up the test I'd missed.

My paper sounded like someone else's voice. To be fair, it was, and the professor could tell. I was just lucky he didn't find the woman from his last semester class who I paid to write it.

The coach convinced him to give me one more chance and not take me off the team. Assigned me a tutor to babysit me and make sure I use my own words this time. Being on the team is the only thing paying my way through college. The pain lingering in my shoulder acts as a reminder that football careers are not long. I should start taking the academic parts of college seriously. Before my body fails me.

There is a job waiting for me with my uncle's commercial construction business. If I wanted it. I just needed to make it to graduation without any major injuries because it involved physical labor. At least until I can become a licensed general contractor. We are hoping his crew wont cry nepotism when they see me rise in the ranks if I have a degree under my belt.

"You must be Owen." His voice was higher than mine but had a slight rasp as if he had been singing for hours.

"The one and only." I admit my instinct when meeting people is to lay on the charm. His facial expression remained stagnant. I rubbed the back of my neck. "And you are."

"Lucas." He tapped his pen against the table and gave me the kind of once-over that made me feel like I was about to be taken apart, piece by piece. "So," he said, "do you actually care about passing this class, or are you just here because your coach told you to be?"

I grin, leaning back in my chair. "Does it matter?"

Lucas did not grin back. "It matters to me. If you're wasting my time, I'd rather be working on my own assignments."

He was a stereotypical nerd straight out of an 80's movie. Thick rimmed tortoise shell glasses and a sweater that he probably picked up on vacation judging by the palm trees and words 'San Diego' in neon letters. This was not the first time I had noticed him. I liked him immediately. He is the teaching assistant in my history class. And if he wasn't constantly pulling my attention from the lecture my grade might be higher. So, in a way, I can blame my need to be tutored on him.

He did not know I was gay. No one did outside of my close group of friends. It wasn't shame that kept me quiet. I enjoyed the shock on their faces when they find out. I was a big black man that played football. Women would flirt with me at parties and wait for me to leave the locker room after games. All through high school I dated girls and even went on a few dates into college.

Our study sessions were a struggle. When he was passionate about a topic his mouth went crooked. The most fucking adorable thing I had laid eyes on, and I needed to capture those lips soon or I would burst.

He never seemed to notice the way I looked at him. Or maybe he just wrote me off as another clueless jock. Between the two of us, he was the real catch. Good thing I've always been good at playing the long game.

Weeks went by, and I ran into him at a party. Well, technically, I stumbled into him. It was late, I was more than a little drunk, and suddenly, there he was, wearing these sharp-looking loafers and a T-shirt tucked into jeans. I had accidentally pinned him against the wall.

My size blocked his escape. Although he didn't seem like he wanted to flee. I could have sworn his body arched into me. Like I said, I was drunk. It could have been my fantasy. He looked up at me like he was waiting for something.

I assumed he was waiting for a kiss and this was my moment.

I was too smitten and drunk to become a coward.

I decided to take the chance. Leap. Be brave. I lean into him and pause, giving him time to pull back. He does not. His cheeks flush and I swear his eyes are daring me to do it. Begging me to kiss him. Just before our noses touch. I feel my stomach churn; my body pivots and I vomit all over his shoes.

"My Jack Spade." He yells.

Gabriel sits across the table from me with his jaw slack and his drink straw paused an inch before his lips. "You vomited on a pair of Jack Spade loafers?"

"Yep, that's exactly how he said it. I stumbled home like a lovesick idiot. Days went by. When I finally showed up for our next tutoring session, he handed me this neatly typed list of 'tasks'. Things that he believed matched the value of the shoes I ruined. Total setup. It was his version of asking me out without actually asking. I knew he just wanted to see if the way I acted at the party was only booze related. Almost kissing him, not vomiting. Spoiler alert: it was real. The first time I got him alone, I kissed him. Game over. We were inseparable ever since.

After college, I got my general contractor's license. Paired that with a Business Management degree, and I was set with my uncle's company. Lucas taught middle school History, but all he really wanted to do was remodel old houses. Anyway, enough about him. Let's talk about something happy."

Gabriel tilts his head, his expression gentle. "That really is a happy story— just beautiful. I'm a little envious. It sounds like the kind of love that only happens once. I've been single so long, I'm starting to forget what butterflies feel like."

Gabriel mentioning a love that only happens once mirrors a conversation I had with Lucas last year. Except he was trying to tell me that all love is different, and I shouldn't cut myself off from the world. I should find a new love. I strongly disagreed then. Now, I am not sure what I want.

"It was happy."

Gabriel's blue eyes softened. For a moment I thought he was going to reach over the table and grab my hand. Part of me wanted him to. The idea of being comforted by a kind, gorgeous, redhead is very appealing. I tighten my lips and gaze down. Now is not the time to feel any level of desire towards Gabriel—not when I'm talking about Lucas.

I could feel his eyes on me, but I was too scared to meet them with my own.

"Correction, it *is* happy. The feeling you had, and the memories won't change. Not even with time. Whether you live in that house or move across the country. If you have a new lover or never date again. The memories will not change. What Lucas meant to you will not change. Ever. Death cannot impact that." He finally takes a sip of his drink that has been waiting patiently.

I have a small urge to hug him. It's been a long time since I talked this much about Lucas. I usually hold it in. My grief is too heavy to ask someone else to bare the weight. I never want to be the person who drags a conversation into a dark place. People tend to pull away when you do that. But Gabriel doesn't do that. He stays. He listens like it matters to him. Like he knew Lucas. Like he knows me.

I clear my throat. "You sound like you have also lost someone."

He moves food around on his plate before looking up. His deep blue eyes lock onto mine and shrugs his shoulders. "My grandparents have both passed in the past five years," He takes a bite of crab cake and plucks his next words out of the air between us. "But my mother was a grief counselor. Our family bookshelves were filled with books on death, grief, and other grim topics. I had a healthy understanding of death from a young age. Probably too young. A child should not be learning about the healthy and nonhealthy habits of grief until they are at least a teen. I was consoling my friends when their pets died like I was a counselor myself."

"I wish I was that emotionally mature when I was young. I was an idiot until-" The sentence died on my tongue. Then I remembered Gabriel did not seem to mind hearing about Lucas. I am so used not saying his name aloud. Afraid I will be a Debbie downer.

"Lucas." Gabriel finishes my sentence for me.

"Yeah." I gulp down the last of my beer and see the

waiter walking over with the bill in his hand. He places it on the table. Gabriel already had his credit card in his hand and slapped it on top before I could reach for my wallet. The waiter promptly walked away to process the payment.

"I will repay you for my half."

"Nonsense. I am staying at your place for free. I intend on helping with food. Whether it's at the house or if we eat out. That is if you want to eat out again." His cheeks pink. "Not that I am assuming you want to go out with me again. As friends. I will probably try all the restaurants at least once while I am here, and you are welcome to join me. Just dinner. Not a date."

His fingers twist around a copper curl, and I can't stop the smile tugging at my lips. He's flustered, and it's adorable. I might just lean into this a little. Lucas is egging me on like it's his full-time job. Thankfully, I don't have to worry about breaking Lucas's heart. He's the matchmaker after all.

Do I want it to be a date? Do I like him or am I just lonely? I should probably figure that out.

"I would love to show you other places in town."

"Awesome." He smiles.

"Awesome." I smile back.

After dinner, we step outside to find the street filled with people. The sidewalks are filled with locals for monthly gallery stroll. I glance at Gabe. "Do you want to walk a bit before we head back to the house?"

He nods.

We wander, peering into windows, commenting on what styles we like. Neither of us are fond of abstract unless it has mid-century-modern influence. He points out a few brass and gold frames to me so I know what would look good on the new dark green wall. He says I can either find the frame first and then find art to fill it or find pre-framed art. I let him do most of the talking, and he has seemed to get used to it. Some people think I am rude when I don't have much to say. In reality, my head is very loud. Concentrating on what someone is saying helps me focus. Allows my mind to calm. Lucas used to have that effect on me. He was a talker when he was passionate about the subject. Gabriel seems to be passionate about life in general.

I hold the door open for him as we step into a gallery. Gabriel is drawn to a painting within seconds. I watch him from across the room as he examines the soft lines. It is a house on a cliff with a lone person standing on the edge. The entire painting appears to be covered in mist and the skies are overcast. The tone is somber.

I move to stand behind him, my height allowing me to look over his head.

"It's sad." I whisper.

He speaks without turning around. "A bit, but it's a beautiful kind of sad."

"The person looks like they are thinking of jumping off."

"Or." He turns to face me. Our eyes lock with only a breath between us. "They are welcoming a new day. It feels like starting over to me. I like it."

Gabriel walks to a statue of a paper crane made of concrete. I watch him examine the piece and whisper to myself. "Starting over? Is that what this looks like?"

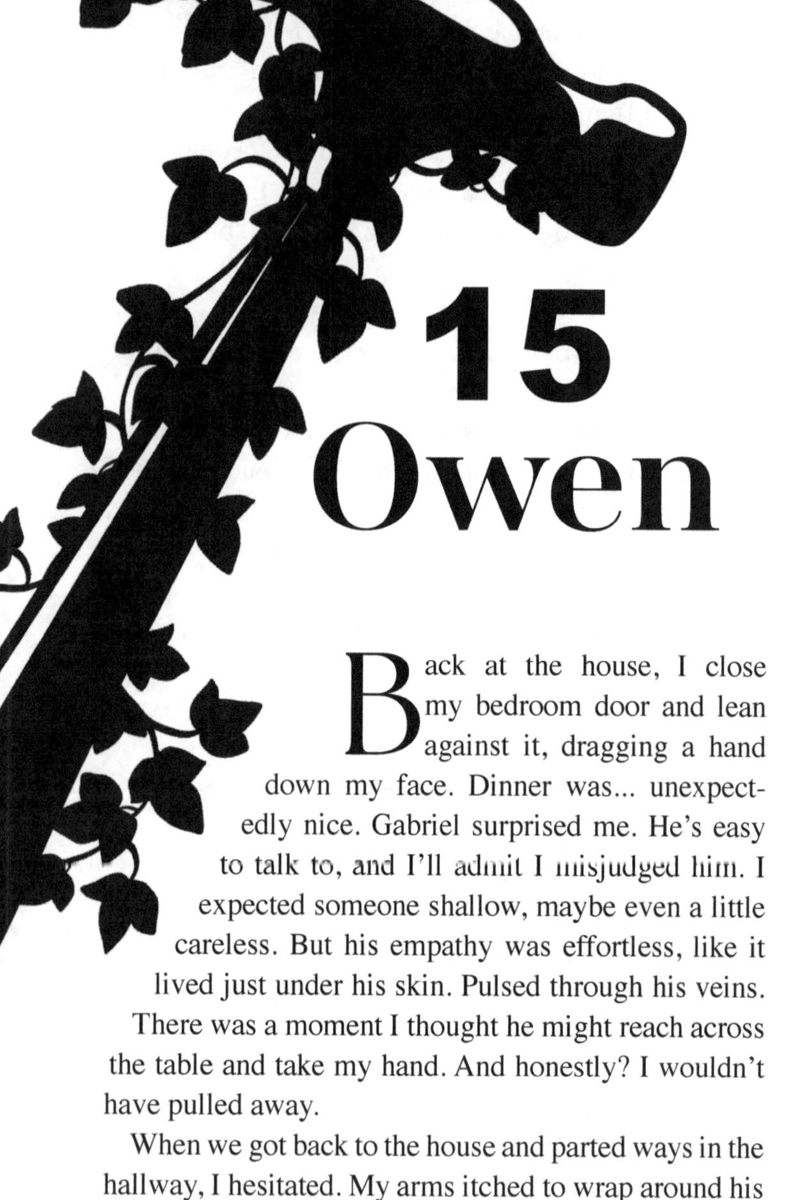

15
Owen

Back at the house, I close my bedroom door and lean against it, dragging a hand down my face. Dinner was... unexpectedly nice. Gabriel surprised me. He's easy to talk to, and I'll admit I misjudged him. I expected someone shallow, maybe even a little careless. But his empathy was effortless, like it lived just under his skin. Pulsed through his veins. There was a moment I thought he might reach across the table and take my hand. And honestly? I wouldn't have pulled away.

When we got back to the house and parted ways in the hallway, I hesitated. My arms itched to wrap around his waist, to pull him close. I haven't kissed anyone since

Lucas. For the longest time, I couldn't even picture it. But tonight... tonight something has shifted. And now, it's all I can think about.

I want to run my hands up the back of his neck and grip his red curls in my hand. Tilt his face up to mine and kiss the constant smirk on his face.

"What the fuck am I thinking? That felt like a date." I mumble into my palm.

I rip off my sweater and toss it onto the chair before heading straight to the bathroom. Gripping the edge of the sink, I examine at my reflection. My hair's a mess, my jaw tight under unkempt facial hair, my eyes slightly wide like I just woke up.

Maybe I did wake up.

This is what Lucas wanted. To open my heart again. To take a chance on myself. Lucas has said many times over the past few years that I deserve to be loved. He wants me to have a companion. A partner. Even if he had to watch me fall in love, he said he would be fine. He encouraged it.

I fought against it. I am still fighting. Fighting the urge to kiss Gabriel. To ask him on a real date.

With a groan, I grab my toothbrush and brush my teeth furiously, as if I can scrub away the longing. I bend over to spit, and when I stand up Lucas is right behind me.

I yelp, nearly swallowing toothpaste in the process.

Lucas gives me a feline grin and leans on the doorframe. Hovers actually. He would pass through the frame if he tried for real. *"Well, I haven't heard that sound from you in a long time."*

"Jesus, Lucas!" I clutch my chest, my heartbeat hammering. "My love, you can't sneak up on me."

"I am literally a ghost. I can do nothing else. It's in my nature."

I move out of the bathroom and collapse onto the bed, my face buried in a pillow. The air grows colder as Lucas moves closer, and I scent something familiar, his cologne, maybe. I know it's not real, but I breathe it in anyway.

Lucas sits beside me, or at least, hovers beside me over the bed.

I roll over onto my back and stare up at his hazel eyes that used to shine in the light. Now becoming duller with each day passing day. *"You seemed happy when you got home? What happened?"*

I consider telling him how I feel. That I enjoyed my time with Gabriel too much and wanted to kiss him. But there is this ball of guilt lodged in my chest. Putting pressure on my limbs to not touch him. A reminder that I was not divorced. I did not choose to be single again. If I had my way, I would still be married to Lucas. We would be looking for a surrogate and running our queer friendly Bed and Breakfast.

I sigh.

"Dinner was fun." I say flatly.

"Are you going to ask him out again?"

"Ask him out?" I bite my bottom lip. "You ask like it was a first date."

"Was is not?"

I sit up on the bed and lean down to take my boots off. I usually leave them by the front door, but my anxiousness had me rush up to my room. The only place I could be safe from what I really wanted to do. My boots thud to the floor. I swing my legs onto the bed and stare at

Lucas. He has moved into a cross-legged position and is hovering over the edge of the bed like a genie. Or a sleep demon. Maybe a bit of both.

"We have decided to be friends. That's the label. Nothing more. Just friends." Even though I am starting to want more. The idea is expanding in my mind every minute moving further from the dinner. I haven't felt this since I had a crush on my nerdy tutor in college.

He tilts his head like a cat watching a mouse. The movement shows curiosity, but there is almost nothing behind his fading hazel eyes. *"Are you happy?"*

The question lands hard. I exhale slowly through my nose, my fingers finding my temples like I could hold in the pressure rising in my skull. "That's a loaded question," I murmur. "I can't give you a short answer."

"Use as many words as you need. I have nothing but time." Lucas says softly.

His pause spoke volumes. He has nothing left worth sticking around. We have no marriage, I know that. I ache when I see him. I cannot answer his question. It's a confession I am not ready to say out loud. So instead, I deflect, throwing the question back towards him like a coward.

"Are you happy?"

His lips draw into a tight line. A moment passes before he shrugs, almost apologetically.

"No."

My heart caves in. The weak walls finally giving way to the conversation we have been avoiding. A collapse I won't recover from.

Of course he's not happy. He's here. Stuck between worlds, tethered to a house we were supposed to finish restoring together. Where we were going to build a life and create decades of memories. And I know it's my fault. My unwillingness to let him go or move forward, that is keeping him here. Trapped. He lingers because I can't bear the thought of life without him. Although I don't have him. I am clinging to fragments. Fighting against time. Against fate. Just to keep him close—and for what? To force him to watch me go on living without him. To make him suffer. That is not love. That is cruelty.

Even now, knowing it's costing him whatever bliss waits in the afterlife, I am selfish. I would trade everything, my breath, my soul, for one more day with him. I would challenge Heaven or Hell alike if it meant bringing him back.

I force the word past the lump in my throat. "Same"

It's barely a whisper, but he hears the pain woven in the cracks of my voice.

Lucas nods then straightens his shoulders. I expect him to comfort me but the expression on his face goes firm.

"You're alive, Owen, but you're not living. And I'm breaking. It's like dying all over again, every day. Watching you, just out of reach. We can't keep going like this. I'm not meant to stay, and you're not meant to stay stuck. You need to move on, so I can move on."

And there it is. Laid before me. Everything I didn't want to hear. My instinct is to fight it. To wallow in my denial.

"I don't want to move on."

"Bullshit." He crossed his arms over his chest. *"I see the way you and Gabriel have been looking at each oth-*

er, and that was before tonight's dinner, which was not a date. You are afraid." He put air quotes around the word "Date."

"Of course I am afraid." I grip the blanket at my sides until my knuckles pale. "The only man I have ever loved died. I thought I lost him forever. Until he returned as a ghost, and I can talk with him again. If you leave it will be like watching you die all over again. And you speak of Gabriel like he is the answer to all our problems. This is not a Disney movie. You are not cursed by a spell that can only be broken by true love's kiss. And if that was the case, YOU are my true love."

My breathing is quick and choppy. Lucas nods his head towards the door, and I remember I have a house guest. My voice is inching close to a volume that could easily travel through the walls. I fall back on the bed. My head sinking into the fluffy pillows that Lucas preferred. He moves to lay next to me, but the bed does not shift under his weight. He props his head up with a hand and frowns.

"I love you too. I always will. But you must believe people can fall in love more than once. You are thirty-five. You have so much more time on this earth." He fades a bit. Talking uses a lot of energy. *"Although it is adorable that you don't want me to leave, there must be something waiting for me. I don't know what is keeping me here, but we need to be on the same page. The best thing for us both would be for me to move on. And for you to open your heart to friendships or love. Whichever finds you."*

I let his point build pillars in my collapsed heart. They are shaky but his intention is clear. Etched in the stone like tiny promises. There is no one else who could talk me through this grief. No one could convince me to move on. If he would have died and stayed gone, I would have retreated into a dark corner never to see light again.

I sigh.

"I know you are right, but it hurts."

Lucas leans in a breath away, but I feel no movement of the air next to my ear. *"I need you to try…For me."*

Then he vanishes.

16
Lucas

The Victorian house sleeps, wrapped in the blanket of midnight. I am restless. Left to wander the grounds, never able to sleep. I stand outside, unable to feel the soil beneath me. My body mimics a scarecrow. Arms wide—untouchable to the elements. The moon hangs high above me, casting grey light over the remnants of a pumpkin patch long since abandoned. The neglected vines snake through the brittle stalks, their decay mirroring the ache in my chest.

I want to disappear. To unravel like the mist that curls along the ground and vanish into nothing. I too should be forgotten.

But I remain.

Every night, I linger.

Every night, I haunt.

I tip my head back and glare up at the moon, its cold face distant. My voice cracks when I speak.

"I was never a religious man," Murmuring into the wind. "I don't know how to start a prayer, or even what an answer would look like. But if any Gods are listening, if something beyond this hollow existence can hear me," My throat tightens, as if I still have breath. "Have I been forgotten?"

The wind shifts causing the trees to rustle around the yard.

"Why was I left here?" My voice shakes, laced with pain. "Is my spirit not worthy of the afterlife? Did I make decisions in life that chained me to this place? Please, take me. Take me from here. All I can do is haunt Owen, the man I love, like a curse."

The silence after I speak is heavier than my words themselves. No divine hand reaches for me. No light pierces the darkness. Just the same stillness, the same aching void I speak into every night.

I lift my arms up to the sky and wait for sunrise, desperate to feel warmth. Hoping, praying, that this will be the time, I will fade.

This time, I will be free.

But I know better.

Dawn will come.

And I will remain.

17
Gabriel

How have I developed a daily routine already? Less than a week in this house, in this town, and yet I feel settled. As if I've always belonged here, nestled between the quiet streets and the shore. Smiling faces everywhere. I walk to the coffee shop where I no longer have to say my order aloud. Then I find a place to sketch outside. A bench by the fisherman's dock or the single remaining bench in Owen's garden. Well, his sad excuse for a garden.

I barely miss my work. The endless emails, the back-to-back meetings, half of which should have just been emails in the first place. The deadlines, the pressure, the feeling that I was always trying to keep my place on top at the firm. In Oxford, time moves differently. I can breathe.

I missed sketching by hand. Missed the scratch of

pencil against paper, the slow emergence of a vision shaped by my own fingers instead of a screen. And I missed being outside, though I have to lather myself in enough sunscreen to become pale as a ghost. My ginger skin was not made for sunny spring days, but I'll take the sunburn if it means I get to sit here, beneath the budding branches, doing something that feels like mine again.

Days like these take me back to art school when life felt lighter, simpler. We'd sprawl out on blankets across the campus lawn, books open, the world buzzing with possibility. It felt like living in a movie. This town carries that same quiet magic, like something out of a fairytale. As if the ocean could grant wishes, or planting a seed here might grow a tree bearing fruit imbued with joy.

Everyone is so happy. Content with their small lives. And if they ever get bored they are two hours or less to a big city. It's kind of perfect.

Owen always wakes before me. When I come down the stairs, breakfast is already waiting in the kitchen. Over the past few days, I've come to see this as his quiet way of saying, "I thought of you." He doesn't linger or push for small talk. Just leaves a plate behind, like a gentle reminder that I'm welcome here. I eat slowly, savoring each bite, then pull on my coat and head outside to my favorite bench.

It's ridiculous how quickly I claimed it as mine. Like a freshman in college finding their spot in the library or the best table in the café. I settle in, pulling out my sketchbook, letting the pencil move over the page.

First, it's just to relax. I usually pick something in my view. Today it's a loose sketch of the pumpkin patch in its current state. Twisted vines, abandoned gourds that have almost been completely absorbed into the earth. Echoes of something once loved but now left to wither. But my mind shifts, imagining what it once was and what it could be.

I sketch elaborate hedges framing a central fountain. Then I erase it, trying a simpler design, just neat rows of pumpkins with space to walk between them. My pencil glides over the page, shifting the decrepit hot cocoa stand to a better position, adding hanging lights over a rock-lined seating area. It starts to take shape. Every bush placement is intentional, thoughtful. From above, the layout forms a pattern.

I try a pumpkin shape. Obvious, given the place. But after three failed attempts, I give up and instead outline something more familiar on a fresh piece of paper. Owen's Victorian house.

The thought makes my chest feel oddly warm despite the chill over my shoulder.

I'm still staring at the sketch when a voice interrupts. "You've been out here a while."

I glance up to see the neighbor approaching, a steaming cup in her hands. Her medium brown hair is in a messy bun atop her head. Somehow she makes it look chic. The light dusting of freckles on her blush cheeks are the kind women imitate with makeup. Her shirt has rows of pickle jars on it and is tucked into her high waist jeans. She offers it with an easy smile. "Thought you might like some tea. It's honeybush apricot."

"Sounds wonderful," I say, accepting the cup. The warmth seeps into my fingers, grounding me.

"I'm Adrienne."

"Gabriel." Somehow I senses she already knew my name. She settles beside me, glancing at my sketchbook.

"You're staying with Owen. That's nice. He rarely has visitors."

I chuckle softly. "Sounds like I might be his last. He didn't mean to post the vacation listing. I slipped through before he could take it down."

Adrienne hums. "Serendipity, I say. A fortunate accident."

I glance at my drawing, a small smile tugging at my lips. She is the second person to say this. It's either a hint about Owen or a sign to watch the movie. Maybe both. "Yeah. Maybe."

She tilts her head, eyes drifting toward the open sketchbook in my lap. "What are you working on?"

"Just sketching," I say, glancing down at the loose lines beginning to take shape. "It relaxes me. And I'm trying to get better at… letting myself relax." I lift the cup in my hands and take a slow sip of tea. It is Earthy, sweet and grounding. "I'm a landscape architect."

Her eyebrows rise with interest. "Well, if this is how you unwind, I should ask for your help down at the community center. We've been trying to plan a community garden. If you've got a minute this week, I would love your input."

I pause, only briefly, weighing the warmth in her voice and the thought of something small but meaningful. Then I nod. "I'd love to."

And I would.

Because for the first time in a long while, it feels like the kind of project my heart would say yes to. Not influenced by the name related to the project or the size of the bonus. Building something that benefits people who truly deserve it.

18
Owen

Adrienne's house smells like cinnamon and butter, warmth from baking wrapping around me as I step inside. I clutch the empty lasagna dish in my hands; from another dinner she made for me, to keep myself from living off of microwave meals and protein bars.

The scene unraveling before me is not what I expected.

Gabriel stands in her sunlit kitchen, laughing, his red hair catching the light like molten copper. He's glowing, radiant in a way that stops me in my tracks. For a brief, ridiculous moment, I think he looks like a fox god, if that's even a thing. Walked out of the forest to fill our lives spontaneous joy.

And then he locks eyes with me, and I melt.

The two-year-old is perched on Gabriel's hip, with one tiny hand gripping his shirt while the other helps stir a bowl filled with cinnamon-sugared apples. His voice is soft, patient, giving her small instructions. Beside him, Adrienne has flour on her cheeks, the older kids giggling around the counter as they roll out dough. Adrienne's husband passed on his darker features to the twins rolling dough. Eight-year-old boy and girl with warm olive skin and thick dark lashes, a nod to his Puerto Rican heritage. But the two-year-old clinging to Gabriel's side is all Adrienne. She's like a tiny garden fairy here to bless the spring, with the same delicate features and ethereal softness that glows off her mother.

It's chaos. It's domestic. It's intimate.

For a moment, I see the future I thought I'd get to build next door, before everything changed.

And I don't know how to feel about any of it.

I enter the kitchen like I have many times before. Feeling comfortable, even with the noise.

"Oh, hi, Owen," Adrienne says, beaming at me like I haven't just walked into an alternate universe.

I swallow hard. "What is going on here?"

Gabriel gives me a small smile, his eyes shimmering like sunlight on water. How have I never noticed that before? I thought he was adorable from the moment I saw him, too attractive, actually. I resented Lucas for inviting him into my home. A single, nerdy, sexy redhead who somehow appears to belong here. This is his home, his neighbor, and somehow I became the visitor.

And now he's here, in Adrienne's kitchen, slipping into my life like he was always meant to be.

"I met Gabriel earlier and we just hit it off," Adrienne

says, nudging him playfully with her shoulder. "He likes to bake, and my kids have been begging me for apple pie. So here we are."

I should say something. I should stop standing here like an idiot, gripping this dish like it's my last tether to sanity. Instead, I slam it onto the counter harder than I mean to. The room goes quiet. I frantically check the bottom to make sure I didn't crack it and then shrug in embarrassment. I feel like a giant in her small kitchen. Surrounded by Keebler Elves.

"Wanna bake with us?" Adrienne asks, her voice light, but her eyes sensing the panic building in me. Her eyes flick to Gabriel then she raises her eyebrows in a suggestive manor.

"No." The word comes out too fast. Too sharp. I went back toward the doorway. "I have a lot to do today. I'm determined to knock off a few big things from my to-do list. Starting with the overgrown brush in the backyard. Bye."

Then I bolt. No grace. No dignity. Just a man fleeing a kitchen like it's haunted. Which is ironic, considering my actual ghost is waiting for me.

Lucas appears the moment I step into the shed.

"What is going on?" His voice is calm, but I can hear the amusement under it.

"Nothing." I don't look at him as I grab gardening gloves, shears, a small saw, and a rake.

"Uh-huh." He drifts through the wall and back again, watching me too closely.

I try to push past him, but he blocks the door, not that it matters. I could walk right through him if I wanted to. But I don't. I let him stop me.

"Does your mood have to do with the handsome

houseguest and the date you went on a couple nights ago?" His tone is teasing, but there's an edge to it. *"Not to mention, he's currently cozy with your best friend and her kids."*

I shake my head slowly, staring at my feet. "It's wrong."

"Why?"

I grip the handle of the shovel too tight. "Because you should be the one close to Adrienne. You should be the one picking paint colors with me. I should be taking you to dinner."

Lucas sighs. *"Owen, I was never great with kids. That was the thing we argued about most. Plus, Gabriel has a design background. I'd trust him to pick paint colors over you, love."*

I let out a dry laugh. "Thanks for that." I huff, running a hand through my hair.

"As for dinners, no amount of dinners, adventures, or kisses could take away what we had." Lucas lifts a hand toward my cheek, and for a second, I believe I'll feel it. The warmth of him. The weight of his touch.

But all I get is a chill.

He smiles, sad and soft.

"Have. What we have." I correct.

"No, Owen." His voice is gentle, but firm. *"What we had. You need to let me go so I can move on. I won't be here forever. I can't be."*

My throat is tight. "You assume I'm keeping you here. Maybe you're not ready to move on either."

"I am ready." Lucas frowns daggers into my chest. I have suspected he was ready to go for a while. Last night's conversation solidified my guess. No one wants to be left by the one they love. A wave of giggles float

from Adrienne's house. Followed by high pitched voices cheering on Gabriel. I stare at the wall of the shed trying to imagine the happy scene unfolding inside her house. When I look back at Lucas he is watching me with a flat expression. He forces a smile, and I wonder if he is only saying what he thinks I need to hear and does not believe it himself.

I shake my head, stepping through him without another word. Without looking back.

And then I start my yard work.

Because if I stop moving, if I stop doing, I might start to think.

And my thoughts are heavy enough to bury me.

19
Gabriel

Back at Owen's house I attempt forced relaxation. Pie warms my stomach, and a mug of tea steams beside me on a delicate, timeworn side table. I should feel at ease, but there's a hum beneath my skin. My fingers itch for movement, for purpose. I have never been good at sitting still.

I stare at my phone like it's judging me, thumb hovering over the call button. I'm supposed to be on vacation. Supposed to be relaxing. Recharging. Letting go. Instead, I cave, pressing the button and lifting the phone to my ear like an addict hiding a quick fix.

I glance around the room, half expecting Carlton to pop out and catch me in the act. The whole thing feels like a teenager sneaking to call their crush after curfew. Shameful and desperate.

Jeremy picks up after two rings. "Well, this is a surprise." I can hear him typing in the background, voices murmuring somewhere behind him. "Aren't you supposed to be off the grid or whatever?"

I sigh, dragging my hand down my face. "This is just a call between friends. It's not like I'm checking my email or logging into project files."

The typing halts. "Friends hang out. friends talk outside work. We have never done either. What do you need Gabe?"

I feel a tug of absurdity. Two weeks. I couldn't make it two weeks before calling the most annoying person in my office for an update. Jeremy was the only one I knew would pick up. I knew he would give me an update without telling Carlton. Because although we work together, he is very competitive and wants Carlton to think he is the most hard-working person in the firm.

"Gabriel." Jeremy is always shortening my name. I hate it. Gabe has bitcoin and a fantasy football team. Gabriel spends time in art museums and updates his wardrobe with the trends from NY Fashion week. I am not a Gabe. "I had a feeling in my gut that I should check in."

Jeremy lets out a dry laugh. "Yeah, perfect timing. We might be circling back to the Kent Golf Course project. Remember that one? Turns out part of the site's protected wetland. They 'forgot' to mention that when we started. Now we're trying to smooth things over with wildlife preservation. We gotta find a solution fast. Kent doesn't the want to postpone the groundbreaking."

I groan. "You're kidding."

"Wish I was. The state is literally voting on whether

the land can even be developed. Carlton is furious. We wasted months working on the Master Plan just to be back at the beginning."

I can feel the pull of the office. The weight of unfinished work, the urgency of a problem that I know I could fix. I was waiting for the Turatello project to start, but if Carlton is scrambling to salvage Kent, I wouldn't be surprised if he calls me back to the office early.

I should be stressed. I should be packing urgently to return.

But as I glance around the cozy living room, the soft afternoon light filtering through lace curtains, the warmth of old wood, the scent of cinnamon still lingering from earlier. I realize something.

Maybe I don't want to go back.

Maybe I don't need to go back.

Oxford, Maryland, with its slow mornings and quiet streets, is starting to feel… nice. Comforting. Like a place where I could build a life. I could go freelance, work from a home office, take on projects I actually care about instead of being stuck in Carlton's never-ending projects for wealthy people and corporations. The kind of clients that would destroy a nature preserve.

I could find an apartment nearby.

I could ask Owen on a real date.

The thought slams into me like a freight train.

Date? What am I even thinking?

Owen is not only way out of my league but also grieving his husband. It would be wildly creepy if I just moved to his town after staying at his house and ogling his muscles every morning over coffee for days.

God, I'm an idiot.

"Hey, you still there?" Jeremy's voice pulls me back.

"Yeah. Yeah, I'm here." I hesitate, then sigh. "Tell Carlton he can contact me if he needs help. And for the love of all things holy, please unlock my email."

Jeremy laughs. "You're impossible. I'll see what I can do."

We say goodbyes, and I hang up, letting my phone slip from my fingers. Then I curl up on the couch, pulling my sketchpad onto my lap.

The Kent project is not what I focus on.

A dozen ideas for the pumpkin patch flood the pages; layouts, structures, pathways winding through imagined rows of orange. I picture Owen in a flannel plaid shirt greeting children from the town as they search for a pumpkin. I see myself dropping mini marshmallows into mugs of hot cocoa in a fabulous concession stand. Made to look like a gingerbread house.

I stare at them, tracing the lines, feeling something settle inside me.

Maybe it's not just the town that's comforting.

Maybe it's one person in this town and the possibility I envision.

After all, this fantasy is not as alluring without Owen's beaming smile.

20
Owen

Early morning light creeps through the single round window in my bathroom the razor glides over my jaw, scraping away weeks, months of neglect. I watch the transformation in the mirror, the sharp angles of my face reemerging, the weight of grief peeling away with each stroke. For the first time in too long, I recognize myself. I wipe the stray shaving cream from my chin and glance over my shoulder.

"Lucas?"

Silence.

I turn a full circle in the bathroom, heart pounding. "Lucas?"

Nothing.

I swallow hard, my fingers tightening on the handle of my razor. He usually comes when I call. Even when

I don't call, he lingers. Haunting me like a thought. But maybe…maybe, he's gone. A pit opens in my stomach, regret curling in my chest. Was yesterday in the shed the last time I would get to speak to him? Did I push him away for good? I should feel relieved. It's what he wanted. What he says I need. But all I feel is hollow. Like a novel with the last chapter torn out. This can't be the end. He said he wanted to give me space. That's what this is. Lucas is giving me space. I collect my breath and clean up the sink.

The scent of coffee greets me as I make my way down. That's new. When I step into the kitchen, the sight before me nearly makes me stumble.

Gabriel, standing at the oven, pulling out a golden batch of apple turnovers. My red plaid apron tied snugly around his waist, the bow in the back making him look like a perfectly wrapped present. He must have sensed me standing in the doorway because he spoke before turning to face me.

"Adrienne had extra filling," he says cheerful as usual, carefully setting the baking sheet on the stovetop. "I saw you had all the ingredients, so I thought, why not?"

I blink at him. At the apron moving with him like a blur. I gawk at the morning light catching in his red hair.

"I hope you don't mind." He says with his back to me.

Not at all. I clear my throat. "Not at all."

He turns with a grin and hands me a cup of coffee. Black with one spoonful of sugar. Just the way I like it. I hesitate before taking it. How does he know how I take my coffee? Has he been paying attention to what I like? Has he been trying to figure me out just as I have been him.

"Your face." He shrieks.

I rub my soft skin. "Yea. I shaved."

His eyes widen like he's discovered I'm a different species. I rub my jaw, still getting used to the smoothness. It's like a spotlight is on me and I cannot hide. Completely exposed to his blue eyes scanning me.

"Wow jawline. I mean I knew you had a jawline under your beard. It was a short beard. I could tell the shape of your face. It's just nice to see." He takes a sip from his mug. "You look good. That's what I am saying." He takes a desperate gulp of his coffee.

I bite back a grin. The compliment fumbles out of his mouth. Relief settles over me. Part of me was worried he was not attracted to me. Large black men are not everyone type.

I chuckle. "Thanks. You look good too."

"I haven't changed anything."

"Still," I say, shrugging as I enjoy the slight squirm he does as my eyes narrow on him. "I can still say you look good."

His lips part. I wink. I fucking wink. A gesture so unlike me but I could not help myself. He stares at me over the rim of his mug, but I can tell he is hiding a smile. The air shifts with something unspoken between us. I look away before I make it any weirder.

"Thanks." He says quietly.

I grab a plate from the drying rack and stand close enough for our arms to touch, but I reach behind him. The apple turnover is still hot as I lift it onto the plate. He has not moved from where he stands. Heat from the oven warming his back. I smile down at him. "You don't have anything that needs changing."

With a wink I take my plate and leave the kitchen. Grateful when he joins me.

He sits across from me at the dining table, already digging into a turnover. The pastry flakes against his lips, one stubborn piece clinging to the corner of his mouth.

I motion to the spot. He licks it away, tongue darting out in a quick flick. Heat surges through me. I shift in my seat, looking away. Everything he does is adorable and sexy. I am as cooked as these turnovers. Delicious perfectly backed turnovers. They might be the first thing baked from scratch in that oven in years.

Gabriel is distracted this morning, tapping away at his phone between bites. Work, probably. He has mentioned a few times that he has a huge project coming up. The entire point of his stay here is to go into the new project with a clear mind. He needs a distraction, and I have full intention to make myself just that.

"I'm driving to Easton today," I say. "They have a few antique stores I want to check out."

He nods absently, still scrolling.

I clear my throat. "I want you to come with me."

His fingers still. His blue eyes lift to mine, wide and surprised. His cheeks flush.

I frown. Why does he look so caught off guard? My attraction to him should be obvious by now. It's radiating off me, burning hot under my skin. Even Lucas saw it. He should not be shocked.

He nods. "That sounds like fun."

The day passes in a comfortable rhythm. We wander

through antique shops, picking through trinkets and old art. Gabriel helps me choose a set of gold frames. Some empty, some filled with paintings of Maryland's coastline, or fishing boats bobbing in harbor scenes. We have become a montage of laughter and sharing nostalgic references from our childhoods.

We had very different upbringings. He was raised in a house with support and encouragement. In a quaint town outside Boston, called Braintree. I remember because I made him repeat the name for me three times. Braintree, what an odd name for a town.

I however was adopted by a Mormon family in Salt Lake City, Utah. All four of my siblings were adopted. My parents wanted a big family. For a while in my youth, I expected to have a new sibling every few years. Like collecting limited edition action figures. They wanted one of every shade. I became the token black kid in my home and my school. When I had the opportunity for a football scholarship my father was appalled that I picked Illinois State University over Brigham Young University. I needed to distance myself from Utah. From their religion. There was a hidden side of me that I needed to explore. Find where I fit in.

The idea of starting a family with Lucas once meant everything to me. It was more my dream than his, and I buried it when I lost him. Or so I thought. But this past week stirred something I didn't expect. It's not that I'm planning to marry Gabriel or raise kids together, but for the first time in a long while, the future doesn't feel like a closed door. Maybe, once he's gone, I'll even consider downloading a dating app.

I watch him sort through a stack of mismatched Pyrex lids; his brow knit in focused determination. He's mentioned in every antique store we've visited that he's hunting for a medium round lid to fit a dish he has back in D.C. When he comes up empty again, he lets out an exaggerated pout, like the universe is keeping them apart on purpose.

I consider for a split-second nipping at his bottom lip. His lip taunts me in a way I haven't felt in a long time. A deep longing grows in my gut. Maybe I'm getting ahead of myself, but I don't want this to be where it ends. I hope—no, I want—him to want more. To want me, even after his vacation ends. When he goes back to his world, a part of me stays with him. The impact he has made in just a few days has changed me. And I mean more than motivating me to shave. I have looked forward to waking up since he arrived. A small thing that felt like a struggle the past three years.

Maybe I am jumping the gun, but I hope this is not the end. I hope he wants to see me after his vacation ends.

We walk into another antique store. This one has a rainbow flag in the window and Chappell Roan playing over the speakers. We both look at each other and smile. An unspoken gay understanding that this is the best shop yet.

He's particularly taken with a pair of robin's egg blue lamps, running his fingers over the tassel shades like he has found treasure. They aren't my taste, but he's thrilled. Gabriel explains how small his apartment is and that he has no space for them, but claims they had a vibe that spoke to him. That's all the convincing I need. I tell the shop owner to wrap them up.

"You are really buying them?" He beams.

I hand my card to the person behind the counter. "I am buying them for my house. We can discuss visitation rights later."

And I wink. Like a fucking creep. I cannot help it around him. Making him blush has become the highlight of my day. When he bites his bottom lip, it sends a jolt straight through me. He must know what he is doing to me. I have never been great at hiding my emotions on my face. I've been fighting the urge to press my face into the curve of his neck all afternoon, to inhale him like a secret. Whatever cologne he's wearing should be outlawed. It's dangerous. I want it to be on me. Transferred the only way that matters. Skin to skin.

The shop worker walks around the counter with a large box. They wrapped the lamps in brown paper. I take the box and leave the store. My view slightly obstructed by the tops of the lamps pocking out of the paper. Gabriel notices my struggle to maneuver.

"I will guide you back to the truck, so you don't run into anyone." He hooks his arm in mine. We walk two blocks to where I parked. When we arrive at my truck, Gabriel unhooks himself from my body. My arm suddenly feels empty. I stand awkwardly next to my truck. Worried how the next few minutes will play out.

"Ummm." I say.

He raises one eyebrow. "What's wrong?"

"My keys are in my pocket." I shift showing how I cannot hold the box with one hand.

"Oh. No big deal." He takes a quick step behind me, and I interrupt.

"The front pocket." I heard the coy tone in my voice and hope it wasn't too playful. This was not planned. I am not that smooth.

He pauses with his hand hovering over my lower back about to slide into my pocket. The moment lasts a lifetime. Both of us mapping out what this means in our heads. He will have to slide his hand into my front pocket. Pockets that are deep enough for a large phone to hide. My keys are currently tucked behind my phone in my right front pocket.

Gabriel takes a sidestep to be next to me. I look down at him. My lips are in a firm line. I am afraid to smile. It would be too creepy if he knew how much I was going to enjoy this. So much so that I am mentally telling my cock to behave. Now is not the time to get a hard on.

Could I put the box on the sidewalk? Yes. Do I suspect Gabriel knows that? Also, yes. Neither of us are suggesting it. This is a dance that I am hoping he will enjoy as much as me.

"That's no big deal either." He looks down. I cannot see his hand over the box. Moments later I feel the tips of his fingers sliding into the pocket. He goes over the phone first and does not feel the keys. Rather than remove his hand, he wiggles under my phone until I hear a jingle. His hand grasps the keys just in time for my dick to twitch as he pulls his hand. We stare at each other. A goofy smile painted on my face. His cheeks flushed all the way to his ears.

My truck beeps twice before he opens the door to the back seat. I set the box inside. Gabriel jumps into the cab, but I stop the door with my palm and don't allow him to shut it. He looks up at me with wide eyes. I lean in.

"Where do you think you are going?"

"Back home. I mean back to the house. Your house."

Gabriel looks like he's on the verge of overheating. I should get him water and food. Move him out of the sun.

The door swings open and he hops out, the height of my trucking making his 5'8" frame look even smaller next to my 6'4" build. He lands with a soft thud on the sidewalk and pauses, waiting until we're side by side before moving. There's a part of me that half hopes he'll grab my arm again. Holding that box was the perfect excuse for him to touch me, and I didn't realize how much I missed that kind of contact until he let go.

Apparently, I'm more starved for touch than I thought. I used to swear my love language was Quality Time. Now? I'm reconsidering. With Gabriel this close to me I am leaning more towards Physical Touch. Being touched by Gabriel feels like a shot of caffeine. It energizes something within that has been dormant.

We stop for a late lunch at a quiet restaurant, steam curling off our soup as we eat. He is still working on the soup when I have moved onto the bread bowl.

Gabriel keeps checking his phone, thumb twitching like he's waiting for a message that matters more than this moment. I tell myself it's just work. He's got deadlines and clients and a whole life outside this little bubble. But deep down, I can't help wondering if he's already tuning out. If I'm losing him before I ever really have him. Because I want to have him. In many ways.

As we walk back to my truck, I make a split-second decision.

I reach for his hand.

He lets out a soft, startled sound. "Oh."

I glance at him. "Oh?"

His lips curl into a slow grin, blue eyes bright under the afternoon sun. "We're holding hands." There's a warmth in his voice laced with a hint of amusement.

"It appears so." I keep my tone flat, as if my pulse isn't thrumming wildly beneath my skin. As if I'm not freaking out inside.

I've only been openly affectionate with one man in public before. And I married him.

This is a new territory.

I'm putting myself out there. Offering a piece of myself for Gabriel to either accept or destroy.

And as I look at him, at his freckled cheeks glowing pink, I realize something terrifying.

He could destroy me.

"Is that okay?" I ask.

He answers with a simple squeeze of my hand.

We walk the last block in silence, fingers locked, hearts racing faster than our steps.

21
Gabriel

I should have kissed him. The thought loops in my head as I lay in bed, staring at the ceiling. My hand still tingles from holding his, my palm burning with the memory of his touch. I could've sworn Owen wanted me to kiss him. His gaze dipped to my mouth, lingering there like he was weighing the risk. He even squeezed my hand a little tighter before letting go. As if he didn't want to. But after dinner, he kept himself busy, darting around the house like idle hands were a problem he was trying to avoid. I stayed out of his way.

He replaced a broken light switch. Tightened a loose doorknob. Halfway through patching a golf ball-sized hole in the wall, he stopped glancing at me altogether. Like I was invisible.

It was hard not to take it personally, but something

changed during dinner. His eyes barely met mine, flickering around the room like he was waiting for something or someone to interrupt us.

It stung.

I reminded myself of what my mother always said, "grief takes many forms and has no expiration date." Maybe it was all too much. The antique shopping, the lunch, the hand holding. Maybe he wasn't ready.

Maybe I'm not either. I can feel anxiety forming with the thoughts of something new. This time away from my job has made me question what I want for my life. Where I want to be in five years. And if the city is the right place for me. And if I want to be eating ice cream out of the tub while I watch TV alone after a long day.

Still, when I reached into his pocket for his truck keys, my fingers grazing the warmth of his thigh, the urge to push him against his truck had nearly consumed me. The image made my lips twitch upwards. It would be like a hyena pouncing on a lion.

I rinsed my teacup, whispered a quiet goodnight, and disappeared into my room. Sleep found me quickly, but not before I drifted through thoughts of him, and all the ways today could have ended differently.

The next morning, I find a note pinned to my drawing bench, right where I drank my coffee yesterday morning. Adrienne's number and a few drops of what

I assume was coffee, along with an invite on the paper: **Meet me at the future Oxford Community Art Center – 11:30 AM.**

Curiosity replaces what remained of my sleepy haze. I finish my coffee, showered, and dressed. Anticipation creeping in with each step. I like Adrienne. She treats everyone like an instant friend. The type of person who would give you the shirt off their back or stay up and bake cookies while watching Gilmore Girls.

I linger in my car, the engine idling, as I triple-check the address.

In front of me stands an old bank building, proud and unmoving as the town has evolved around it. It's brick façade weathered by time but still stands stubborn with dignity. The red bricks, faded in a few places, hold stories in their cracks. Above the entrance, a grand white stone arch frames an imposing wood door, it's keystone stamped with Est. 1871, like a badge of honor. For a building that has seen more than a century of change, it's remarkable well preserved.

Half of the parking lot has been torn up, replaced with fresh dirt. I assume that is why I am here. When I tell people of my job they often ask me what plants to buy for their garden. Yes I can make great suggestions, but my expertise is in design, not horticulture. A small garden sounds cute to work on, but my heart is leaping at the idea Adrienne could want my help with the building also.

Before I can overthink it, Adrienne emerges, clipboard in hand, her smile bright and full of energy as she hurries toward me.

"Just on time." She said. "I knew you were the punctual type."

"This building is incredible." We start to walk together up the cracked path. Dandelions rising up from the spaces in the concrete.

"Isn't it? Some residents wanted to have it removed from the historic registry because it sat empty for many years. They wanted to put in some fast-food place. A group of us from the PTA came up with an offer to the city. Let us find a new use for the building. They gave us one year to raise funds and get grants. And voila! I present the home of the OCAC. Oxford Community Arts Center. I picked up the keys just last week." She grabbed the brass door handle and struggled to pull. The heavy door creaked as it slid open. I stepped in first while she held the door.

Inside, the space was filthy, but still stunning. Parquet floors hidden under a layer of dust. Art Deco light fixtures tangled in webs. One side is still lined with teller booths, their wooden dividers intricate and detailed, a relic of another time. At the back of the room, a massive vault door hangs open, revealing rows of copper safe deposit boxes inside.

Adrienne moves through the space with a bounce in her step, her excitement infectious as she explains her vision.

A community garden outside. Inside, space for art classes and a gallery to highlight local kids' work.

"I want it to be something special," she says. "Something that puts this town on the map. Draws people in from the neighboring areas. We're small, but we have talent. We just need a place to show it. And the benefits for the kids are endless. We could have after school programs. Maybe even bring in a pottery teacher."

"You could put a kiln and vent out the wall." I add pointing to the back corner.

"Yes." She scribbles on her clipboard. "I love it."

I spin in a full circle. Inhaling more dust than I should but in complete awe with the space. She's right. It's bursting with potential. My background is not is renovation, but I will enjoy the short week I have to work on this project with her. Who knows, maybe I will come back to visit for their first gallery opening.

I eagerly agree to draw up some concept plans. A few options she can present to the city for permits and final approval. Because most of the funds come from a state grant, the city gets the last word. She was thrilled with my quick sketches that she threw her arms around me and squeezed.

"This is just ten minutes." I say through strained breath. She pushes off and squeals. Actually squeals. "Give me a couple days. I will have something more. Do you know of any art supply stores nearby?"

"There's a Michaels in Easton. It's about a fifteen-minute drive."

"Perfect." I tuck my sketch pad in my messenger bag. I leave invigorated, my mind buzzing with ideas. I head towards Easton making a list in my head. I need colored pencils, a drawing compass, and some stencils. Items I left at my apartment because I was not supposed to be working. This project, however, does not feel like work.

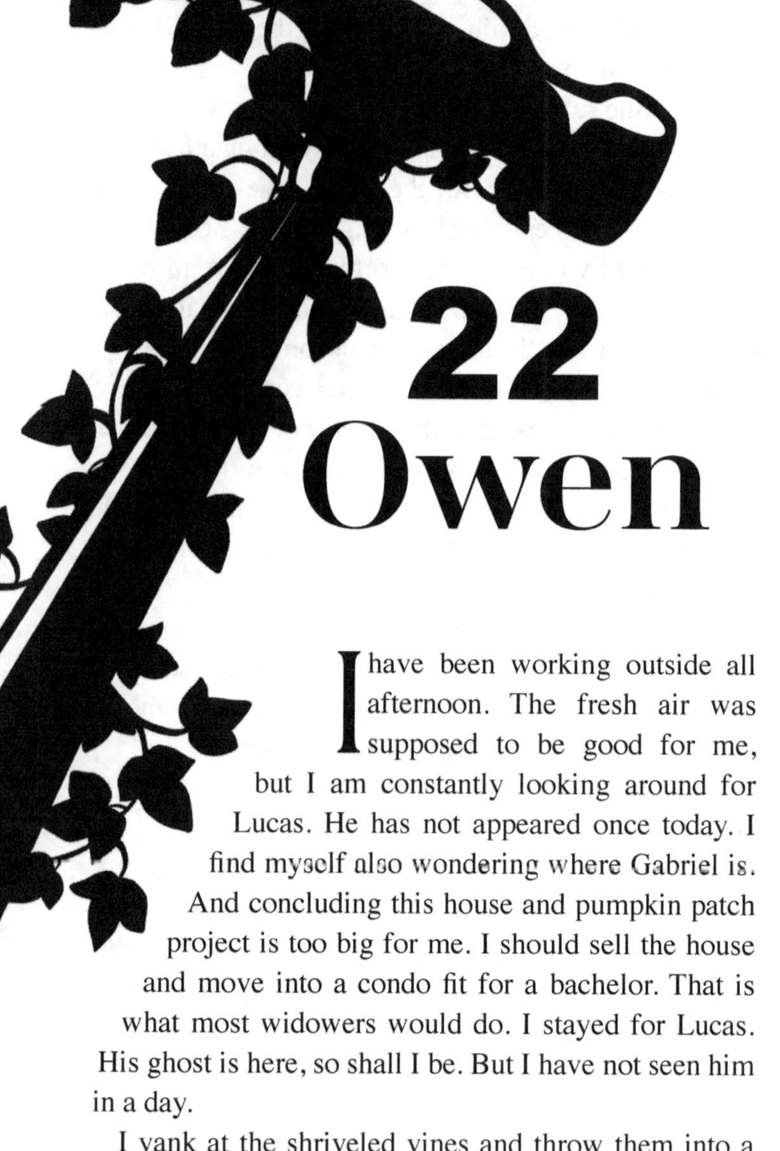

22
Owen

I have been working outside all afternoon. The fresh air was supposed to be good for me, but I am constantly looking around for Lucas. He has not appeared once today. I find myself also wondering where Gabriel is. And concluding this house and pumpkin patch project is too big for me. I should sell the house and move into a condo fit for a bachelor. That is what most widowers would do. I stayed for Lucas. His ghost is here, so shall I be. But I have not seen him in a day.

I yank at the shriveled vines and throw them into a pile, my breath coming in sharp bursts. My chest is tight. Too tight. I should slow down. I should take a break, maybe drink some water. But I can't.

Gabriel is in my head, filling the spaces that belonged

to Lucas. It's wrong, isn't it? But Lucas wanted this. He told me to move on. So why isn't he here? Why has he left me?

I yank at a stubborn root, my fingers digging deep into the soil, searching for something to hold on to. The seams of my shirt strain with the effort, my muscles burning as I pull with everything I have. I drop to my knees, the damp earth soaking through my jeans. My breath hitches, and before I realize what's happening, tears streak down my face.

"Lucas," I whisper. My voice is raw. "Where are you?"

Nothing. Not a chill. Not a flicker of his image. Not the faintest whisper in the wind.

He's gone.

Panic spreads through me like a contagion. I shouldn't have been so affectionate with Gabriel. Shouldn't have grabbed his hand. Shouldn't have let myself wonder what his skin would feel like under my hands. What he would taste like against my tongue. My body aches for Gabriel, but my heart rests in an urn filled with ashes.

I claw at the oversized root, my hands trembling. My breath coming too fast. Too shallow. My fingers scrape against the rough bark as I wrench it free, the force sending me sprawling onto my back. My hands burn where the root tore against them. My chest heaves, and the sky above me swirls, dark at the edges. I notice most of the root remains and I have only ripped off the top.

I stumble to my feet, my legs weak beneath me, and stomp toward the shed. The door slams against the wall as I grab a shovel, my grip white-knuckled around the handle. Back at the root, I stab the blade into the ground with everything I have, again and again. My gasps turn to ragged sobs. My vision tunnels. I can't breathe. I can't think.

The root has to go.

I can't plant anything new here until it's gone.

I thrust the shovel into the dirt, over and over, until it's nothing but splinters and mulch. My hands shake as I toss the shovel aside and dig with my fingers, scraping away the remains. Tears drip onto the soil. My breath shatters against the weight in my chest. I dig with my bare hands. Sharp chunks scrape my palms, reminding me I did not put on gloves.

But I do not slow down.

I can't stop.

I dig faster. Tears seeping into the earth.

Someone calls my name.

I can't breathe.

I can't-

The world narrows to a single point. I fall to my elbows and roll onto my back. The sky faded into view. A face comes into view. Red hair and freckles.

23
Gabriel

I park on the side of Owen's house, clutching my messenger bag to my chest. Excitement hums beneath my skin as I think about all the ideas I have for the community center project. I can't wait to run them by Owen. He may not have an interest in design, but he listens to me, even when I ramble.

As I approach the porch, something stops me. A cold friction in the air blocking me from climbing the steps. Goosebumps raise on the back of my neck. A sound floats on the wind.

Soft crying paired with ragged, heavy breathing.

I freeze, my fingers tightening around the strap of my bag. The sound isn't coming from inside the house. It's coming from the side of the house. I move cautiously, stepping off the porch and make my way toward the side yard. Nervous with what I might be walking into.

That's when I see him.

Owen.

He is on his knees, frantically digging into the earth with his bare hands. Clearly lost in a maze within his own mind. He does not shift at my approach. He continues to dig and scratch into the earth. Dirt clings to his dark skin, streaks of it have smeared across his face where he wiped at tears. Tears that continue to waterfall down his cheeks. His shoulders shake with every gasping breath.

His face is tight with pain, but he does not let it slow him down. Owen is drowning in a storm raging within.

I hesitate. Should I interrupt? This battle is personal, and I've known him for a week.

A part of me thinks I should get Adrienne; she knows him better. She might know how to pull him out. But what if that makes it worse? What if calling her exposes his struggles that he has tried so hard to bury?

My feet move in two slow hesitant steps. He is sinking with a ship, and I am watching from the shore. Perhaps I can help. Perhaps I can help gather the wreckage.

Then I notice the blood. His fingertips are raw, the skin torn from the vigorous digging.

Shit.

I step forward. "Owen."

He doesn't respond. His fingers keep clawing at the ground, but the movement is weaker now. His arms tremble before he suddenly collapses onto his elbows, rolling onto the damp grass.

I run to him, dropping my bag. His arms lay limp at his sides, his chest rising and falling too fast. Tears have carved clean paths through the dirt on his face.

"Oh, Owen." I lift one of his hands, turning it over to

see the damage. His skin is so dirty I can't tell how bad the wounds are. He doesn't look at me. His eyes are lost in the sky, like he's not here at all.

I press my palm to his chest, feeling the frantic flutter of his heartbeat.

"Do you need a hospital?"

He shakes his head slowly. My gut is telling me it's not a heart attack. This is years of emotion coming out in the form of a panic attack. I hope my presence has not added to his stress. I want nothing more than this wonderful man to be happy.

"Owen, can I take you inside? We gotta get your hands cleaned." I say gently, "You don't have to talk to me. Just let me take care of you."

He sucks in a jagged breath, his gaze finally meeting mine. His brows knit together as if he's trying to place me, like he isn't sure if I'm real or if I'm a figment of his imagination.

I start to pull my hand away, but he stops me. His fingers cover mine. No words, no warmth in his expression, but the touch is enough.

"Okay," I say exhaling a quiet breathe. I sit back on my heels. "I can't lift you, so I need your help."

He moves like a puppet, his body responding but his mind distant. When I hook an arm around his lower back, he leans into me. Not completely, but enough that I can tell he needs me here.

We move together, step by step, up the porch. The front door swings open into the house, and I lead him inside. His breathing has slowed, but he still look hollow.

The kitchen sink won't be enough to clean him. I need to get him into the shower.

I guide him up the stairs, into his room. One side of his bed is perfectly made, the other flipped open like an envelope, the sheets still wrinkled from sleep. It feels too intimate, stepping into this space, but I don't stop. He needs me.

At the master bathroom, I finally let go of him. He remains in the doorway, dirt crumbling from his clothes onto the tile floor.

I grab a wooden chair from the bedroom and set it down. "Can you sit and take your shoes off?"

He nods. Slow. Deliberate. He unlaces his boots with stiff fingers, then peels off his socks. I walk to the shower and turn on the water, waiting for it to warm. When I glance back, he's watching me. Silent. Expressionless.

I approach him like he is a timid animal. He says nothing. I step closer, stopping inches from his knees.

"Put your hand up like this." I signal a flat palm. Recalling a technique my mother uses with nonverbal children in grief counseling. "If you don't want my help, okay? I will stop and leave you alone."

He nods.

I reach for his wrists and pull him to stand. I have to step back, he's massive, still built like the football player he used to be. When I grip the hem of his sweater and lift, he instinctively raises his arms, like a child waiting to be dressed.

"Um, I can't reach over your head." I expect him to smirk, maybe tease me. But there's nothing.

He sits back down, arms still lifted, waiting for me. I pull the sweater over his head, the fabric heavy with sweat and dirt. When he stands again, he doesn't move to undress further.

I gulp.

This isn't how I imagined removing his clothes for the first time.

I unbutton his jeans, sliding the zipper down. He doesn't stop me. His jeans are loose enough that they slide easily over his hips. He steps out of them, one leg at a time. I look around the room and try not to stare at the beautiful broken man standing in his underwear before me. The room has filled up with steam coating the mirror.

I turn, searching for a fan. "Is there a-"

Before I can finish, Owen takes three slow steps toward me. My back hits the counter. He looms over me, his presence suffocating. My heart hammers. This is it. I've crossed a line. He's going to shove me away, tell me to get out.

Instead, he reaches past me and flicks a hidden switch behind the hand towel. The fan hums to life. His arm brushes mine as he pulls back, his fingers gliding down my skin. A shiver runs up my spine.

I wrap my fingers around his wrist and gently guide him toward the shower. He steps in, still wearing his boxer briefs. If that's what makes him feel safe, I'm not about to change it. He's grieving, and I keep hearing my mother's voice in my head: "Be kind. Be patient. People need compassion when they're hurting." All those morbid books about death she kept around the house, turns out they were training me for moments like this. To be exactly what Owen needs.

The water starts washing away the dirt, peeling back the layers. He tilts his head back, letting the spray soak his tight curls. Never before has a symbol of such strength looked so vulnerable. Like the water could carve him away. I want to help him. I want to know him. Most of all, in this moment I don't want to be anywhere else.

The glass shower door softly closes behind me. At my feet, a pile of dirty clothes rests in a heap. Serving as a reminder of everything Owen just felt. Laundry should be the next step. Somewhere in the house there is a laundry room, and I need to find it, get these clothes cleaned before he sees them again. He doesn't need that kind of reminder waiting for him.

There must me something comfortable for him to wear in his bedroom. Those gray sweatpants he always wears around the house must be here somewhere. I could set them on the bed. Would that be weird? Am I overstepping? He is currently in his underwear behind me. Clearly lines have been crossed between host and guest. Maybe I should make him tea, if he likes tea. I have only seen him drink coffee. I don't think coffee is a good idea after a panic attack.

My mind is reeling. I'm snapped into place when a wet hand grabs my wrist. Owen leans out of the shower, dark eyes pinned on mine.

"What?" I ask.

He tugs once. Face pleading.

"You want me to join you?"

He nods.

My conscious whispers in my ear loud enough that it could be in the room with me, *stay with him*.

"Okay."

I strip off my hoodie and t-shirt, kick off my shoes, peel off my socks and jeans. Keeping my underwear on to match him. Owen watches through the glass door, his face unreadable. His hand rests on the handle, ready to invite me in.

"I know, compared to you, I look like vanilla pudding." I force a laugh. I am not nearly as fit as him. My edges are soft where he is hard muscle and sharp lines. His skin is dark and perfect. I am pale and dusted with freckles.

He doesn't react to my self-inflicted jab.

I step into the shower, the water spraying against my shoulder. Owen grabs a washcloth and a bar of soap. He hands them to me.

I start at his shoulders, rubbing the suds over his skin. He rinses them away. We repeat the process down his chest, his back. Minutes pass in silence.

Then I look down at his hands.

I take one, lifting it closer. The skin is torn; his nails are packed with dirt. It looks like he clawed his way out of a grave.

I clean his hands carefully, using the corner of the cloth under his nails, tracing over his cuts. When they're finally clean, I do something reckless. Involuntarily.

I press my lips to his knuckles.

It's instinct. An unspoken declaration that I am here for him in whatever way he needs. I wish I could take away the pain, erase the torment that led him here. An echo of himself.

A tear slips down his cheek blending with the shower spray.

"I'm sorry," I whisper. My breath blowing over the sores on his hand. "That was bad timing, I just-"

"You have freckles on your shoulders."

I freeze. His voice is hoarse, a deep raspy whisper. My stomach flips.

"Yea." I frown.

He pulls me into his arms, wrapping me in his warmth. His lips brush my shoulder, lingering on my freckles.

"I like them," he murmurs.

24
Lucas

It almost felt like my own hands were on him, steadying his shoulders, whispering comfort the way I would have. Gabriel cares for Owen. That was clear. I watched Owen collapse in the yard, grief overtaking him as he clawed at the earth like he could dig his way out of the pain.

I stayed back, like I've been doing these last few days. Giving him space. He needs to learn how to live without me. I keep telling myself that. But it doesn't make the distance hurt any less.

My hand rests on the place where a heart once beat, expecting that familiar ache. But there was nothing—I'm hollow.

I am no longer part of this world.

No longer his.

Then I heard the sound of Gabriel's car pull in the driveway, and relief swept through me like wind through leaves. He was here. Without thinking, I gave him a nudge. A burst of cold against his skin. A whisper of my presence to get his attention. Don't go inside. I pleaded although he could not hear me. He didn't need much convincing. Once he heard Owen's sobs, Gabriel ran straight to him. He dropped beside him in the dirt, hands moving with the same urgency mine would have.

And for a moment, I let myself have hope. Hope that Gabriel might be the one to pull Owen back into himself.

Gabriel was sweet and empathetic. Despite their size difference, He was the one cradling Owen. Every word out of his mouth was with earnest concern.

It's early to speculate, whatever is growing between them. But it is no longer a seed. Standing in the shower I designed for Owen and me; I watched him invite Gabriel in. Witnessed a vulnerability in him that, in all our seven years together, had never been mine to see.

He never would have allowed me to take care of him like that. He always had to be the strong one, the provider, and I adored him for it. It meant I could break when I needed to, disappear into my anxiety for days, sometimes weeks, knowing he'd keep everything together. I thought moving to Oxford would fix me. A fresh start, a clean slate. I truly believed it was what I needed.

I watched him in the shower with Gabriel. Hidden from his view. Holding in breath I no longer had. It was the most beautiful sight. Water dripped from his thick dark lashes as he watched Gabriel clean the dirt on his hands. Then Owen embraced him. I faded into the wall just as he placed a soft kiss on Gabriel's shoulder.

I have remained in the back yard ever since. Waiting for the sun to set and the night to surround me. What happens between them is not for my eyes to witness.

I look up to the sky and begin my nightly plea to be taken from this place. It's clear I am no longer needed in his life. He is in good hands. Clearly I can move on now.

I've tried to let my body drift upward, weightless and free. But around thirty feet off the ground, something tugs at me. An invisible tether, snapping me back towards the house.

My shoulders drop and I settle on the grass for another night.

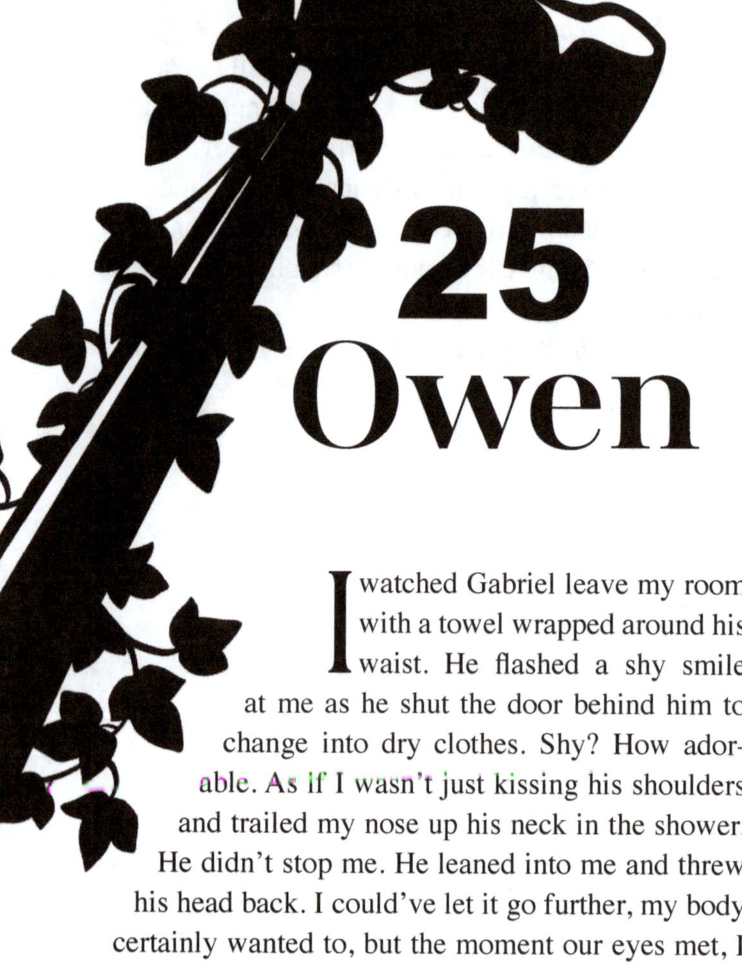

25
Owen

I watched Gabriel leave my room with a towel wrapped around his waist. He flashed a shy smile at me as he shut the door behind him to change into dry clothes. Shy? How adorable. As if I wasn't just kissing his shoulders and trailed my nose up his neck in the shower. He didn't stop me. He leaned into me and threw his head back. I could've let it go further, my body certainly wanted to, but the moment our eyes met, I knew. It wasn't the right time.

Moments before I was catatonic and suffering from some sort of breakdown. Is that what a panic attack feels like? I have only ever experienced something similar once before. After a football game. I remained in the locker room long after all the players were dressed and heading out to meet their families or girlfriends. A college scout had been in the stands that night. We lost, and I played like shit. I walked off the field convinced I'd just blown my last chance at a scholarship.

My mind spiraled with all the decisions waiting before me. Whether or not I would have to take the only offer I had on the table and play football for BYU. A college known for their strict honor code that includes being openly queer. I had not spoken the truth of my sexuality aloud in high school, but I knew my attraction went beyond women. Far beyond. To the point it circled women and landed solely on men by the time I met Lucas.

BYU was my parents' choice for college. They met there and were engaged before the end of their second semester. Which is a long time to date according to Mormon standards.

My stomach twisted violently before everything came up into a garbage can. A thousand tons of worry sat on my chest, making it hard to breathe. No one was there to pull me out of it. I had no Lucas—or Gabriel. Instead of meeting up with my family after the game, I wandered off and walked six miles. A non-direct route home in the dark. It took the full two hours of the walk for my body to settle; every step slowly brought me back to a resemblance of calm.

When I arrived home my family was busy playing board games. I stayed in my room all night. Determined to put the episode behind me and move on to whatever chapter is next for me. It turned out the scout saw a previous game. He was already prepared to offer me a scholarship and was only there to watch another player.

Relief pushed all my fears away when I accepted the scholarship. It opened a door that probably saved my life.

This memory flies through my mind as I think about what happened in the garden. I should have gotten up from the dirt and gone for a long walk instead of letting the darkness consume me. Gabriel found me at my worst. My most pathetic. Most helpless. Unable to speak and barely functioning. He stepped in without hesitation and gave me everything that I didn't know to ask for.

He told me to change into comfortable clothes and meet him downstairs. I pull on my grey sweatpants and a crew neck sweatshirt I got in NYC when Lucas and I went to see Kinky Boots five years ago.

When I head downstairs I find Gabriel in the kitchen. He is covering a large wooden cutting board with crackers, meat, cheese, and cut fruit. I linger in the doorway for a long minute before he notices me. I smile at his plaid pants and oversized hoodie. I have to restrain myself from picking him up in a tight embrace.

"Hi." He said with a grin on his face.

"Hi."

"I thought the perfect thing for tonight would be wine, charcuterie, and a comfort show." His blue eyes catch the light and my chest warms. He lifts the board of food and hands it to me. He grabs one of the wine bottles he brought and two glasses. I follow him from the kitchen to the living room. The TV is waiting on a streaming service menu.

"Is there a movie or show you want to watch?" I place the glasses on the coffee table. The wine bottle is already open, so I begin to pout two equal glasses. I hide the fact that I don't drink much and know next to nothing about wine. He sets the food down and plops on the couch. First he sits in the middle, then moves to the corner before ending somewhere between the two spots. The corners of my lips tug up. He's nervous again and I find it adorable. His hoodie hangs loose, but my mind fills in the details. I've seen the toned body beneath it, the trail of freckles like a map I wouldn't mind getting lost in—with my tongue making the path.

"Owen?"

"Huh?" I must have been lost in thought. He looks like he was talking to me with no response.

"Are you okay?" His brows knit together with concern.

I sit on the couch. Letting the soft leather embrace my body. "I am fine. Did you say something?"

"I asked what your comfort show is? Ya know, something you have watched before, but you never get tired of the characters or story."

I lean back. What is my comfort show? Lucas loved crime documentaries. Occasionally I will put one on when I am leaving the house. So, he can have entertainment. I never cared for them. I am more of an action-comedy guy myself. There is one show however, that I will watch on the days I feel blue.

"The Great B….ish …king Show." I mumble out.

"What was that?"

I exhale. "The Great British Baking Show." He smiles and begins searching for it on the TV. "I don't even like to bake but I like watching them cook. And all the contestants are so nice to each other."

"Well, I love to bake. I have seen the latest season already. I hope it doesn't bother you if I might work on a few sketches. I will still be here." He finds the show and clicks on the latest season. "You can interrupt me all you want though if you want to comment on flakey crust or bread sculptures."

"Bread week is my favorite."

He presses play and sets the remote down. He pops a piece of sliced strawberry into his mouth. Takes a long sip of his wine and pulls a pad of paper from his messenger bag.

By the time the technical challenge starts, Gabriel's practically melted into the couch. His legs sprawled, knees bent, and toes slowly migrating toward my thigh. I catch a glimpse of his polish, soft pink and glossy, and it makes me smile. Somehow, without even realizing it, I've fully settled into the moment. Peaceful. At ease.

Involuntarily I slide my hand behind his ankles and pull his feet onto my lap. Gabriel peaks around his paper with wide eyed. I begin to massage the bottom of his feel with my thumbs.

"Is this okay?" I ask.

"Yea, umm, yes." He says with the nervous tone I have come to really enjoy. As usual, it's followed by his cheeks turning pink. I smile but keep facing forward to the TV. Minutes pass and I have moved from rubbing his feet to his ankles, to his calves. He continues to sketch. His face is blocked, and I am curious what it would take to make him stop drawing. What do I need to do to get some attention?

My palm slides over his flannel pants up his thigh. I reach his hip and rub back down to his knee. He does not stop me or flinch under my touch. I repeat with my hand shifting a few inches to press on the front of his leg. A small moan escapes him.

Again, I rub starting at his hip, but I curve my hand

to the inside of his thigh. My thumb grazing his cock on the way down. This causes his hand to freeze dropping the pencil. It rolls onto the floor. I watch him from the corner of my eyes. Attempting to control my smirk and failing. He places the paper flat on his stomach and watches me. He is waiting for me for me to react. To show him the touch was on purpose.

I dare to touch him again. Making sure my intentions are clear, and my wandering hands are by no accident. He holds his breath when I reach up once more. This time when I glide along his cock he is semi hard. He shifts to sit up and I grab his legs, holding him in place.

"Stay." I look him deep in his blue eyes. "Please. I will stop if you ask me to."

It is obvious now that his body does not want me to stop. The bulge in his pajama pants has significantly increased in size. I have to restrain myself from pouncing like a lion.

"I don't want you to stop, but-" He lets the sentence die.

"But, what?"

"But I know you are hurting, and I don't want to take advantage of you." He bites his bottom lip and my dick flinches in my sweatpants. I reach for the remote and pause the TV. I grab both his ankles in one hand and lift his legs. I place them back on the couch and kneel with one leg on each side.

"It looks like I am the one taking advantage of you." Finally, he drops the sketch pad to the floor removing the barrier between us. I lean down until my nose is nearly touching his. "Gabriel?" I say softly.

"Mmm hmm."

"It has been a long time since I have wanted to kiss anyone. I would like to kiss you."

"Okay." He places his hands gently on my waist, and I crash onto his mouth. We start slow. Lips finding each other. Mapping each other out. Then he arches his back under me and parts his lips. I take my chance and slide my tongue in. He tastes like wine and berries. I brace myself with one arm and tangle my fingers into his copper curls.

Why does this feel so perfect? His heat, his size, the way he is moving under me, it's exactly what I need.

But I need more.

When we separate, his lips are pink from our kiss. I stand up quickly and pick him up with a quick swoop of my arms. He lets out the cutest noise then turns bright red and covers his mouth from embarrassment. I laugh and sit down pulling him atop my lap. Straddling me. His hands wrap around my neck, and we kiss again.

I cup his ass with both hands and grind him onto me. The living room feels like a sauna. Our breaths are hot and labored between kisses. I kiss along his jaw to his neck while moving my hands from his ass up his back.

"Can I take this off?" I tug on his hoodie.

He grabs the hem and pulls it over his head taking a T-shirt with it. I hold back a growl. He is bringing out a side of me that has been dormant for a long time.

Our hard cocks are pressed together between us. I spot his freckles and delight in kissing them again. Curling his body into mine until there is no gap between us.

It's still not enough.

I break from touching him long enough to remove my shirt. I need to feel his skin against mine this second or I will explode. We grind together. The friction driving me crazy. He reaches between us and slides his hand around my cock through my sweatpants. His breath hitches.

"What's wrong?" I make him look me in the eyes.

"Absolutely nothing." He bites his lip again. "You're uh… ummm… huge."

I chuckle. There is tension in his shoulders now. I pull him into a slow kiss. Giving us both a moment to hold each other and ease into the moment. It does not take long for him to relax against my body once more. He continues to palm me through my pants but does not take it any further. I moan into his mouth.

It feels great but that is not what I want right now. In this moment I need to take care of him. I slide my hands down his back and under the waist of his boxer briefs. This time when I cup his ass grateful there is no fabric in my way. Using his body to create the friction I crave. His hand no longer fits in the space. He grips the back of the couch like handles on a motorcycle. I bite and lick his neck. A whimper escapes him.

My last bit of self-control fades.

Hands still on his ass I flip him to lay on his back once more. Then tug his pants until the tip of his cock can be seen. His breaths are labored. I pause to watch his chest rise and fall. Wondering if it's from lust or the desire for me to stop. I open my mouth to ask for consent when he reaches down and slides his pants to his mid-thigh. Leaving himself bare before me like a buffet.

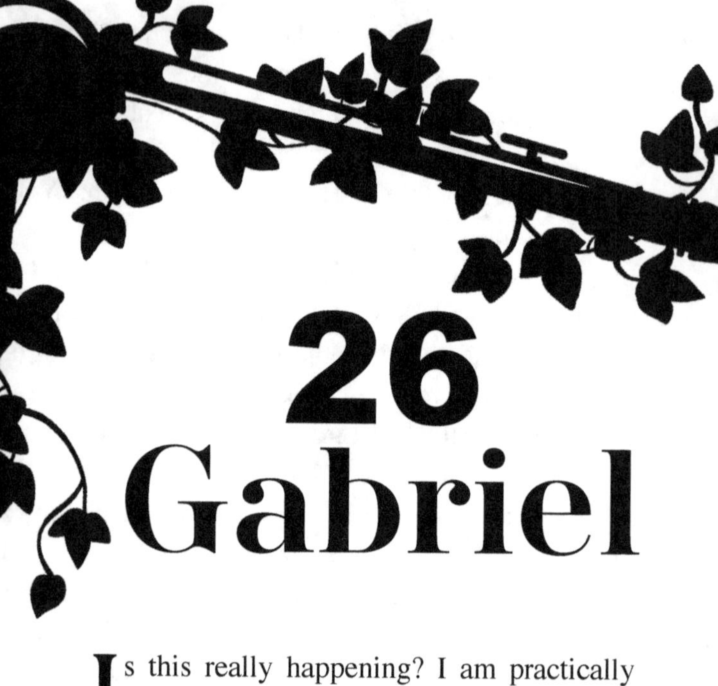

26
Gabriel

Is this really happening? I am practically naked on a gorgeous, oversized soft leather couch. With the hottest man leaning over me. Looking at my body like it is his last meal.

I swallow. My saliva tastes like wine and him.

"I am not sure how to explain this, but this feels new. Like I am exploring again." He frowns then turns it into a smile. "I just want you right now. I want to touch you. But am not sure it can do-um do everything."

"I understand." I interrupt. "We can do whatever you are comfortable with."

With a slow nod, he leans over until his body completely covers mine. Shading me from every lamp in the room like a lust filled tent made of hard muscle. Gently he presses a kiss to my lips. The passion grows between us. The kiss becomes more frantic.

I almost forget that I am exposed from the waist down

until his hand wraps around me and begins to stroke me slowly. My hands run up his chest tracing his abs. They are flexed from propping himself up on one arm. He breaks our kiss, and I try to move on my elbows, but he pressed a palm to my chest holding me in place.

With a crooked smile he moves down my body. Kissing my collarbone, my chest, my stomach. I suck in a breath when he grabs me again. One smooth motion he strokes me and takes me into his mouth.

My hand grips the side of the couch while other reaches down to his hair. Not to stop him, but to hold him there. I gasp. "Fuck."

My voice doesn't sound like me. Full of heat and already at a breaking point. It's been so long that I don't recognize myself in the moment, and let's be honest, in my last relationship I was primarily the giver of blow jobs not the receiver.

Owen devours me. Taking me fully into his mouth. Spit from his mouth drips down my crack. He pauses his sucking but continues to stroke me. I look down and watch him take a single finger from his left hand and suck it into his mouth. He has a question in his expression. Giving me time to stop him. I do not. Instead, I slightly widen my legs as an invitation.

His hesitation is brief. The wetted tip of his finger nudges my hole. A breath catches in my throat. Owen's mouth is on me again and the duel sensation of his warm mouth and a finger sliding inside is overwhelming. I cry out his name and he presses deeper in response. I am so hard. So close.

His finger begins a steady rhythm pumping inside me all while my cock disappears in his mouth. The beats line up and my stomach tenses.

"Owen, I'm gonna cum."

Instead of removing his mouth he speeds up until I begin to shake and spill in his mouth. He hums. The vibration sends a jolt. I clench around his finger. He licks up every drop.

27
Gabriel

The next five minutes happened in slow motion. I laid on the couch in a daze. Owen slips my pants back up my hips. Kisses my stomach. Gets up to wash his hands. Refills both our glasses of wine and then un-pauses The Great British Baking Show. He leans back sipping the red wine and rubs my ankle like nothing just happened.

Like he didn't just suck me off.

He must feel the weight of my gaze, because his lips slowly curve against the rim of his glass. A Smile that's filled with secrets and satisfaction, like he's tasting something only known to him. I suppose he is. It has been a long time since I have felt close enough to someone to be intimate. We have leaped over hurdles in a fleeting time.

The air between us hums, thick with both of us pretending nothing happened. Not out of shame, no—the energy is purely playful.

I reach down, deliberately casual, and pick up my sketch pad and pencil from where they fell to the floor. My hand stutters a little. I control my breathing. If he is going to play pretend, then I will too. I'll sketch like nothing's changed, like I don't still feel the imprint of his hands on my skin or the ghost of his mouth on my cock.

We settle back into a rhythm that almost passes for normal. Almost.

Beneath the quiet, under the steady scratch of pencil on paper and the slow sips he takes of his drink, my body remembers. It buzzes and aches from the images of just being ravaged by Owen. He devoured me in the best way, turned me into a puddle under his touch. Took me in his mouth and swallowed me whole.

And somehow we are both pretending nothing has changed.

Thirty minutes pass, Owen rested a hand on me the entire time, never breaking out connection. I look around the room and remember who he was meant to share this home with. I remember his grief. People often make reckless decisions when they are grieving. Hooking up with a stranger who originally rented a room from you is defiantly reckless behavior. I can't let myself read too far into this. We enjoy each other's company. We are becoming friends. It's nothing more than that. It can't be.

This is unlike me. I am never quick to catch feelings. It usually takes me weeks or months. There must be a deeper connection or the start of one before I let it get physical. Usually.

The spark I feel for Owen came on fast and is growing rapidly. Burning brighter with every day that passes. Is this how most people feel? People who develop feelings almost instantaneous. Does he feel this way?

I shift until I am sitting crossed legged. He notices me pull my feet away and gives me a look of concern.

"Owen?" My voice trembles slightly as I tap my pencil's eraser against the paper, each beat echoing the quick rhythm of my heart. He sets his wine down, his eyes flickering between warmth and something more cautious. He's trying to read me. I take a breath. I owe him honesty. I like him. Really like him. And I don't want this to be a fling. If he's open to more, I am too.

He places a hand on my knee and pauses the show. "I ruined things didn't I?" A wrinkle forms between his brows as he scans my body from where his hand rests up to my face. Our eyes meet and my chest warms. His usual stoic expression is soft.

"No. Trust me. Nothing is ruined."

"I made this uncomfortable for you. You didn't come here for a hookup," He nods to the living room as if the house is in on the conversation. Quickly he removes his hand. "And I made it weird."

"What happened was… unexpected, but not unwanted." I bravely grabbed his hand and place it back on my knee. "But we should talk about-"

My phone rings.

We both look down at my screen lighting up on the coffee table. The name Carlton with a bag of money emoji flashes on the screen.

"It's my boss." I pick up the phone and rise from the couch. Out of the corner of my eye, Owen presses play on the TV but lowers the volume to a whisper. I slip into the dining room and find a quiet corner, tucking myself against the wall for some privacy. "Hello."

"Gabe, I hope you're feeling rested. I need you to take over the Kent Golf Course updates." A car horn blares in the background, he's clearly driving. Of course he is. It's well past office hours, but boundaries have never been his strong suit. No wonder I came so close to burning out. I have been following his lead. Running on fumes for years, hopping from one project to the next without a real break.

Once again he is telling me to jump, and I can only respond with "how high?"

"I only have four more days."

"Nope. I need you in the office tomorrow. Can you drive back tonight?" The phone switches from Bluetooth to handheld. I can hear him talk to a valet attendant.

"Why the hurry?"

"We have seventy-two hours to get a new Site Plan approved." Carlton gives his name to a hostess. His voice lowers as he walks through what I can only guess is a restaurant where his wife is waiting. "Kent agreed to keep part of the land in conjunction of the wildlife preservation people. We were able to prove only part of the land was used for migration of birds or whatever."

I roll my eyes at how casual he is on things that actually matter. Yes I design beautiful long-lasting outdoor spaces, but you know what was there first—nature. Carlton is not unique. Most in my industry are more concerned with profits and timelines than bird migration patterns.

"Sounds great for the birds."

"Sounds great for us. All your hard work won't be for nothing. I just need you to tweak the design to include the preserved area including accessible paths around it and mock-ups of nature marker. Maybe a small gazebo for the bird watching nerds."

"That shouldn't take me that long." I peek out the dining room to make sure Owen is still watching his show. "Are you sure they won't let us have a bit more time?"

"You have seventy-two hours Gabe. Hi beautiful, sorry I'm late. Ya know how traffic is." There's a pause after he greets his wife before he continues. "Stay one more night if you don't want to drive in the dark, but I expect to see you by noon tomorrow in the office."

He hangs up before I could agree or disagree. I slide my phone into my pajama pocket and slowly turn around. Owen stands in the doorway with the picked over charcuterie board in his hands. His shoulders nearly touch the frame, yet his expression makes him feel small.

"Everything okay?"

"Yeah, it was my boss. A project I thought was over needs me to fix something and it's on a tight deadline. I have to return tomorrow." I walk towards him, but he steps backwards into the kitchen. I follow him and rock on my heels while he cleans up.

"So," He places the cutting board in the sink and stands with his back to me. "You are leaving tomorrow."

"Probably after breakfast."

"I see." When he turns to face me, my arms ache with the urge to wrap around his waist, to hold him there and not let go. The words are right there on the tip of my tongue. This could be my only chance to say something. To tell him I want to see where this could go. That whatever is growing between us feels important. Special. I'd drive two hours from D.C. every weekend if he asked me.

Maybe it's too soon to have these feelings, but the spark cannot be ignored.

My chest tightens, heart pounding like it's racing to get the words out but hitting a wall of fear. I open my mouth ready to speak, but he cuts me off.

"Is there really a landscaping emergency that requires you to leave right away or-" Owen cocks an eyebrow filled with skepticism.

"Or what?" I brace my hands on my hips. "You think I am running away or something."

"Maybe."

I narrow my eyes at him. Suddenly feeling exhausted. And my mind is already racing with ideas how to fix the Kent project. "Listen." I step closer until our toes touch. "That was my boss, demanding my return by noon tomorrow. I am not making shit up to get away from you. Trust me. That's the last thing I want to do."

The overhead light flickers, making light dance across the ceiling. We both glance up, then back at each other. His lashes are dark and thick, shadows spilling over his cheeks as his eyes flutter closed. He's thinking. Debating. Searching for something to say.

But the silence stretches. Too long. Too heavy.

My chest tightens. I shift my weight. Nothing. He doesn't speak.

I swallow down the knot in my throat and turn on my heel.

"I'm going to pack," I murmur, more to myself than to him.

He doesn't stop me.

Upstairs, the guest room feels colder than before. I hesitate at the door, my hand resting on the knob a second longer than it should. Maybe if I left it open… maybe he'd follow. Maybe he'd say something.

But he doesn't follow.

I close it gently behind me and crawl into bed.

28
Owen

This could be my last morning with Gabriel, and I want us to part on good terms. I have been pacing in the kitchen since 8am. The coffee pot if full. I even filled one of those tiny pitchers with cream and set it next to the matching sugar holder. I have ham cheese and eggs already mixed in a bowl, ready to be scrambled.

I still have not seen Lucas. It has been days, and I was convinced he was gone until he started messing with the lights last night. No doubt alerting me that I was saying all wrong things to Gabriel. I handled that phone call terribly, and I don't know what is wrong with me.

I think I crossed a line last night. I'm not even sure anymore. I gave him plenty of chances to stop me.

Didn't I? But the way he grabbed me, the sounds he made when I kissed him, it didn't feel like hesitation. Every pass of his tongue over mine felt like a green light.

At least, that's what I thought.

It's been a long time. Maybe too long. What if I misread everything? What if he felt like he couldn't say "no" because of me. Because of my size, my energy, the way trapped him into staying in this house with me.

First I pin him to the couch, then I snap at him for taking a work call. What the Hell is wrong with me?

But something in him shifted during that call. That wasn't in my head. I'm sure of that. Still, I've been cooped up too long, and it's obvious I'm rusty when it comes to reading people. For all I know, he was relieved to have an excuse to leave. To get away from the six-foot-four stranger who acted like he was competing in some kind of Super Bowl level make out session.

God. I went from calm to chaos in less than a week.

Maybe I should check on him. He has a long drive ahead this morning. He could've forgotten to set an alarm. I'll knock. Let him know breakfast is ready. Then I'll back off. Give him space.

He deserves that much.

I scrub my face with my hands. The first man I have had interest in for the past three years and I have turned into a clingy horny creep.

Ugh.

I tiptoe upstairs in my socks. Making a mental note to tighten the creaky boards. When I reach his door it is silent. I am convinced he is still sleeping. I knock gently and wait.

My heart begins to race.

I knock louder. Perhaps he is a heavy sleeper.

There is no answer. No groan from the mattress. No patter of footsteps. I hang my head and turn to leave until an image flashes in my mind. He could be lying on the ground. He could be unconscious. He could be-

I grab the doorknob violently and thrust the door open. I scan the room in a panic.

"Gabriel!" I shout.

No answer. I rush to the other side of the bed hoping not to see him on the floor.

The space is empty.

"Gabriel!" I shout again. Lucas appears. His face is somber, and he hovers near the dresser. His hand is motioning to a piece of paper.

"He's not here." Lucas frowns.

I grab the letter and give Lucas a pleading look. "Why didn't you tell me?

"I was outside when he drove away. Then I watched you prepare breakfast and pace in the kitchen. I wasn't sure what to say." He reached out for me and his hand passed through my arm. I shivered.

"He just left." My voice is barely louder than a whisper. I folded the letter. Lucas most likely already read it, but I wanted to be alone before I take in his words. The words accusing me of coming on too strong and he has no intention of seeing me again. I began to slowly walk out of his room. Lucas floated by me to hover in my path.

"You care for him." It was a statement not a question.

"Huh." I avoided giving him a direct answer. My head feels hazy.

"I have been watching you. Trying not to interfere." He pointed to the letter. *"Gabriel cares for you too."*

My face snaps up. Technically I am taller than Lucas, but he is hovering, so we are eye level. "This is not a conversation I can have with you."

"*Why not?*" He crosses his arms. "*I am not really here remember. My body lies in a Cemetery next to my grandparents in Illinois. What you see here is an echo. Don't let an echo hold you back.*"

"I didn't hold back." I mumbled.

Lucas tilts his head. "*What was that?*"

I sighed. "I didn't hold back. That's the problem. Nine days with him is all it took for me to stop holding back. I practically jumped him on the couch. Then he freaked out and left."

"*I don't think that is what happened.*" He points to the letter again while floating away into the hallway until he is partially in the wall. "*Read the letter.*"

I sigh and look down at the paper ripped from a sketchbook.

Owen,

I'm sorry to run out without saying goodbye. ~~My time with~~ This week has been amazing. I am not sure what last night meant to you, but I fear it meant more to me. I am not in a place to be ~~used~~ hurt right now. I think you could hurt me; I like you too much.

~~If you want~~ If you are open to more. If you want to grab dinner or are in the city give me a text.

I hope to hear from you. Good luck with the house.

Gabriel

I read the letter four times. Rubbed my thumb over the phone number scribbled under his name. Could I have found it on his reservation? Yes, but it's more rewarding having him write it down with intention to give it to me. I saved his number in my phone and went downstairs to clean up breakfast.

29
Gabriel

Two days I have been drafting and re-drafting site plans for the Kent Golf Course and newly designed Nature Preserve. An anonymous tip informed the news about the project. The public instantly put the needed pressure on the city to approve something. Suddenly citizens were overly concerned about the migration of the Brown Pelican.

In the end I am incredibly happy with my design. And my next clients are excited to be working with me after seeing my name pop up in the news. I am not sure how I feel having my name attached to private golf course for the wealthy and elite. Who would have preferred to fuck over the Pelicans or any other wildlife in their way.

My phone buzzed in my pocket and my heart jumped. I have been waiting for Owen to text me or call me. It has been two days. Two days! That's it I am convinced he is over it, whatever we started. When I pull out the phone I see Adrienne's name.

> I loved the design concepts you emailed. I forwarded it to the city council. You made them excited about the project.

> I am happy to help. It was fun.

Three dots appeared and disappeared a few times before a message came through.

> They are voting to approve the plan based on your sketches Friday. Any chance you could stop by Saturday? I would love to pick your brain on a few things. Lunch is on me.

I looked at my calendar even though I knew for a fact I have no plans. Jackie's brother was still crashing on the couch. When I was not at work I spent it shut away in my room anyway. Before I returned her text I began a search for the nearest hotel. Oxford had none, but I did find a cute guest house available. On the opposite side of town from Owen. Good, he won't think I am a stalker. After all, Adrienne is inviting me, and I have my own reasons to be there.

> Yes I can be there. I just booked the Sanderson guest house on Strand Rd.

She responded quickly.

> I know the place. It's cute. Why
> are you not staying with Owen?

How do you explain to her that we lived a year's worth of emotions in less than two weeks? We cycled through it all, annoyance, curiosity, empathy, desire, concern, lust. Then it all came crashing down in one sharp gust of rejection.

How do you find the right words for something that hit fast and hard, and feels unfinished? This wasn't like those flings from my early college days. This felt like the start of something that mattered. Something that could've lasted. If I wasn't a coward.

Maybe it can still be something. Because I haven't stopped thinking about him. And every day that passes, I regret walking out with nothing more than a note.

If I had stayed I would have word vomited all over his shoes. Feelings were on the tip of my tongue. Begging to be made into solid words. I denied them life. Denied myself the opportunity to discover what we could have. Or maybe I saved myself future heartbreak.

> Things ended weird. Don't tell
> him I am coming. I will reach out
> to him when I am in town.

Okay

> See you Saturday.

I tucked my phone back into my desk. An alert popped

up on my computer for a meeting starting in five minutes. I grabbed a notepad and filled up my travel mug with fresh coffee.

Carlton and Jeremy were already in the conference room when I arrived. The floor-to-ceiling glass walls framed a sweeping view of Lincoln Park, reminding me just how high up we were. The energy buzzing through the room felt like the opening bell at the stock exchange. Sharp, fast, and money focused.

It was clear this meeting would be finance-heavy, and for once, I was glad that wasn't my lane. Jeremy would handle the budget proposal. My job was to make sure the design worked and looked damn good.

I take my seat across from Jeremy. He types on a laptop with two energy drinks next to him. One is already open with the other one waiting to be guzzled. He is always chugging them and then will be shaking by the end of the day like a junkie.

Carlton is on the phone. He holds up a finger to me as if I was about to speak. I hold my pen at the ready to take notes.

"Got it," he says to the person on the phone. "Yes. We will be ready for a site walk in two weeks. Mid-May is a beautiful time of year in Lake Como."

Hearing Lake Como mentioned lights a fire in me. This will be my first international project. It will require me to travel to Italy multiple times in the next two years. This project is huge. The Turatello family is loaded. They own many mansions on Lake Como. Or they did. Four years ago, two of them were damaged in a fire that spread from one to the other. The historic homes were lost. Now the family wants to combine the properties into a resort. The kind of place where billionaires visit by invitation only.

If I can make the clients happy it could lead to referrals amongst the exact type of people who hire landscape architects. Rich eccentrics that want their back yard to look like a rose garden and hedge maze straight out of Alice in Wonderland.

Secretly I am hoping it leads to freelance work, and I no longer have to work for Carlton. I would love to have control over the clients I work with and the projects I put my name to.

Carlton sets his phone down. He has a wide smile on his face. Like a child waiting for you to ask a question so they can brag. Jeremy and I both give him our full attention.

"Well boys." He smacks the table. "You are going to love this. Less regulation, no obnoxious wildlife loving hippies. Clients with impeccable taste. Just wait until you hear their wish list, Gabriel. And Jeremy, the budget is- well let's just say there is no budget. I just need you to handle the permits and other boring stuff."

"Boring stuff, got it." Jeremy continued typing after a long swig of his energy drink.

"I am ready." I held my pen at the ready. "What are they asking for?"

"A pool in the shape of the Madonna Lily. Whatever that is. Luxurious cabanas on their private beach. A courtyard garden in the center of the resort. I sent the head architect's contact info to your email, as well as satellite images of the property. That will have to do until we can get you out there in a couple of weeks to survey the property. I hope your passport is up to date."

Carlton was taping away on his phone with one hand and waving the other one in the air as he named off the first list of client requests.

With every project, the client tends to add more as we move through each stage. I'm almost certain that once they see my initial concepts, they'll want to scale up and add even more features. That's exactly why I always start my proposals on the simpler side, leave room to grow without overwhelming the clients.

Carlton ends the meeting, and I head back to my desk and immediately start researching Madonna Lilies.

30
Owen

"Have you texted him yet?"

Lucas sits crossed legged in the air floating next to me as I kneel to replace an outlet. I had an electrician out yesterday to add ground wires to the outdated electrical system. It is a miracle this house hasn't burned down in the past century. I sigh and tighten the last screw. I scoot down the wall a few feet to the next outlet. Lucas hovers along with me. I love him. I always will, but he has been nagging me for two days about Gabriel.

"What am I supposed to say? Sorry I made it weird at the end. I want to see you again." I pop the old outlet off and reach inside my plastic shopping bag for a new one.

"Yes love. That is exactly what you say."

I groan. "I waited too long. It will be awkward now." I look down at my phone where I saved Gabriels number. I keep opening the messaging app and staring at the screen. I have not typed a single letter. I open it, feel like I am going to vomit from nerves, then close it.

After replacing the next outlet, I repeat the unhealthy cycle. I open my phone and stare at a black text box. Lucas moves closer as if his chin rests on my shoulder. I hold back a shiver. My thumb hovers over the screen. Should I just send "hi"? Would that be weird? Or is that casual enough?

"Text him."

I close my eyes. If I move on with someone else will Lucas leave for good. I cannot expect him to stay forever and watch me live on without him. Invite someone besides him into our home. Love them in front of him.

I hear the fainted click. The sound my phone makes when I send a text. I look down and I see a single letter sent to Gabriel.

O

"What did you do?" I shriek. Standing up and shaking my phone at him. The image of throwing his ashes into the ocean fills my mind. Not in a farewell-my-love way, but a ugh I-can't-believe-you-did-that kind of way.

"God that was hard. It takes so much energy to touch things." He fades a little like mist. *"I have been trying to tap your phone since last night. Being a ghost is rough."*

"You sent him the letter 'O'! What does that even mean?" I stare down at the message scared that he will respond. Or maybe I am scared he won't respond.

"It means nothing. It was just the only thing that worked. I was poking at the screen until something

clicked." Lucas faded more. *"You might not be able to see me for a while. I don't know the logistics but after I do poltergeist shit I struggle to-"*

And on a breath he was gone.

I marched into the living room. Head down waiting for a text bubble to pop up on my phone. Tripping on the plastic bag full of outlets and covers. They scattered on the floor. I set my phone on the tall new accent table I got for the entryway. As I picked up the supplies I heard my phone ding.

I looked around for Lucas, but he was nowhere in sight. I set the bag on the table and swiped to unlock my phone. Gabriel's name appeared in my notifications. My thumb hovered over the screen. I need to sit down. I am about to embarrass myself and prefer to be comfortable while I did it.

After a deep breath I opened the message.

I assume that was an accident.

Yes sorry.

I waited for him to respond. Why isn't he responding? Well, I guess that answers my questions. There's my closure. He killed the conversation. I put my phone down and immediately pick it back up. Or did I kill the conversation. I told him it was an accident and asked nothing to keep the conversation open. Geez, I am bad at this. I used to be so charming, at least both men and women in college thought I was charming.

I was meaning to text you anyway. Maybe it was serendipity.

The lack of immediate text bubbles indicating he was typing had me ready to turn my phone off. I think I am sweating. This is crazy. What the fuck is happening to me? What the fuck did he do to me?

...

The dots disappear, before reappearing after a few moments.

...

This is torture.

I love that movie.

What movie?

I respond way too quickly for it to be cool. I must sound eager and thirsty. He could be texting me from bed next to a gorgeous rich lobbyist. Isn't the life of attractive gay men in Washington D.C.? At least that's what I picture. Men lining up to take Gabriel to expensive restaurants and seduce him into bed.

I look around the room expecting to see Lucas judging my poor attempt flirting. I do not see him, but I feel the chill in the air. A chill I have grown accustomed to for the past three years.

Serendipity, the 2001 Romantic Comedy starring Kate Beckinsale and John Cusack. It's one of my favorites.

I decide to grow some balls and take a chance.

Maybe I will watch it tonight

I said over text before adding.

We could watch it at the same
time and chat on the phone.

Does this count as a date? Did I just ask him on a date, a remote date? It has to be a real thing. People have long distance relationships all the time. And I understand a two-hour drive is hardly a long distance. Not to mention, Gabriel and I don't have a relationship per se. I'm spiraling. Why is he taking so long to respond? I knew that was a weird thing to say. Who says "chat"?

We both press play at 8pm. I will
have my wine ready.

I thrust my fist in the air. Then I look around because this enthusiasm is too much. I have not been this excited to talk to someone in a decade. In the early days with Lucas when I was building the courage to tell him I was attracted to him, and he thought I was a dumb straight jock.

Perfect.

A smile blooms on my face. It is perfect. I might have rushed things when he was here. I wanted him to stay, but maybe this is exactly what I need. To dip my toe into the dating pool and feel the water slowly.

I slide my phone in my back pocket and stand. Before

I jump back into my projects, I pause in the middle of the living room. Lucas is here. I can tell by the chill in the air although I cannot see him.

"Before you hassle me more about Gabriel, just know, I am not giving up on him. I am taking things slow. I need you to let me set the pace. Okay? No more interference." The only answer I receive is the graze of cold fingers up my arm. Instead of shivering I lean into it. His cold has become my comfort. Even though it should not be. He should not be. "And thank you."

31
Gabriel

Jackie and her brother are gone when I return home from work. I take my time spraying the couch with air freshener. It reeks of old socks and that is not the environment I want when I watch a movie with Owen. Even though he will not be here in person.

I clean up the living room and throw his duffle bag into the hall closet. After I make a snack tray and grab a full bottle of wine I settle on the couch at 7:55pm. Five minutes away from a virtual date with Owen. When I open the streaming menu I picture Owen in his house. Grey sweatpants on. T-shirt tight on his body. I message him.

Pressing play now.

I take a big drink of my red wine. The opening pro-
duction credits begin along with the opening song. My
phone buzzes.

> Me too.

> ...

My phone rings and I see Owen's name on the screen.
He's calling me. And it's a video call. Fuck. I have been
anxiously playing with my hair and my curls are in every direction. Also, I am wearing a hoodie that Jackie
got me. I never wear it out of the house because it says
"Looking for my next book boyfriend" on the front.

"Hi." I attempt to hold the phone at a good angle, but
this lighting is doing me no justice. I end up hiding behind my glass of wine with as nervous smile. Owens'
face fills the whole screen as he holds the phone too
close.

"Hi." The warmth of his smile reaches me through the
screen and wraps around me like a hug. I sink deeper
into the cushions. Melting under his gaze. Thank God
I have a blanket over my lap, and he cannot see the
Christmas pajamas pants I am wearing even though it
is spring. "Sorry, I hate texting. My thumbs are big and
clumsy."

"Calling is fine." I reassure him.

Calling is in fact not fine. I hate it when anyone other
than my mother calls me. Everything is better in text.
If I could text to make doctor appointments I would.
This call, however, is making my insides twist and my
stomach flutter.

The image of Owen become shaky as he moves the

phone around before it settles in one spot. "Can we just set our phones down and talk like we are sitting next to each other?"

"I would love that."

By the angle of his body, I assume he placed his phone on the coffee table propped against something. I place my phone in a similar way. Hoping I don't look like a disgusting couch potato. I can see him eating popcorn and sipping on a beer bottle. The movie starts and we don't say anything for the first 15 minutes. It's not awkward though. I find just knowing he is there strongly comforting. He finally breaks out silence with a comment on a character playing the jazz flute.

"No one looks cool playing the jazz flute." He says with a furred brow.

I cannot help but chuckle. "I bet you would look cool playing the jazz flute." I don't think he would. I agree with his statement about jazz flute not being inherently cool, but the look of exaggerated doubt on his face was perfect. He is relaxing and becoming more playful. I really like this side of him.

"Do you play any instruments?" He asks while I fill up my glass of wine again. The movie is reaching a point where the two main characters are separated, and it has been over a year. Both of them are still thinking about the one romantic night they had together in NYC.

"I played the piano when I was younger. My mother forced all of us into lessons. I had keep going when my siblings went into sports. It was required for me to be in some sort of class. I wanted drawing, but art didn't count in her eye."

Owen was silent again. I assumed his attention was

on the movie until I looked down and saw the couch empty. He returned in view a moment later with a new beer in hand.

"Do you hate sports?" He asked casually as if I didn't know football was a huge part of his life. I debated how honest to be.

"I wouldn't go as far to say I hate sports." I took a drink of wine. "I don't mind going to games in person. I can always enjoy myself in a stadium filled with excited people. Would I trade a sports-ball game for a Taylor Swift concert? In a heartbeat."

He looks at me through the camera with a serious expression on his face. I get nervous when he puts the beer down and picks up the phone. He brings it close to his face and raises an eyebrow. I hold my breath with my wine glass resting on my lips.

"Sports-ball? Did you really just say that?" His tone is dry.

I shrug. "Yes"

Laughter fills my living room. A booming joyful sound that is strong enough to shake the phone in his hand making it appear he is in the middle of an earthquake. It's contagious and I can't help but join in. We watch the rest of the movie making commentary throughout every scene. Until it's the end and the camera is zooming in on a cashmere glove landing on the ice. It's the moment I have been waiting for. This is when they confess they have both been obsessively looking for each other and although they never say they love each other it feels like the start of something magical. A once in a lifetime kind of love.

I reach down to fill my wine glass and frown when I realize the bottle is empty. How did I drink an entire bottle? I didn't even notice. Oops.

The credits start to roll, and Owen is clutching an empty beer bottle to his chest like it's tethering him in place. In the soft amber light of his living room, his dark eyes shimmer. I can't tell if he's crying or if it's the reflection of the screen. Either way, guilt rolls through me like waves. Great job, me, you made a grieving widower watch one of the most romantic movies ever. Smooth—real smooth.

Owen clears his throat, voice rough but steady. "That was great. I really liked it."

"Really?" I responded with a bit too much enthusiasm. The wine is definitely starting to hum in my head. "I know it's nearly Hallmark level cheesy, but what can I say? I'm a hopeless romantic."

He gives the usual stoic "hrm" and lifts the phone closer so I can see his face more clearly. Owens' face fills the screen. Soft, amused, and a bit unreadable. I am still trying to figure out if he finds me cute or annoying. I mirror him by bring my phone closer. Suddenly hyper aware of how intimate this feels. "A hopeless romantic." He says slowly. Lingering on each word for long beats. "What exactly does that come with?"

The way he says "come with" sends a tiny shiver down my spine. I scramble for something cleaver to say, but what comes out is shaky and breathy. "it's not very romantic if I tell you what I find romantic."

God. What even is that sentence?

My cheeks are burning now. I pray the blue light from

the TV is balancing out my color. "You'll have to figure it out yourself." I add. Mentally I face palm, but I attempt a charming smile for Owen.

Owen chuckles, low and warm, and I feel ten years younger and completely out of my league. Flirting with the hot jock. Before he can say more or laugh at me I blurt out, "It's late. I have to work in the morning."

His lips twitch as he pulls in his bottom lip, biting it for a second too long. It should be illegal for that motion to look so good. So inviting. The silence becomes static between us. The movie's over. Both our faces are illuminated with the same glow as we sit in opposite living rooms.

"Gabriel." His deep voice makes my name sound velvety. "I accept that challenge."

I blink like a dope. "What challenge?"

His smile turns sly. "Figuring out what you find romantic."

I'm pretty sure I'm going to combust. My face is on fire, my heart racing in my chest, all I can manage is a nod. A dumb. dopey, please-jump-through-the-phone-and-kiss-me kind of nod. "Okay." I whisper, because the heat has burned my ability to function.

"I'll let you sleep. We'll talk soon."

Damn this phone. I want to kiss him. My whole body is buzzing with the need to feel his lips on mine. Soft. Warm. Everything about our last night together still lingers. I'm desperate to return the favor. I'm ready. At least...I think I am.

But then the doubt creeps in. I barely know him. Distance is good. Healthy. That's what I need to keep reminding myself. I've always needed time to build something real, to let connection grow beyond instant chemistry. But God, the attraction? The attraction is not the problem. If anything, it's overwhelming. Clouding my thoughts.

"Okay." I say again, forgetting how to have a conversation.

"Goodnight, Gabriel."

"Goodnight, Owen."

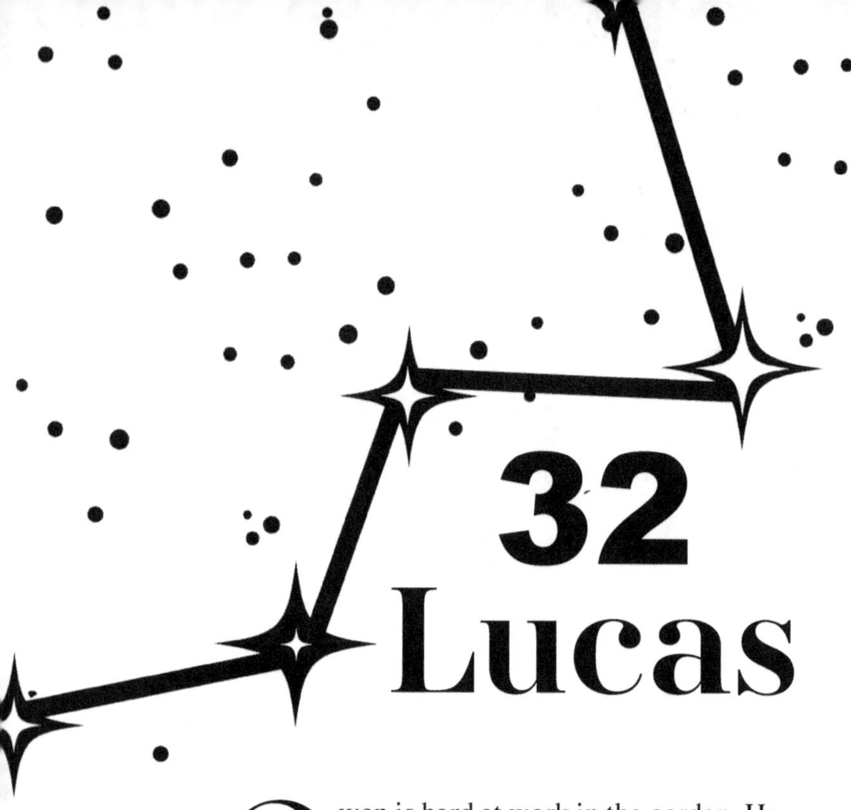

32
Lucas

Owen is hard at work in the garden. He finished tilling new rows for pumpkins. The shape is odd, and I am not sure of his vision, but he keeps checking a picture on his phone to make sure he is doing it right. I have continued to give him space. He had such a wonderful night with Gabriel last night. I have not heard him laugh like that in three years. This morning, he was humming while cooking breakfast. I even saw him make a grocery list. With ingredients to make dinners, not just beer and frozen meals for the nights Adrienne does not feed him. My old Owen is coming back and although I should be jealous I'm not responsible for bringing him into the light. I'm thrilled he has found Gabriel. Grateful even.

Just like a rose bulb coming back to life after a long winter. He is blooming again.

"I know you are watching me." Owen says without turning around. I move to hover in front of him and act like I am sunbathing on the grass. He kicks up some dirt with his shovel and playfully throws it through my body. I flinch out of habit, but it falls right through me.

"I was trying not to bother you."

"You could never bother me." He sits back on his heels and holds the short shovel across his lap. "You could haunt me until my last breath, and it wouldn't bother me."

I frown. *"It should."*

"I see no point being bothered by something I cannot change. Especially when that something is seeing your face every day."

Owen thinks he is being sweet. Being a loving husband even after my death. It's tragic. He is the most amazing man, and I am holding him back from a full life. He could be driving to D.C. right now to see Gabriel if it weren't for me.

"Did you text Gabriel today?"

"Not yet."

I smile. *"But you want to."*

"Yes, I want to." His shoulders drop. "Don't you feel weird encouraging me towards another man?"

"Owen, my love, it's been three years. As much as you hate to admit it, the truth is we are no longer together. Because I am, you know, dead." I motion between us. *"I don't understand why you can see me. Nothing makes sense. I feel like I should not be here. I should leave but I have no sense of direction. No guide. No compass. No path before me. I am in an endless space of limbo. And*

yes, I'll admit, watching you shower has been a high-light, but even that's not enough to justify this. And as much as I love talking to you every day, we both know... I'm not supposed to be here."

"I knew you watched me shower." He smirked.

"I am being serious."

"Sorry. I know." He stood and looked down at me. "What should I do? Call a psychic or a priest. Perform an exorcism."

I float to be at eye level. *"Maybe."*

"You cannot be serious." Owen turns and stomps towards his shed. I watch him toss his shovel inside and lock it up. No longer in the mood for yard work. He starts to walk away from me, and I use the last of my strength to make my voice loud. I want it to echo. I want it to imprint itself on him, even if it hurts.

"Owen!" He turns to me with wide eyes. Birds fly out of the trees as if my voice vibrated enough for them to feel. I narrow my eyes at him and cross my arms over my chest. *"I am no longer yours and I no longer have claim on you. You need to fully accept our lives are separate. I could vanish at any moment. A ghost from your past has no place in your future. Go be free. You need to ask yourself, what would you do if I wasn't here?"*

He let my question go unanswered. Got in his truck and drove away.

33
Owen

It's early Saturday afternoon, and I'm driving without a destination, just circling the town while the weight of my conversation with Lucas lingers like a storm cloud. His heated words keep echoing in my head, each one sinking deeper, pressing against my chest like sandbags I can't shake off. His frustration grows as the days go on.

"A ghost from your past has no place in your future."

He's not wrong. I've spent three years keeping my heart locked away, convincing myself that moving forward was a form of betrayal. But Gabriel—he makes me want more. Makes me crave the warmth of something real again. He has me stepping out ready to take a chance.

I grip the steering wheel of my truck tighter, debating

whether to text him. Ask if he wants to hang out. Hell, I'd drive to the city, book a damn hotel room, just to sit next to him and watch a movie instead of being stuck on the other end of the phone.

As I turn onto Main Street, a familiar Jeep Renegade comes into view. Parked outside the old bank building. The green snake decal on the rear window, some kind of family crest, tells me it's Gabriel's. A smile tugs at my lips, half-convinced I conjured him here just by wanting to see his face. But the smile fades just as quickly as I realize he didn't tell me he was in town. If he wanted to see me… he would have let me know.

I pull into a spot behind him, kill the engine, and head inside.

The moment I step through the door, I spot him. He's standing on a chair, arms stretched high, while Adrienne steadies him from below. The chair has wheels and it's shifting under his movements. My stomach tightens.

"What the Hell are you doing?" I ask, voice sharper than I intend.

Gabriel startles slightly but keeps his balance. "Checking to see If these need new light bulbs or if the wiring is bad." He gestures toward the row of columns.

"I needed help making a to repair list." Adrienne said in her cheerful tone.

He looks down at me and grins. "And I needed a project to inspire me. Take my mind off work."

I exhale through my nose, ignoring the warmth in my chest at the sight of him. Too distracted by the unexpected worry I had seeing him messing with old wires on a rickety rolling death trap. "And you decided to climb onto an old office chair instead of getting a ladder?"

"There isn't one here," he says, as if that justifies his recklessness.

I turn to Adrienne. "Why did you let him do this?" I heard the possessiveness in my tone the second the words left my mouth.

She narrowed her eyes on me. "I was here to keep him from falling."

"He could have been electrocuted." I point to the antique wall sconce.

"I turned off the breaker." Adrienne playfully put one hand on her hip and kept the other braced on Gabriels back. I trust Adrienne. I do. My imagination just got the best of me when I walked in. She raised her eyebrows at me and tilted her head towards Gabriel. She was behind his back and hid her movements from his view.

"Please, get down."

Gabriel gives an exaggerated eye roll but moves to accept Adriennes outstretched hand. I step in smoothly, catching his hand myself and placing my other on his lower back. Adrienne snorts and moves to busy herself across the room. I know Gabriel is a grown adult and he's barely eighteen inches from the ground, but the last thing I need is him falling and getting hurt. Or worse.

"Happy?" He said. With big innocent blue eyes looking up at me once his feet were planted safely on the tile. I nodded. He walked over to his messenger bag and grabbed a notebook. It had a long to-do list that was growing with every movement of his pencil. I watched him add *Call-Electrician to the bottom. Followed buy, *Adrienne should buy a ladder.

"I'll head home and grab a ladder." I stand close to him and try to keep my voice low, even though I know Adrienne is listening. She is doing a poor job looking like she is inspecting the old teller stations.. "Go get your luggage from your car and put it in my truck. I'll drop off at my house."

"My suitcase is already at my rental, the Sandaway Suites."

I step back and study to see read him. Was he avoiding me? His blue eyes with a quick smile. No, he's not avoiding me. This is the same nervous energy I find adorable in him. He needs assurance that I want him near me. I need to take this opportunity to express my interest. In college I wasted time not telling Lucas I was interested in him. I don't want to waste any time with Gabriel. Who knows how long we have anyway. My time with Lucas was cut short.

I can feel my thoughts spiraling into dark corners. Gabriel notices me take a calming deep breath. He rubs a hand down my arm once and softly over the back of my hand.

Once grounded, I ask.

"You're staying at a rental?" The words slip out sharper than I mean them too, shock laden in my tone. When our eyes lock, he does not flinch. Instead, he smirks. Satisfied with how worked up I am that he is not staying with me.

"Well-" Whatever he was going to say dies on his tongue as I step forward, closing the gap between us. The edge of his notebook presses into my chest. The dust filled air tightens. Coiling around us. Holding us in place. The tips of my steel toed boots tapping against his canvas loafers.

I flick a glance toward Adrienne. She's distracted, thankfully, but still in the room. If she wasn't, who knows what I might do. Every instinct in me wants to throw Gabriel over my shoulder and haul him home like he's mine. Because he should be mine.

But I stand still, jaw tight. I remind myself he is in Oxford for a project. For Adrienne, not me. Not yet at least. I need to make myself the reason he wants to come back.

I know Gabriel wants to take things slow. Maybe he wanted to stay under another roof to keep distance from me. Although, the way he is staring at my lips now contradicts that thought. He is begging me to kiss him and if we were alone I wouldn't hesitate for a second.

"Yeah," he says, clutching the notebook to his chest. "It's a cute guest house."

"I know the place," I say, frowning. "It's on the other side of town. That won't do."

Gabriel raises a brow. "That won't do?"

"Yes." I fold my arms. My heart will ache if I know he is in Oxford and not near me.

"You'll stay with me."

I need him close.

I want him close.

Gabriel's mouth hangs open like he wants to argue, but Adrienne clears her throat, barely hiding a grin. "If you stay at Owen's house we can talk over coffee in the morning. It would make things easier on me. I wouldn't have to use my in-laws for childcare."

I nod. "See? Even Adrienne agrees. You'll stay with me."

"Okay, if it would help." He says to Adrienne but keeps his eyes on me.

"Glad that's settled." She looks down at her buzzing phone and walks off to answer a call.

I couldn't resist reaching out to wrap a copper curl around my finger. It bounces when I release it. With a finger under his chin, I force him to look deeper in my eyes. I need to know he wants this too. "Tell me if you don't want to stay with me."

He swallows. "No-I mean yes. Yes I want to stay with you. If you want me there."

The corners of my lips twitch into a toothy smile. "I want you there."

"Okay." He says on a breath.

"Okay." Removing my finger from his chin, I step back. "Okay."

"Okay." Gabriel echoes.

I swiftly turn and head towards the front door. "I'll be back with a ladder. After I pick up your luggage. Promise me you'll stop trying to get injured while I'm gone?"

I glance over my shoulder to find his amused expression has softened. "No promises."

I shake my head, but he just rocks on his heels, a triumphant smile on his face. Somehow I got exactly what I wanted but it feels like he is the victorious one.

It took all my charm and a text from Gabriel for Gayle, the owner of Sandaway Suites, to let me take the suitcase with me. I gave her my credit card and told her to charge me for two nights.

"So, this Gabriel is a friend of yours?" She purred as

she ran my credit card. We were standing in her lobby, which was also her living room. Transformed with a narrow table that she used as a check in desk. To her left was a rack painted to look like weathered wood that held brochures for the area. Her family immigrated to Canada from Japan in the nineties and somehow she ended up here. Her husband is runs a boat rental company. They met in their forties. Evidence that love can find you at any age.

"Yes, a friend." I gripped the handle of the suitcase tighter. Please leave it there. Don't ask any more. I plead in my head.

"A special friend?" Gayle winks while emphasizing the word "special."

Biting back a groan. "He's special to me. That is all you get." I make sure to flash her a warm smile. I'm not trying to me rude, whatever is developing between Gabriel and myself is new. I want to keep it private for now. Sure, I don't mind holding his hand in public. That's all the residents of Oxford get to feed their gossip addiction. For now.

I tip an invisible hat and make my way to my truck parked out front. She watches me leave with the screen door clouding her face. "I'll just ask Adrienne for details at church."

Ignoring that comment, I place the luggage in my truck and head home for a ladder.

34
Gabriel

Adrienne and I stroll down Main Street toward the coffee shop, the midday sun warming the pavement beneath our feet as we make our way to an outside bistro table. She's grinning at me over the rim of her coffee cup before we even sit down.

"I only have one more hour of childcare before I need to be back," she says, setting her cup down with a clink. "So, spill the tea."

I feign innocence, blowing on my coffee. "No tea. Just coffee.

She gives me a look. "I suspected something was going on between you two. And it's obvious you've been talking after you returned to D.C."

I shift in my seat. "Talking, yes. Just talking."

She snorts. "Owen practically demanded you stay at his house. With him."

I wave a dismissive hand. "He's just being nice."

"No." She leans forward, smirking. "He wants you close. Like, in-the-same-bed close."

I turn into a statue with the coffee mug resting on my lower lip. In-the-same-bed close. My cheeks flush. "Oh." Is all I can get out. I slowly drink my coffee ignoring that it is still a bit too hot. I need to focus on something else. The burn on my tongue is the perfect distraction from the fact that Owen might be expecting me to sleep in his bed. Could I sleep next to him and not let it lead to sex? Do I want it to? Am I ready for that?

"I'm just saying," she sings, wiggling her brows.

My mind had automatically assumed I'd be sleeping in the guest room, but now she's put the thought in my head, what will I find when I walk into his house? Will I find my luggage in his room? In his space? Or the guest room?

My leg bounces under the table, sending tiny ripples across the surface of my coffee. My phone buzzes in my pocket, and when I check it, Owen's name is on the screen.

Heading back to the bank now.

I exhale, rubbing the back of my neck. "He's on his way back."

Adrienne grins like she knows something I don't. "Good."

We finish our drinks, and by the time we return to the old bank, Owen is already on a ladder, replacing the lightbulbs in the sconces on the columns. He pulls a rag from his back pocket, his broad shoulders flexing as he wipes the frosted tulip-shaped glass clean. He's focused, determined, like he's been doing this for years.

I suppose he has. He spends every day fixing up the Victorian house. Patching holes. Replacing broken tiles. He told me he spent months tracking down doorknobs to match the originals. He genuinely wants to restore it and not give it the flipper remodel treatment.

Adrienne checks her phone. "Alright, I gotta go," she says. "But I expect updates. Don't forget to lock up." There it is. She was planning on leaving me alone with him. I wonder if her childcare time is actually up or if she is making excuses for me.

I roll my eyes while jingling the janitor size key ring at her.. "Yeah, yeah."

Once she's out of sight, Owen climbs down the ladder, dusting off his hands. "So, how long have you two been working on this place?" he asks, glancing at the worn walls.

I lean against the nearest counter, letting the memories wash over me. "Honestly, since the first day I met her. It's been growing on me—this place, this project. I used to take free art classes as a kid at a community center, a lot like this. Or at least what she's hoping to create here. Lately, I catch myself thinking about it at work. Daydreaming about building a community garden, all the different art classes that could happen here. It's important to me in a way I didn't expect. I love what she's building, and I'm just... really grateful to be a part of it. I know that probably sounds cheesy."

His expression softens and he lifts his hand like he is going to grab me but then notices how filthy his hands are. He rubs them on his jeans and smiles. Bright against his dark skin. "You'll be here every weekend, then?"

"Probably. Until it's finished."

He nods once, decisive. "Then you'll stay with me."

It was not a question or a true invitation. I should be alarmed. I should hate him being so bossy and demanding. Truthfully, the idea of spending weekends with him doesn't feel as terrifying as it probably should. It feels right.

"Okay."

We spend the next few hours working side by side, and by the time we're done, we're both exhausted, covered in grime, and in desperate need of a shower. At least we can cross changing lightbulbs, polishing the brass door knobs, and scrapping paint so the windows will open off the list. Adrienne brought me in to help her design the community garden, but my enthusiasm for the space keeps spreading. Plus, she needs help. Most the parents on the PTA who supported the endeavor are busy during the school year and can't pitch in until summer break.

"Let's head home and get cleaned up," Owen says, stretching his arms over his head. "I'll make dinner."

I arch a brow. "What did Adrienne leave you for tonight?"

He shakes his head. "No. I'll make dinner. I've been doing my own cooking for the past few days."

My lips twitch. "Oh? Mac and cheese?" As I walk past him I feel a playful slap on my ass.

He winks. "Watch your mouth and get in your car."

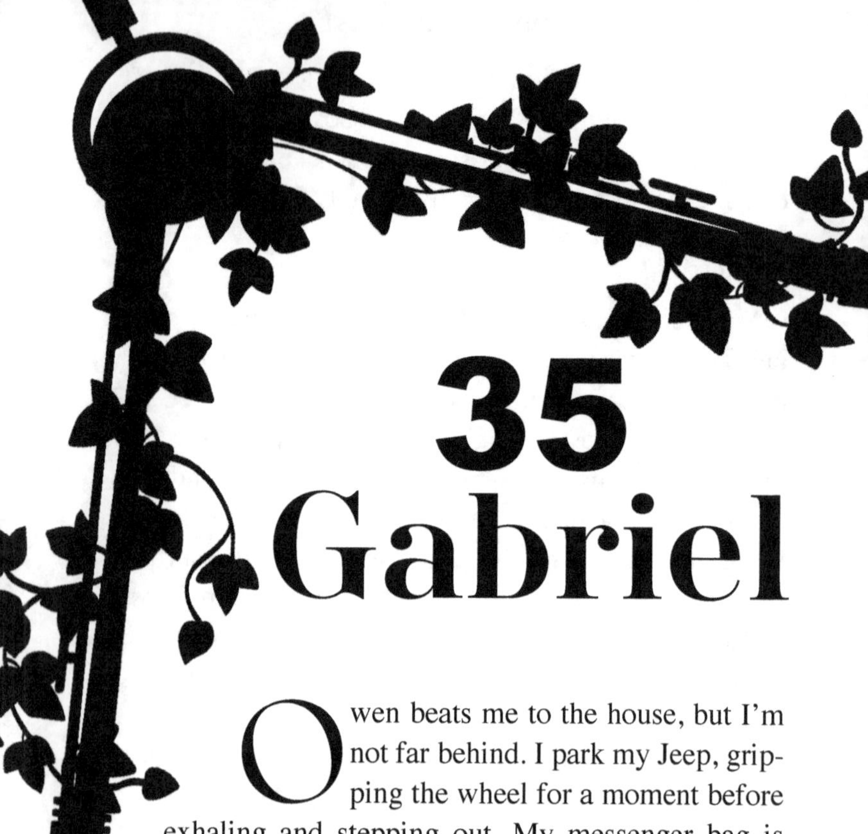

35
Gabriel

Owen beats me to the house, but I'm not far behind. I park my Jeep, gripping the wheel for a moment before exhaling and stepping out. My messenger bag is slung over my shoulder, feeling heavier than it should. Carrying the weight of expectations.

Every step slow as I cross the threshold. My suitcase isn't in the entryway, which means Owen has put it somewhere. The question is, where?

I hear his voice drifting from the dining room, low and steady as he talks to someone about matching antique drawer pulls for the kitchen. I hesitate, then tiptoe upstairs, my heart hammering against my ribs.

When I step into the guest room, I spot my suitcase against the foot of the bed. A breath in my chest finally drifts free. So, this is where he put me. I don't know if I feel relieved or disappointed. Maybe both.

Do I want to share a bed with Owen? Yes, God, yes. I want to be held in his large arms, wrapped in his warmth, surrounded by the scent of flannel and whatever it is that makes him so irresistible. Probably fumes from wood stain, but I have grown to like it.

But I can't change who I am. I need more assurance. More than heat. We already know that's there. The night on the couch proved that. But I need to know this isn't just a fleeting thing for him. That I'm not just a momentary distraction as he grieves. My heart is already tangled up in him, and if I fall any further, I need to know he'll catch me.

I set my messenger bag down on the wingback chair and wander to the window. Late afternoon sunlight spills across the side yard in a warm, golden wash, casting long shadows over Owen's progress. It's still rough. With piles of dirt and scattered debris, but there's movement, signs of effort and intention. Where the old, crumbling shack once leaned, a neat stack of wooden planks now waits, full of promise. I can almost see it complete: Owen in one of those rugged tan work jackets, handing out steaming mugs of cocoa crowned with marshmallows, while kids dash around in search of the perfect pumpkin.

That little shack was an eyesore, and I'm glad to see he's rebuilding it. He will make this place his own. Put his stamp on this town. Similar to what Adrienne is doing with the community art center. One of the things that inspired me to go into architecture was the idea of having my name on a building. Proudly showcasing my designs for the world to enjoy. A legacy. I wanted to design parks, schools, hotels, and other gathering places. It feels like the direction my career is heading will lead to only designing for a specific group. The ultra wealthy who are out of touch and do not care one bit about building a community. They would rather I design a space to keep the average person out, than invite them in.

"I hope you don't mind I put you in here."

I jump, whirling around to find Owen standing in the doorway. I hadn't even heard him come in. His lips twitch in amusement before he rubs the back of his neck. "To be honest, I wanted to put your stuff in my room. But that choice is up to you." His voice dips slightly, a quiet invitation. "Just know my door is open."

Then he turns and walks out, leaving me standing there, heart pounding from the jump scare and the invitation to share a room with him.

He wants me in his room. Wants us to share a bed. The thought sends heat racing beneath my skin.

I glance down at my dirt-streaked clothes, suddenly hyper-aware of how much grime clings to me. I need a shower. Desperately.

Without another thought, I head into the bathroom, hoping the hot water will do something to steady me. Because no matter how much I try to brace myself, I already know I'm falling for Owen. And there's no stopping it now.

36
Owen

My insides are vibrating while I cook dinner. Focusing on the motions to steady my thoughts. Chop, stir, and don't forget to season. Growing up in Utah is no excuse to have bland food. The scent of smoked turkey sausage blends with caramelized onions and red peppers. Spicy rice simmers in a blue ceramic Dutch Oven, almost ready for me to mix everything to complete the jambalaya. It's nothing elaborate. Just comfort food that I learned from a roommate in college. Cooking tonight does not feel like a chore or necessity. It's meaningful. Laced with intention.

It's been years since I cooked a real meal from scratch. Longer since I felt reason to. Feeding Gabriel feels like a good reason. Not because he is starving or incapable of feeding himself. He's sharp and independent. In no way does he need me to take care of him, but I can't fight the urge to. I love to watch him go quiet. It's not that I don't enjoy hearing him talk. I do. But I love the feeling when the words fade, and he just looks at me. His blue eyes take me in. Flaws and all. Despite my messy life and sad existence, he likes what he sees. Obvious by the flush in his cheeks. Acting as my own personal barometer—letting me know if he is embarrassed, nervous, or turned on.

From across the kitchen Gabriel hums along with a pop song playing on the Bluetooth speaker, a beat far too bubbly for my usual tastes. But damn if I don't enjoy the way he moves his body. Hips swaying and curls bouncing as he bops.

The ease between us follows to the table. The small distance between us feels like miles. I stretch my legs out and pin his between mine. Momentarily quenching the craving I have to touch him. Hunger lives behind every glance he sends across the table. Desire looks good on him. Smoldering in those ocean blue eyes, and it feels even better knowing it's for me.

Gabriel eats up every bite and washes it down with a glass of red wine. The same wine he brought with him the last time he was here. Picking out wine is not one of my strengths. The other day, I showed a liquor store employee a photo of the wine label from my phone. On the off-chance Gabriel would return to my house, I wanted to have the wine he likes. I also stocked the pantry with the gluten free rice crackers he liked. He is not allergic to gluten but told me once he loves the way they snap. While he was up in his room one night I tied one. It was oddly satisfying.

After dinner, we clean up together, shoulder to shoulder, hands brushing as I pass him a soapy dish. He nudges me with his hip, playful, testing the waters. I press back, watching him grin up at me. The tension is thick, warm, buzzing under my skin, making my fingers itch to touch him.

When we settle on the couch, I put on a show we've both seen before, something to fill the silence but not enough to distract from the pull between us. I switch from beer to whiskey, hoping it'll steady me, but instead, all it does is make me hyper-aware of him. The way he tucks his feet under him, the subtle curve of his mouth when he speaks, the animated gestures he makes when he's caught in a story.

I've stopped listening. His lips have a hold of me like a hypnotist uses a coin. I just want to taste him. The need overwhelms me.

I reach for Gabriel, cupping his face in my hands, cutting him off mid-sentence. His breath hitches, but he doesn't hesitate. His lips match my rhythm; all heat and urgency. I taste wine on his tongue, and it makes my head spin. His hands grip my shirt, pulling me closer, and I groan when he shifts, straddling my left thigh without breaking the kiss.

With a strategic roll of his hips, I lose any pretense of control. His arousal grinding into me. I grip his waist, pulling Gabriel flush against my chest, and when he moans into my mouth, I curse the layers of fabric between us. My hands roam, sliding over his back, down to the curve of his ass, pressing my hardening cock against his. A whimper sneaks past Gabriel's lips, and it sends a jolt of heat through me. I want to swallow that sound and save it for later.

We break apart slowly, our foreheads pressed together, sharing breath. The look in his eyes roots me in place. Our thoughts are perfectly aligned. Our bodies buzzing at the same frequency. Without words we scream for the same thing—bed—now.

Gently I move him off my lap. Aching to feel his warmth again. I stand, offering my hand. He hesitates only a second before slipping his fingers into mine, with a slight tremble. I lead Gabriel upstairs, stopping outside his room. It feels like a date, that agonizing pause on a porch when you don't know if you'll be invited in. When you are not ready to end a date.

I cage him in against the wall, dragging my lips over his jaw, down his neck. His hands clutch my shirt, like a lifeline.

"Invite me in," I murmur, lips brushing his skin.

He laughs, breathless. "What are you, a vampire? This is your house."

"The room is currently yours. I won't pressure you," Pulling back just enough to lock eyes with him. "Last time you were here, I was intense. I practically attacked you on the couch. I don't want you to think—I am using you. I like you, Gabriel."

His lips crash into mine, deep and desperate. "I like you too, Owen." Gabriel presses up onto his toes and links fingers behind my neck. Fireworks ignite when he kisses me again. "Use me…please."

I groan, reaching for the doorknob.

We don't bother turning on a light. Both stripping clothes off as we stumble to the bed. I trip taking my second sock off and fall onto the mattress. Leaving only my underwear remaining. Gabriel has stripped enough layers to match me. His light skin inviting me to touch it under the moonlight pouring in from the window. He crawls over my body. Slowly like I am his prey. I welcome it. My body begs for it as I find myself so fucking hard. I fear my cock will bust through my briefs.

I prop myself up on my elbows. Meeting him halfway with a slow kiss. Full of need. Only breaking our lips apart when he wants to explore my body. My chest and stomach are tense from the pose, and he peppers the flexing muscles with kisses. The kind that lets his tongue slip out with each press of lips. I stare down at him. Begging, pleading him to go lower. Gabriel presses a kiss just below my belly button and runs a finger along the waistband of my underwear. I have to stop myself from holding my breath.

This is real. I'm giving myself to him, and somehow, it's freeing. Not because of the act itself, but because it's with Gabriel. Right now, it's just my body I can offer. My heart remains timid and frozen. Each moment with him removes a brick from the wall. If only he knew the control he has over me. How obsessed I have become with his freckles. How blue has become my favorite color.

Gabriel touches me and my chest begins to thaw.

For three years, I've been stuck. Stagnant. Hiding from the world. Haunted.

And now, somehow, Lucas guided the very person that might heal me. Every kiss gives feeds the restoration. Piece by piece, he's putting me back together. Into something that almost feels like a whole person again.

I close my eyes and throw my head back. Gabriel slips his hand under the fabric and pulls me out. His warm breath on my cock makes me drop from my elbows until I am flat on the bed. At his mercy. My body has become a puddle, melted by the heat of him. When he takes an inch of me into his mouth I grip the comforter. "Fuck."

It's been too long. I focus on the carven medallion on the ceiling, hoping the distraction with let me last longer.

He hums as he lowers his mouth further down. Taking me in more, inch by inch. I watch his cheeks hollow out as he sucks as he lifts up. I might die. This feels so good it might kill me.

His movements quicken. His head moves up and down on my length. At this pace I'll spill into his mouth before I get to have my way with him. His mouth is not where I intend on finishing. I need more of him than just his mouth. Gently I reach down to touch his shoulders. He pulls off of me with a pop of his lips. I instantly miss the feeling of his mouth, but I need more.

"Is something wrong?" He licks the corner of his mouth as if he just ate dessert and was savoring every bit of frosting. I sit up until we are face to face and he is straddling me once more. I kiss his lips that are wet and slightly swollen.

"Absolutely nothing is wrong." I whisper. We kiss again, this time Gabriel grinds over my painfully hard cock. "I want you."

"You have me." He says between kisses.

I run my hands down his back and under the waist of his underwear. While he is distracted with our kiss I slide a finger down his crack and press the tip to his hole. I speak with my lips barely touching his. "I want all of you."

His back stiffens. I move my hands, afraid that I have

made him uncomfortable. Gripping his chin with my thumb and finger, I force him to make eye contact with me.

"Okay." Gabriel whispers.

"Okay?" I narrow my eyes. "I need more enthusiasm than that. I need more than an okay."

He presses his palms to my chest and gives me a shy smile. I cannot see the color of his cheeks in the low light, but I feel his skin getting hot under my touch. After a deep inhale he answers me.

"Yes. I want that." He bites his bottom lip. "But I didn't bring anything for that."

The athlete in me comes alive, flipping him swiftly, so his back is on the bed and press a kiss to his forehead before walking towards the door. "I'll be right back."

I tiptoe into the hallway and look around for Lucas. I have not seen him since Gabriel came over today. Lucas said he was giving me space, but I wonder where he hides when not around.

In my room there is a very neglected box in my top drawer. I purchased condoms and lube about a year ago when I thought I was ready to date again. Spent three days looking at profiles on dating apps and got overwhelmed. Deleted my profile completely.

Lucas even gave me a hard time. Teasing me about expecting the perfect man to just knock on my door. Little did he know that exact thing was going to happen. Because laying in the next room is a man that could very well be as close to perfect as I could find. He has pulled me out of my shell and a future without him is becoming harder and harder to picture.

37
Gabriel

I knew Owen wouldn't be gone for long. Every second without him felt deliciously drawn out, giving me just enough time to catch my breath, and carefully consider the best way to greet him when he walked back in. I tried a few poses, each one more tempting than the last, until I finally settled on lying on my stomach. Legs stretched out straight, ass on display. Arms folded under my head to keep my hands from shaking.

I was about to change positions for the twentieth time when Owen walked back in. A greedy grin filled his face when I looked over my shoulder at him. He tossed something on the bed and covered my body with his. Owen blanketed me with kisses. On the back of my neck, behind my ear, over the freckles of my shoulders.

It felt like he was taking his time introducing himself to each freckle on my skin. Mapping their placements in his memory.

He slowly slid my underwear down my legs and threw them on the floor. My breath hitched when he presses a kiss to one ass cheek then the other. "I will go slow."

"Why are you whispering?"

He paused his kiss and let out a sigh. His breath was warm on my thighs as he gripped them and spread them apart. I have never felt so exposed. Even though the only light was from a small tiffany lamp in the corner, I felt as if being lit by the midday sun. Spotlit and on display for him to do as he wishes.

"Habit." Owen nestled his face against me, and I felt his tongue trace circles before pressing in slightly. A moan escaped him causing vibrations into my core. "Fuck. I am going to make a habit out of this."

His tongue darted in and out of me. Savoring every flick of his tongue. I heard the plastic snap of a container and moments later felt a lubed-up finger glide into me. I clenched around it.

"Gabriel." He came up on his knees and presses my legs apart. Owen nestles between my thighs. "Relax. I will take good care of you."

I nodded with my face pressed into the blanket. He was right, I needed to relax. I am so nervous of what happens after this. After I give him my body will he never call me again? Will I never stay here again? The last thing I want is for this to end before it can really start. Owen wanted me here this weekend, but what about next weekend? Will he have his fill of me and want to move on?

I take a deep breath and press back slightly on his finger as it pumps in me. Noticing my movements he takes the opportunity to add a second finger. Stretching me. I say his name on a breath. My hard cock presses into the mattress and the friction only makes me more sensitive to the glide of his fingers. The pace of my heart is struggling to keep up.

He leans over me. His lips hover over my ear. "Are you ready for me?"

"Yes."

"Yes, what?"

Yes what? How do I answer this? Yes please sexy huge black man naked behind me—take my body and use it as you wish. Mark me. Lick me. Stretch me around your cock.

I say none of those things. All I can do is arch into him and beg. "Yes, please."

He smiles as he kisses my shoulder once more. "Good boy." His fingers slide out of me, and he steps off the bed. I remain. Legs wide and waiting.

Behind me, I hear the tear of a condom wrapper and them I feel the bed dip again. I want to tense my muscles and brace myself, but I force myself to relax. To let his hands caress me. To welcome his large cock pressing against me.

"Breathe." He presses just the tip. I come undone. My body pleading for more of him. "Fuck, Gabriel you feel so fucking good."

I don't recognize the sounds coming out of my mouth. Breathy and barely words. As he slips a few inches in and pulls out slowly. His force increases. Filling me. Claiming me from the inside.

That's what this feels like—claiming.

I want so badly for Owen to call me his. Intimacy

has always been a big deal to me. It must coincide with emotion and connection. He's deep in me now and I feel the addiction starting. The pleasure pulsing through my body is sealing my fate.

My hardness presses into the bed with each thrust of his hips. Rocking me into the mattress until he is completely seated inside me. He grabs ahold of my hips and does exactly what I asked. He uses me. Slides in and out like I am his toy. Here to serve him. His large hands grip my skin with a fever. I'm on the edge of my own orgasm.

Our sounds blend together in a harmony of gasps and moans. I'm stretched around him. The feeling of fullness causes drops of pre-cum to soak into the bed under me.

His strong arms wrap around my waist, lifting me against his chest. Owen sits back on his heels. He bounces me with his cock hitting deep inside me. The new angle hitting my prostrate and I curse so loud I fear the neighbors will hear.

I can no longer reach the headboard for balance, so I reach back and grasp his head. Diggin my fingers into the tight coils of his hair. His mouth threatens to bite the curve between my neck and my shoulder. Bruising me with hard kisses. Owen slides a hand around my hip and wraps around my length. Each stroke causing my body to shutter.

"You feel too good. I'm gonna come." I say between heavy pants and screams. Sounding like a tennis player serving. My voice painting the ceiling with high notes of pleasure. He has one hand on my cock and the other rubs up my chest and grips my neck gently. Applying pressure on my veins as he thrusts under me.

"Come for me." He whispers into my ear.

I let out a long moan. Grateful for his command. My body clenches around him. I spill onto the bed and his hand. He uses it to stroke me until my cock is slick and soft. Soon after he bites down on my shoulder and grips both my thighs. His thrusts are rough, but his hands keep me in place.

I feel the condom fill inside me with the last of his violent thrusts.

We both slow our pace. Our chests rising and falling in sync. The room feels eerily quiet. Owen presses another kiss to my shoulder. Sharp contract to what he just did with my body. I lean back into him. Closing my eyes.

"That was amazing."

"My thoughts exactly." He playfully slaps my leg. "Let's take a quick shower, and sleep in my bed. We made a mess of this one."

His hand stays on the small of my back as we walk to the bathroom, like he's not quite ready to let me go yet. Every touch feels like a quiet promise, and I soak it in. If I'm not careful, I'll start to crave the way he holds me. Like I am already his. A title my heart is longing for.

38
Lucas

This is what I wanted, I remind myself, staring down at the two sleeping bodies tangled in a bed that used to be mine. Gabriel is tucked into a ball with his head nestled against Owens' chest. I was never the one who reached for cuddles in the middle of the night. That was Owen, clingy even in sleep. Funny how now I'd give anything to be the one smothered by him, instead of watching someone else fill that space.

I'm standing too close to them. Goosebumps have formed on their exposed skin. Slipping through the outer wall, I drift down to the ground like mist on a breeze. Earlier tonight I was on the porch watching Owen kiss Gabriel. They were in the throws on passion on the couch. Lit up by the TV glow. I tried my best to stay out of the way. Give him the space he needs to move on. I need him to move on. Although his love was the greatest gift I received in my lifetime, it feels like a tether. And I am a ball and chain keeping him from living.

Owen's eyes found me once. Locked onto me as I stood outside in the moonlight. He grimaced at the sight of me. I smiled softly before fading into the dark. Staying out of the house until all the lights were off and I was sure they were both asleep.

This is my future if Owen stays in this house.

The only after life I will know.

I will watch him fall in love.

Watch him fuck.

Watch him live a full life with someone else.

I dig my nails into my palms and feel nothing. The moon taunts me behind the clouds. Tonight, it hides from my angry words and pathetic pleading. Hides from my pain. A pain that has become too bearable for me to tolerate. There must be something I'm missing. A task I need to complete or one step I missed at the time of my death.

I replay the moment.

I don't remember falling.

One second, I was standing in the living room. We were going to watch a show. I think I was reaching for the remote. And then...

I'm on the floor.

Not laying on the floor.

Suddenly, I'm looking down. I didn't understand. My body is on the floor. Sprawled out on the hard wood floor like a discarded puppet. Eyes half-lidded, mouth slightly open. There's no movement, no breath. Just an earie stillness.

But I'm not on the floor. I'm standing. I can feel my-self—no, not feel, exactly. I'm aware of myself. I move, but my body does not move with me.

Then Owen runs in, and I reach for him. My hand goes straight through his arm like smoke. No sensation. No resistance.

"Owen!" I scream, but he does not even flinch.

I shout again, louder. Still no response.

"I'm here. Look at me." I plead. *"I'm here."*

A scream tears out of his chest, raw and cracking.

"Lucas? Babe, wake up. Please wake up!"

He drops to his knees besides my body and shakes my shoulders. His fingers pressing into my shoulders like he can pull me back into myself by force alone. His eyes are flooded with tears.

I try to touch him again. Grabbing at his shirt, his face, anything—but I slip through.

I scream in panic. My chest rises rapidly, but there's no breath. I clutch my throat, gasping on reflex. There's no rush of air. Nothing to choke on. No ache.

I am not suffocating and that is somehow worse. Because all I feel is cold emptiness.

My name bleeds from Owen's lips over and over. His sobs have turned into desperate pleas to a God he no longer believes in.

I want to respond. To tell him I'm right here, watching him cry over my body, that he's not as alone as he feels. But my voice does not reach him.

And then, like a shiver rolling down my spine, the truth settles in.

Harsh and Damning.

I died.

39
Owen

I step into Mr. Garcia's office, plans tucked under one arm, the scent of stale coffee and dust linger in the air. As far as City Halls are concerned this building is nothing to be excited about. The first city hall burned down decades ago. They moved the government offices into the same building as the seventy on duty police officers and park management. A box with white siding and blue awnings. A larger version of the post office that's a block west of here.

Mr. Garcia looks up from his desk with a warm smile, adjusting his reading glasses. He is on the City Council, President of the Historic Society, and Leader of the Tourism Board. Needless to say, he wants my renovation to be successful.

"You have something for me, Owen?" He points to the rolled papers with a napkin and then wipes what remained on his lips from a chocolate donut.

I spread the papers across his desk, smoothing the edges. "A pumpkin patch layout, completed renovation list, and timeline for the rest of the repairs. All the hard stuff is over. Plumbing, electrical, and upgrade in the attic to support the roof."

His eyes light up as he scans the documents. "This is fantastic. Better than I expected. I especially love the design of the pumpkin patch. I have never seen anything like it." He leans back in his chair, stroking his chin with a big grin on his face. "What do you think about a grand opening? A real event to bring the community together? We could advertise it in neighboring towns. I could use some of the tourism budget to make it something really special."

My mind immediately thinks of telling Gabriel only to remember this is not his project. It is mine alone. I force a smile. There was talks about a grand opening when Lucas first met Mr. Garcia over three years ago. They both love pomp and extravagance. Never did I think I would be hosting the grand opening alone.

"I think that would be nice."

"Great when will it be ready?" He moves a plate to reveal a desk calendar underneath it.

I glance at the calendar on my phone, swiping through months. "It will only work if I have pumpkins. So, September. September 24th?" I suggest.

He grins. "Perfect."

Perfect. I echo in my head. I will decide after the grand opening if the best thing for the town is for me to sell it to a worthy host. Someone who wants to be a pillar in the community. Not a barely functioning bachelor, who refuses to give up on his dead husband while simultaneously falling for someone knew. In no way am I what his town needs.

Our meeting was quick, but it filled me with excitement. I have felt like I was screwing up with everything. The renovations. Grieving. Being a good brother and son. My family rarely calls after I freaked out when my brother, eager to serve a Mormon mission, asked if he could do a baptism in Lucas's name. I did not take it well. Having no one but Adrienne to talk to I have evolved into ultimate hermit level one thousand. Moping inside the house with no energy to complete projects. At times it felt like I was the one haunting the space.

Then a cute redhead walked in my life, and I suddenly want to make it perfect for him. Am I nesting? Isn't that what it's called? After all, every repair made on the house since I met Gabriel has been met with the question "would he like it." Thoughts of him have taken root in the front of my mind. Guiding my decisions. Pulling me forward.

Feeling accomplished as I step out into the warm afternoon air. The weight of responsibility sits lighter on my shoulders today. Gabriel is only a block away, helping Adrienne at the future community art center, but instead of heading to him, I go home. Needing to have a conversation with Lucas. I have been avoiding him since I woke up this morning wrapped around Gabriel.

As soon as I walk in, I know I'm not alone. The air has the usual chill that means one thing.

Lucas stands by the window, staring out into the yard, his expression unreadable. His presence is no longer a shock, but the sight of him still knocks something loose inside me. He's wearing the same soft sweater he died in, the one I used to bury my face in after long workdays in Chicago. I set a bag down on the coffee table and the box of screws clang together like coins. The sound does not cause him to flinch or glance in my direction. I approach slowly to stand by his side.

This will be the first time we have spoken since Gabriel, and I slept together. My mind prepares for the worse. He could be upset and have changed his mind about me dating again. If he asks me to break it off, would I? Could I? He wanted me to move on and find happiness with someone else, but it could be too much for him. Watching me become more blissfully happy each day. Longing for someone else's touch.

He looks over at me from the corner of his eye.

"I think a dog saw me earlier," he says, still facing away.

I freeze. It was the last thing I expected him to say. "What?"

"I was outside. A man was walking his German Shepherd. It looked right at me and barked. Right at me."

My throat tightens. "Maybe it just sensed something. Isn't that something people believe? That animals can sense spirits."

Lucas finally turns to me. *"It's getting easier."* He lifts his hand, and the lamp on the side table flickers. *"The more I do it, the less effort it takes to effect things. When I touch something, the recovery time is shorter too."* His voice drops. *"I'm changing. It all feels so permanent."*

Although he has no breath I can feel it when he motions a tired sigh. He looks like he just ran a marathon but is not allowed to collapse at the finish line. He must remain standing with shaking limbs and no rest. I don't know what to say. I don't know how to help him.

"What happens when I go full poltergeist?" He continues. *"Will I be stuck here forever?"*

I shake my head. I have no answers. I can offer nothing.

He fades slightly. *"Maybe I already am."*

The words sit heavy between us, thick with something neither of us wants to name. Fear laced with something toxic. Guilt grows inside my chest. I am the happiest I have been in three years with Gabriel in my life. Yet my husband is miserable. Suffering. Watching me move on as if he is not watching.

I open my mouth to speak but am interrupted by the crunch of tires in the driveway.

I glance toward the window to see Gabriel parking his Jeep, and when I turn back. Lucas is gone.

40
Gabriel

I push open the door, my messenger bag slung over my shoulder and pause just inside. Owen stands in the living room, his back to me, shoulders tense. He's moving like he is in a tough conversation. I fear he is practicing how he will tell me last night was a mistake and I should stay somewhere else. It felt too good to be true. Owen makes me feel safe and I let my guard down. Intimacy happened quicker than usual and now I will pay the price.

I suck in a deep breath that tastes like spring. Blooming flowers and damp air.

The door creaks slightly when I push it open.

"Were you talking to yourself?" I ask, tilting my head.

He turns, and instead of answering, he steps forward and kisses me. It's soft, slow, and savoring. I find myself blanketed in the scent of sandalwood clinging to his skin from his morning shave.

Compared to him, I must look and smell atrocious. I'm covered in dust from the bank renovation, dirt caked into every line of my hands from digging in the future community garden. It's been years since I was the one getting dirty. My job as a project manager meant watching others do the labor, directing from the sidelines. But today, I was in the thick of it. Wondering why no one told me how good it feels to get dirty. How rewarding it is to work with my own hands. To be both designer and creator.

I used to dream of a corner office, of big promotions, of having my name on the wall at a prestigious firm. But now? Now it all feels… superficial. When this project is done I will be able to say, with pride, that my own hands helped to build it. I cannot think of anything better to create other than something that will enrich a community for generations to come. Not a place to showboat wealth or be exclusive. A space to teach, strengthen a community, and celebrate art. Something with meaning behind it.

Owen pulls away and smiles at me, brushing a stray curl from my forehead. "Want to help me replace cabinet pulls?"

"I would love nothing else." I squeeze his torso as I kiss him. When did this happen? This undeniable urge to be close to him. I dread leaving tomorrow. It's been such a short time and a crazy part of me would pick up my life and move in with him if he asked. If it meant having his arms around me and these tender kisses every day. And the not so tender way he took my body the last night. Filling me. Griping me tight. His hands and tongue everywhere. He is gentle with my heart but not my body. In the best ways I could imagine.

Heat pools low in my stomach when I replay it in my head.

After we eat dinner, I drag myself to the guest bathroom, exhaustion weighing heavy in my limbs. My eyes are sunken, and my muscles are beginning to resist movement. Gardening turned out to be more of a full body work out than I expected. I squeeze toothpaste onto my brush and start scrubbing.

Owen walks in, his own toothbrush in hand, and without hesitation, uses my toothpaste. We brush while watching each other through the mirror.

"Hey," he says, voice warm and playful, toothpaste foam on the corners of his lips. "I want you to sleep in my bed again. If you want. It's bigger than the guest bed."

I pause to spit and rinse, and in that moment of silence, I see something flicker across his face. His shoulders stiffen slightly, bracing for rejection. There's a chance he is just as nervous as I am. Every second I wait for him to realize how gorgeous and amazing he is and kick me to the curb in search of a hot replacement. But he is looking at me like I hold all the cards. Owen wants me. Me.

I touch his arm, grounding him. "I'd love that," I say, then cringe. "But can I be completely honest?"

His eyes widen, and I realize I'm freaking him out. He is as anxious as I am. I give his arm a squeeze before continuing. "Nothing weird. I'm just exhausted. Like, my muscles feel like Jello. I'm not sure if I can… ya know." My face heats, and I look down, suddenly shy.

Owen hooks a finger under my chin and lifts my gaze to his. His smile is warm, reassuring. "Want a massage?"

I laugh. "Oh, I remember the last massage you gave me."

He grins. "Well, this one won't turn into more unless you instigate it. Deal?" He kisses me once on the lips, then once on each cheek, still warm with embarrassment.

"Deal."

In his bed, his hands work over my sore muscles, kneading away the aches and tension. I melt into him, curling into his warmth as his fingers stroke lazy circles along my spine. Even when I'm on the edge of sleep, he keeps touching me. His hands are gentle, soothing. He presses kisses to my shoulder, and it works like a lullaby. Luring me into a deep sleep.

41
Lucas

The air tonight is different. Thick with mist rolling out of the forest tree line behind the house. I came out in a ritualistic manner. Longing to feel the crisp air on my skin. Saddened when I feel nothing. I manifested on the back lawn with the overwhelming sensation of being watched. My hollow chest rumbled with anticipation. The vibration was not the stars above or a heartbeat in my chest. This was a foreign sensation.

A wave of energy hits me. In the darkness of the trees a woman walks out. Her dark skin and long black leather coat gives her the illusion of being a shadow. Long braids hung in front of her shoulders, bleeding out from an oversized hood. I should wake Owen, who is sleeping alone upstairs, after Gabriel returned to D.C. days ago.

I should warn him of the intruder, but her posture is calm and her strides slow. She is not prowling towards the house. Instead, she is looking directly at me. I point to myself in confusion.

"Yes, you." Her smile is steeped in sadness. There is an absence of life behind her eyes. "You are the soul I seek."

This is it. It's time. My wait is over. They have come to collect me. A chill runs through me as I narrow my eyes, suddenly struck that stranger can see me and does not feel human. She stops a few feet from me. Hands still in the pockets of her coat that billows behind her like a cape. I see no angelic wings. Which makes me feel uneasy. Although, I see no horns either. So, that must be a good sign.

"You are here for me?"

She nods once. "I am."

I look up towards the second-floor window. Behind it my husband is deep in a peaceful sleep. I cannot leave like this. I cannot just vanish. I take a step back. She flinches and pulls her hands from her pockets. The only piece of jewelry she has is a round ring on her middle finger. A six-pointed star in the center.

"Where are you taking me?"

"Calm down, you look like you're about to run from the cops." She puts her hands up with palms out, like she is attempting to talk me off a ledge. Perhaps she is. I am seriously considering flying upstairs and screaming until Owen wakes. I cannot leave without saying goodbye. Without giving him closure. "I don't know what waits for you. That is the truth. I am here to collect your soul and guide you to a gateway. That is all. I know nothing of judgement or what comes after."

I relax for a moment. But only a moment. My gaze flicks from her to the second-floor window and back again. My hands shake frantically at my side. All I can think about is Owen.

Behind me the back porch light flickers. The bulb grows bright and pops. We both flinch and then stare at each other now covered in complete darkness.

"So, you collect souls. Who are you?"

"We have had many names from the beginning of time in every language spoken. Your culture would call me a reaper." She holds the edge of her long coat and bows dramatically. "We are not evil. I am not here to cause pain for you or whoever lives in the house you keep looking at. I'm assigned as temporary guardian of your soul. Like a chaperone."

"And you are going to collect my soul right now?"

"That's the plan."

I cross my arms over my chest. *"Why now? Why not when I died?"*

She begins to walk towards the bench, speaking to me over her shoulder. "You are a case of bad timing." She waits for me to sit on the bench before she continues. "A man died in New York the same time as you. Let's just say outside influences interfered. He cut you in line. Took your spot. Confused the reaper assigned to you, and poof, you became a ghost. We can usually sense a ghost if not collected quickly, but something about you is special. I was unsure what I would find, but I feel it now. A deep pull within you like gravity."

"My husband. I feel tethered to him and this house." I say looking down at my hands in my lap.

"People with husbands and houses die every day." She shrugs. "I know that's not comforting. I'm a reaper, not a therapist."

"I understand I'm being selfish. I've been haunting him, holding him back. It wasn't my death that stopped him from living—it's me. My presence is the chain he can't break."

"Then it's time to set him free."

"Can I say goodbye?"

The reaper stands. She stares down at me. "Reapers are not in the business of bartering."

"Please. I beg of you." I get on my knees. They do not sink into the soil or become moist from the grass. *"He will wake in a few hours. Let me say goodbye. He deserves that."*

Closure. The word kept repeating in my head. He needs closure. I can't just vanish from his life. Closure. He deserves closure.

She looks me over before scanning the house. Her shoulders drop. "Fine. I will be back at sunset tomorrow." She taps my chest and it's solid. Her finger does not pass through me. I gasp.

"Can I be touched now?"

"No." She frowns. "That's a reaper thing. He will not be able to touch you."

I nod and float up from kneeling. She moves a few feet away in the blink of an eye. Her finger is still pointing at me. In a promise that she will be back. I nod once more. Then the reaper is gone. The air feels light once more.

I float up and through the exterior wall of the house. I

pass through the bathroom and enter Owen's bedroom. The sheets are pushed down low on his hips. His bare chest rising slowly with each breath. I mimic sitting on the bed but do not touch him. My cold presence will wake him if I get too close. He has always been a furnace at night threatening to overheat. I used to playfully nudge him away from me or I would find myself waking covered in sweat.

I think back to how he was wrapped around Gabriel's body the other night. They looked perfect together. Truly puzzle pieces who found their match.

The reaper could not have come at a more perfect time. There is no longer a place for me here. He has someone to hold and share his heat.

42
Owen

The house waits patiently for Gabriel's return. The air is stagnant, as if the walls have been holding their breath since he left. And I am the beating heart keeping an anxious rhythm. I did not expect to miss him this much. He burst into my life bringing the sunshine that was missing. I text him when I feel low and he lifts me up. Our evening calls have become my comfort. When I close my eyes I see the freckles on his shoulders, begging to be kissed.

The pillows on the couch are still slightly indented from our bodies. I've been afraid to touch them. Unwilling to erase any proof that Gabriel is real and not just my dream manifested. It's ridiculous how empty everything feels when he's not here, how every shadow seems darker, every meal feels lonelier than before I knew him. The gap after Lucas died and Gabriel showed up on my porch. I was alone. It was my belief that I deserved to be alone. I never minded it before—before him. But now? Now, it feels wrong.

I sit at the kitchen table, staring at the last few sips of coffee in my mug, trying to ignore how hollow the place feels. Upstairs my sheets still smell like him. I haven't wanted to wash them. Couldn't. I'm a mess. Falling hard—fast.

I pull out my phone and type out a message.

> Are you coming back this weekend? I want to see you.

I set the phone down and run a hand over my face. I know he has a life in D.C., work, responsibilities, but Hell, I miss him already. Is it terrible that I want to take him home and lock him in my house for good? Okay, I don't want to lock him up. I just want to see him at the end of the day. And in the morning. And the occasional lunch wouldn't hurt.

A minute later, my phone buzzes.

> I would love to, but I have a thing on Saturday. Why don't you come with me?

I sit up straighter. This is unfamiliar territory. Spending time together outside of Oxford. This is something a couple would do. Are we a couple? I push my thoughts aside and type out a response.

> What kind of thing?

A Fundraiser. Do you have a suit?

I smirk. Does he think I don't own a suit? I have multiple, all pressed and ready to wear, hanging in bags upstairs. Most of them never worn. Purchased years ago, when Lucas and I made a deal to trade watching football games with attending Broadway plays. He kept a tally of every college and NHL game that graced out TV.

The suits have hung neglected for the past three years.

Yes.

Not a track suit. A black-tie suit?

I roll my eyes.

Yes. It's bright yellow with matching alligator shoes and a fedora. The feather is a nice touch.

He responds quickly.

Please tell me that was sarcasm.

I have a great black suit, tailored and everything. I just haven't worn it in a while.

Text me your address. I'll drive up Saturday afternoon.

My phone pings again with his location. I stare at it

longer than necessary before locking the screen and setting the phone down. It's happening. This is more than dinner in Oxford. We have hit up most restaurants and the coffee shops a few times. Gossip has spread fast, and everyone knew Gabriel's name by the end of last weekend. Even today I went into the grocery store and the cashier asked me where the cute redhead was because they had not seen him in three days. She knew exactly how many days it has been since he left.

I take the last sip of my coffee, now gone cold. Out the window, the street is still damp from an early morning spring rain. Tulips are trying to bloom in Adrienne's yard.

Oxford really is something special. Quiet, charming, the kind of place that feels like home the moment you breathe it in. And Gabriel fits effortlessly. Like he was meant to be a part of a cheerful seaside town. Meant to be here. Meant to be beside me.

If only there were a job here for him, something permanent to anchor him here.

Not everyone has the freedom I do. Owning a share of commercial property in Chicago means my life is flexible. I can settle wherever I want, live comfortably without compromise. But Gabriel's rooted in D.C. His career, his world, it's all there. Would he uproot everything for me? Am I worth it for him? That's a big ask. Too big. I am getting ahead of myself.

Still, I can't help wanting it. Wanting him to stay.

I sigh and lean back from the table, already counting down the hours until Saturday.

43
Lucas

I paced around the house all afternoon. Passing through walls until I didn't notice I was doing it and found myself hovering several feet above the ground outside. I decided it was best to rip the band aid off right before I have to go. Owen was in such a great mood. Something to do with the texting this morning. He had the biggest smile on his face afterwards. I've stayed out of the way while he played music and worked in the yard.

The pumpkin patch looks amazing now. Owen diligently planted rows of pumpkins in a unique design with walking paths throughout. In the center is a pumpkin shaped fountain with an empty plaque. He had a crew on the property yesterday running a water line. When they tested it the water sprayed from the top like the stem of a pumpkin.

New benches were added, and the frame of a larger cocoa stand was finished. It was more than I had ever imagined. More than I could have designed. It was all very impressive. He has come a long way from the college jock that tacked a sheet to his wall instead of buying curtains.

It was one hour until sunset. One hour until my last goodbye. Owen has finished eating and retired to the couch. Before he could turn on the TV and browse streaming menus for way too long, I appeared before him. My expression was flat, and I kept my hands behind my back.

The atmosphere changed into something cold and dark. He has been so happy the past few days. I am about to crush him before I vanish into the night. Or whatever happens when your soul is collected.

"Hi." I waved awkwardly.

"Hey." He tapped on the couch to sit down—rather hover like I'm sitting. "You have been avoiding me."

I pretended to sit on the couch. Allowing my body to hover like can touch the cushion and wouldn't just pass through it. His deep brown eyes followed my movements. I tattoo the curves of his cheeks and the sharp angle of his jaw in my brain. I am going to miss seeing his face every day. I am going to miss hearing his voice. I feel the need to cry but cannot form tears.

"Yes. Because you don't need me right now. I think you know exactly who you need." I force a smile, and he frowns in response. *"Stop. That's not a sad thing. That*

is a happy thing. The happiest actually. What you have found is beyond anything I could have dreamt for you. I will leave knowing you are in a better place."

"I do feel happier." He sipped his beer before catching my words and looking at me with wide eyes. "Leave? You're leaving? How? When?"

His phone lays next to him on the couch. I tap the screen once. The action is easier than it should be. The phone lights up and I see the time. 7:00pm. *"I have forty-five minutes."*

"What?" He reaches for me by instinct and his hand passes through my leg. He lets out a frustrating grunt. "That's too soon. How do you know the exact time?"

"A reaper appeared to me last night. I begged for one more day."

His brows knit together while he clenches his jaw. "Lucas, you knew this all day and waited until you had forty-five minutes left."

I scoot closer to him. Wishing with everything I am made of that I can touch his face. Feel his skin. *"I thought it would be easier if you didn't have a lot of time to dwell on it. Ya know, rip-the-band-aid-off-fast method."*

Owens drops his chin until it nearly touches his chest. His breathing is slow and painful. Stuttering as if holding back sobs. "I would have spent the day with you if I knew it would have been our last together."

I knew he would have wanted to spend every remaining minute with me. I denied him access to me. Because I'm broken. Disconnected. A reminder of what he needs to give up.

"Owen, love, we already had our last day together. Or what was supposed to be our last day. Everything

since my death has been an echo. My presence has only held you back. It's time for me to find peace and for you to pursue more of what makes you happy. I think we both know who I am talking about. Who has brough a smile back to your face and warmth to your bed. You've been afraid to hurt my feeling. But what hurts has been watching you without love. Without appreciation for just how amazing you are. I see you holding back because I am still here. Now I am leaving, at last. Give Gabriel all of you. Show him the Owen I fell in love with."

My words hung on the air. He pressed the pads of his palms to his eyes. Creating a dam for his tears. I was worried I said too much. Laid it on too thick, but he started nodding. Owen lifted his shoulders as if an invisible weight was lifted.

He cried when I died. It was violent and messy. He held my body and screamed until the paramedics showed up. The red sweater I was wearing became stained with his tears. I look down at myself in the same sweater and see no water marks, because I was already gone. I had left my body when he sobbed over it.

Now, his tears form slowly and do not run down his cheek until they can no longer fit in the rim of his eyes. I reach inside myself and imagine pulling energy. Soaking it up like a sponge. The same thing I do when I want to touch something. But this time I imagine the pull stronger. Latching onto the house as my energy source. I picture a wide circle around myself sucking in energy like an orbit. I must become the sun.

The lights in the room begin to flicker. I raise my hand to his cheek and say a silent prayer.

When my hand stops against his cheek we both gasp. I can feel the damp lines from tears on my palm blending with five days of stubble. Fear washes over me that it won't last. This is my only chance. A brief window. I lean in—press the softest kiss to his lips.

For a few seconds we are connected. Touching for the first time in three years.

Then I feel myself go weak. The lights return to their normal glow. And we pass through each other like clouds. I move off the couch. And stand in the center of the room. The kiss was both too much and not enough.

Owen stares up at me. He sucks in a quick breath. "What do we do for forty-five minutes?

"Will you sit with me outside while I wait. I'm ready but also terrified." Owen wipes his face with his shirt. Gives me a short-lived smile.

"Yes, Lucas, my love. My husb-"

I hold up a hand to stop him from more. *"Husband no longer. I will be gone. But you will still be Owen. Bachelor, football fan, carpenter, general contractor, and so much more. Divorce me from your heart and let it be filled again."*

"Divorce you? That sounds so bleak."

I place a hand on my hip. *"I am dead. All I know is bleak. Now come sit under the moon with me and wait. The sky is clear tonight and I want to find all the constellations like we used to."*

"I haven't done that in a long time."

"I know." I float towards the door. *"We have forty minutes to find as many as we can. If you are up for one last constellation naming race?"*

Owen stands. His hands flinch like he wants to touch me and gave up. I memorize the dark glossy pools in his eyes. The cut of his jaw. His thick lashes were made heavy with tears.

"No." His voice is rough. "No, this will not be our last. We will just be looking at the stars from different sides after tonight."

I nod and begin to float outside. He follows.

We pointed to the sky and teased each other when we identified the stars wrong. As usual Owen made up his own constellations. With names and back stories based on his personal heroes and not ancient legends. The last one he named was a row of five stars that he said made a zigzag. He named it for us. For our marriage. For our love.

Tonight is reminiscent of the early days of our relationship. I spent so many nights looking up at the night sky with Owen. Feeling small in the big world. Never wondering where I was supposed to be. My place was always by his side. He did not see the reaper when she appeared before me. But he watched as I faded into smoke and left with her. Leaving a vacancy in his life. A hollow place in his heart. But most importantly, leaving the door open for his future.

44
Owen

The streets of Washington D.C. mirror the fading light, puddles filled with golds and pinks from the setting sun. I check my reflection in the rearview mirror at a red light, straightening my tie. It's red silk and happens to be the only one I own. Left over from graduation from ISU.

I'm late. Well, later than I should be. Gabriel changed our meeting place to the Gala location. He rode along with his roommate instead of waiting, since I couldn't give him an exact time of arrival.

The walk-through with the City Council went great this afternoon. Better than expected, and I finished the brick paths through the pumpkin patch. I couldn't stop myself once I started, not when the layout had come together so perfectly. The bricks, salvaged from an old school, formed the outline of the house, like a blueprint in the soil. Just like Gabriel had envisioned. And the pumpkin-shaped fountain in the center will be a favored photo spot for families in the future. I can't wait to show him. This is his design after all, his dream. Something Gabriel drew in a sketch pad weeks ago that I snuck a picture of. My mind would never have come up with something so whimsical. It brought a sense of magic to the space.

The Gala is already in full swing by the time I arrive, the hum of conversation and the clink of glasses spills out before I step inside. The Willard Intercontinental Hotel is breathtaking. A seamless blend of old-world elegance and modern indulgence. Gilded molding, velvet drapery, and crystal chandeliers cast a warm golden glow over the room. Everything seems to sparkle, even the marble floor.

A cover band plays a delicate rendition of a pop song that I am sure only those without silver hair recognize. The music fades into the background as my pulse picks up. I begin to scan the crowd, the sea of black tuxedos and satin gowns, my eyes darting past strangers in search of one person. Gabriel.

And then—I see him.

At the top of a grand staircase, just as the lights seem to shift to highlight his face, there he is. Like a paused frame for a classic movie. For a second the world around me blurs, leaving only him in focus.

He's descending slowly, with one hand brushing the polished railing. The moment stretches.

Gabriel's dark green suit fits him like it was stitched by the hands of a God. Each line, each shift of fabric, was designed to lure me to him. The sheen of the satin lapels catch light from the chandeliers, leading my gaze unavoidably to his mouth. Currently fighting back a small frown. He has not spotted me yet. But his eyes are also searching the crowd.

And his hair. God his hair. Freshly trimmed on the sides but still with wild flare. Copper curls gleaming like burnished gold, left loos atop his head like a crown.

He doesn't just look good. He looks like royalty.

A prince.

My prince.

The commotion seems to pause, either freezing from the power of his presence or thawing from the warmth of his smile. I can't tell which, but I know I'm caught in it, held in place by the sheer force of him. Wanting to run towards him but held captive by the sheer aw of his smile.

His eyes finally find me. He lights up with a radiant smile.

Then he lets out a breath. So soft it would go unnoticed by anyone else. But not by me. I feel the release, because it echoes the same feeling I'm holding in my chest. Gabriel's steps quicken, and before I know it, we are wrapped in a slow, deliberate hug. We stand like rocks in a river, the guests moving around us. Our hug lingers just a little too long to be two friends finding each other. His scent makes me want to kiss him right here, in front of everyone. But we're in a different city, a different crowd. And my mind thinks back to all the spaces I have been in my life that would not want to see two men being affectionate. I hold back.

We pull apart far enough to look at each other's faces. I gaze down at him. Letting the room melt away so it is just the two of us.

"You made it," he murmurs, his voice a little breathless.

"Didn't want to miss you in a suit. I must say it exceeds anything I could have imagined. You look amazing." I say, one hand still resting on his waist.

"Me?" Gabriel points to himself. "I look like chum compared to you. You look like an underwear model."

"Underwear models don't usually wear suits." I chuckle.

He gives me a grin that is both innocent and sinful. "True, but I know what's hiding under that suit."

I squeeze him once more before we break apart.

"If your memory ever fades let me know." I snatch two glasses of champagne from a passing server. "I will refresh your memory. All night if I must."

His cheeks flush, and he ducks his head, smiling into his champagne flute. "How's the house?"

"Empty." I don't elaborate. The emptiness is mostly due to his absence. Exaggerated by my longing to have him near. But Lucas has been gone for days, and the entire feel of the house has shifted.

Finally, Lucas is in an afterlife that I can only hope is heavenly. Not a version of Heaven that's been described by any religion, but a place where he can be at peace. We spent years blaming each other for his inability to move on and it turned out to be the result of something out of our control. Something we could never have predicted. His exit took with it the cold that lingered in the house. Fueled by my guilt and desire to be close to him. Now when I look out on the bench we sat on during his last moments, I smile. I am filled with warmth with the knowledge he got what he wanted. He wanted to be free from limbo. A ghost no longer. He wanted to know I would be okay without him. Know that I would not be a hermit and be open to the world. Be open to love again.

I stand with Gabriel now, anxious to look in his blue eyes and listen to all the pop culture references I don't understand. My house is empty without his laugh rolling down the hall. I miss looking out the window and seeing him sketching while listening to an audio book. I even miss the way he tucks his socks in the edge of the couch after he takes them off. Claiming it is too warm for socks but then immediately grabs a throw blanket to wrap his legs in.

There have been so many gaps in my life that I ignored. Never attempting to fill or fix. Then he knocked on my door expectantly. He is a gift sent by a higher power. Whether it was fate, an angel's blessing, or Cupid's handiwork, I couldn't be more thankful for Gabriel.

We spend the evening pressed against a wall, fingers brushing against each other, his hand curling behind my back where no one else can see. The champagne is crisp, but the real buzz comes from the quiet moments, the way he whispers while on his tip toes to be closer to my ear, the way he places a palm to my chest when he laughs, the glint in his eyes when he looks at me.

Everything is perfect.

Then his roommate Jackie arrives.

"Holy fuck, this is Owen?" she exclaims, dragging some poor soul behind her by their suspenders. "He's gorgeous and huge."

Gabriel groans, hiding behind his glass. "Jackie, please."

I chuckle, offering my hand. "It's great to meet you."

"I heard you played football in college. You sure are built for it. I have never seen Gabriel play football, but we did participate in a disc golf tournament for Pride last year." She wiggled her fingers. "He's got a good grip. But you probably already know that."

"God, Jackie!" Gabriel buried his face in his hands.

"Gabriel said you helped plan this." I motion to the room. Hoping a change of subject will give Gabriel's cheeks some relief. I place my hand on his lower back, and he leans into it.

"Yea, I run community outreach for the DC Arts Center." Jackie trades her empty glass for a full one of champagne when a server passes us by. "I have been encouraging Gabriel to get in the same business. He has that offer in Oxford on the table and I think he should take it. He is practically beaming with light while he packs for the weekend, and he looks so stressed when he is in D.C. I worry for my ginger."

Gabriel playfully stops her hand before it can touch his hair.

"I wouldn't call it stress, just intense focus. My latest project, the most ambitious one yet, is in Italy. If I nail this assignment, it will put me in front of high-profile clients with serious money. I could be designing islands for Dubai in a few years." Gabriel is speaking clearly but he sounds like he is trying to convince himself.

"What job offer in Oxford?" I interject.

"Gabriel, is that really the clients you want to work for?" Jackie asks before he could answer. "You have been kicking your feet with excitement over The Oxford Children's Art whatever. You planned out a community garden. You even tracked down old school desks with built-in tables for drawing classes. There is a stack of rulers and pencils in the corner of your room to give as donations. I think it is obvious where you want to spend your time. And it's not in a stuffy office with architects that act like finance bros who cater to the wealthiest people in the freaking world."

"Thanks for the life analysis Jackie." Gabriel mumbles. Watching their conversation has me protectively putting my arm around his waist and pulling him into my side.

The person at her back tugs on her arm. She takes two steps back before continuing.

"Well, I won't be coming home tonight. I'll be at Sam's. So, you have the whole place to yourself." She points at both of us and then walks backward into the crowd, wiggling her eyebrows in a way that makes Gabriel's face light up in an even deeper shade of pink.

I let the hum of the conversations in the room fill the space between us for a minute before tilting his chin up and forcing him to look at me.

I try to keep my voice cool. Channel cool guy, Owen. Be cool.

"What job offer in Oxford?"

He hold his breath and swallows the last of his champagne. "It would be a huge pay cut. Like a fifty seven percent pay cut. I would be crazy to take it. And it would involve many hats. Community outreach, event planning, garden maintenance, and more. I don't think I could even afford an apartment on that salary. It's better if I keep my job and continue to volunteer on weekends. Adrienne will find someone to fill the job."

This is what I have been looking for. A reason for him to remain in Oxford permanently. To live with me. My tongue feels glued to the roof of my mouth stopping my ability to speak. Everything I want to say spirals like a tornado in my head. It's loud and chaotic.

My silence does not go unnoticed. Gabriel looks down at his glass when I don't respond. It takes several seconds to calm myself. Between the break of music, I can almost hear Lucas's voice next to me. Begging me to invite him to move in with me. Asking him to take the job. Leave the city. Live a happy small life with me in my Victorian home and help run the pumpkin patch.

This is what I want. So why can't I say it aloud? What am I afraid of?

Words fail me. I try to ease the awkwardness with a smile, but my lack of response does not go unnoticed. The sparkle in his blue eyes dims like an ocean on an overcast day.

45
Gabriel

Owen tried to follow me through the streets of Washington D.C., but traffic split us apart. He will have to rely on GPS to find my apartment. I, however, swerve around cars and cut though alleys to beat him to my apartment. My heart pounds with anticipation. The night isn't over, it's just beginning.

I burst into the apartment, nearly tripping over my own feet as I yank off my dress shoes. Hopping on one leg, I make my way through each room, scanning for anything that might turn Owen off. I want the mood to be right when he walks in.

Jackie's room is a disaster, her bathroom even worse, covered in a war zone of makeup and hair products. I shut both doors quickly, as if sealing away the chaos will keep the apartment from looking like a mess.

I adjust the magazines on the coffee table, then shift

an unlit candle that smells like Christmas an inch to the left before second-guessing and putting it back. My heart hammers against my ribs, and I don't know why I'm suddenly so nervous. This isn't our first time alone. We've already slept together. His hand rested on my back for most of the night at the gala, an unspoken claim in front of a room full of strangers. I know he is attracted to me, but I don't know if this is something real for him. Long term. Or if I'm just a late rebound after losing his husband, or if he wants… more. If he wants me.

There is a soft knock on the front door.

I swallow hard. My chest tightens at the thought of him leaving. Of this being temporary. When I told him about the job in Oxford, he barely reacted. I don't know what I expected, but something more than a casual nod. Maybe an invitation to stay with him. But that's a fairy tale ending. And I shouldn't be expecting a fairy tale when he hasn't even said he loves me.

Oh God. Do I love him?

My vision blurs for a second, and I realize I've stopped breathing. I shake out my hands at my sides, forcing slow, even breaths. Another knock. Louder this time.

I rush to the door and open it.

Owen stands there, a goddamn movie star in a black suit and red tie, his broad frame taking up the entire doorway. My eyes drop to the red and black duffle bag in his grip. My stomach twists. My throat goes dry.

"Come in," I manage to say.

He steps inside with a slow smile, setting his bag down next to my stack of shoes. He toes off his dress shoes, and I realize I'm still standing there, holding the door open like an idiot. I slam it shut, suddenly feeling overheated.

"So," I clear my throat, "let me give you the tour."

It's a short tour. My apartment is nothing compared to his Victorian house. I rush by the open door to my room but don't step inside. I show him the kitchen which is also the dining room. It's not impressive. It's a duplex with a shared wall that reduces the number of windows, so it feels like a box. He nods along, polite as ever, but I can tell he's just humoring me. I have spent very little time decorating the space. It was meant to be short term. A year at the most. But I have been too caught up in work to think about moving and Jackie is the least picky person I know. She would live in a van if it weren't for me.

When the tour ends, Owen grabs his duffle bag. "Mind if I change? Haven't worn a suit this long in years." He loosens the tie.

"Yeah, yeah, of course. I should, too."

I guide him into the bedroom. A neat pile of folded pajama pants and a T-shirt wait on my bed.

We face each other, the bed becoming a barrier between us. Both of us strip off layers with awkward glances and fumbled movements. I yank at my bow tie and get it caught. Owen tugs his pants down, and they bunch at his ankles. He wobbles for a second before they finally pop off, making him stumble back against a wall. I bite my lip to keep from laughing.

Owen raises a brow. "Enjoying the show?"

"Oh, absolutely."

We both chuckle, the tension breaks as we finish changing. I lead him to the kitchen, still a little buzzed from the champagne. "I'm starving," I admit, opening the fridge. "All those fancy appetizers and I still feel like I didn't eat."

"Same," Owen says, joining me at the counter.

We start assembling a snack tray, our fingers brushing as we reach for cheese and crackers. There's a lingering heat between us, something charged, something inevitable. My gaze flicks to his lips, and I forget what I'm doing entirely.

The next moment, I'm against him, our mouths crashing together in a kiss that steals my breath. He lifts me onto the counter effortlessly, his lips dragging over my jaw, my neck. A shiver racks through me. I grip his shirt, wanting more, needing to feel his skin.

And then I lean back to open my neck more to him and I feel a handle under my palm.

A pan crashes to the floor.

I jerk back just in time to see Jackie's leftover tofu stir-fry spill out in a mess of vegetables and noodles. "Oh, crap."

I go to jump down, but Owen grabs me mid motion, lifting me like I'm made of feathers and steering me to the side. Only then do I see the minefield of tofu cubes I nearly stepped into.

Owen, my hero.

"Thanks," I say, my face burning.

Owen shrugs. "We should probably clean this up."

I take one look at him, his dark skin, broad shoulders, the way his sweatpants hang low on his hips, and suddenly, I don't care about the mess. I grab his shirt and pull him against me. "Leave it. I need you now more than I need a clean apartment."

He groans low in his throat and guides me toward the living room. I follow, already dizzy with need.

We stop when my legs hit the back of the couch. I pull off my shirt frantically, whimpering because I have to break our kiss. We both reach for the hem of his shirt at the same time. He lets me take the lead. I stumble back trying to reach over his head. He hooks an arm around my waist to keep me from falling. We share a look fueled with desire. My eyes trail to his exposed chest. He allows me to savor him for a long moment. Soaking in the sight of his taught skin and muscles. He flexes his pecks for me when I lightly touch them with my fingertips. My cheeks heat and he chuckles.

My lips find his chest, my hands exploring, my mouth trailing around his nipples. His body is solid, warm beneath my touch. He hums in pleasure as I worship him.

Then he freezes.

"Uh, Gabriel?"

I pause between swirls of my tongue, looking up at him. His eyes flick to the window.

I turn my head and oh. My. God.

A car sits in the driveway across the street, its headlights beaming directly into my apartment. We are on display for the entire neighborhood.

Putting on a show for the nameless old man sitting in his car.

I scramble off Owen, rushing to yank the curtains closed. In my haste, I don't see the cord tangled at the bottom. The second I tug, the lamp on the end table flies off and crashes to the floor.

I stare at the broken lamp, my stomach sinking. "This is a disaster."

Owen chuckles, stepping beside me. He presses a soft

kiss to my temple. "No, everything is perfect." Bodies pressed together and lips locked we move towards my bedroom. I carefully step backwards, and he holds out a hand to keep me from slamming into the door frame.

In my room I spin him around and thrust him down on my bed. It groans under his weight. I climb on top of him and go to work taking his pants off. He lifts his hips to allow me to slide his sweatpants down. I remove his boxer briefs at the same time. I savor the sight of him completely naked under me. My mouth waters at the sight of him. There is no time to be coy. I need to set this night in a better direction. I kneel straddling his legs and bend to lick up his shaft in a slow long swipe. He whips his head up to look at me and I watch him through my lashes.

I do it again and linger my lips around the tip. Grabbing him with my right hand I lower my mouth until he hits the back of my throat. A trickle of pre-cum coats my tongue as I lift off before lowering myself again. I fill my mouth with saliva and force it to drip down using it like lube for my hand to match the rhythm of my mouth.

His moans hypnotize me as I find the perfect rhythm sucking his cock. Gently I decide to test the waters. We have not had a conversation about preferences, and I have no complaints being topped by him. He is so gloriously large that I have never felt fuller than I have with him inside me.

I slide my spit-covered hand down his crack and am met with a surprise that has me lift off his cock and sit up straight. My hand rests on the end of a silver butt plug.

"Oh?"

I cannot think of anything sexy or clever to say. I cannot even make a complete sentence. Owen lifts his body to rest on his elbow. He widens his legs, pushing my knees apart. I explore the plug more and fuck, is it hot.

"Oh." He repeats with a flirty reassuring tone that is a one-word invitation.

"When did this happen?"

He smiles. "After we changed. When I used your bathroom. Why do you think I can't keep my hands off you? I am so fucking horny. All I can think about is replacing that with you. If you are into that."

"Oh, I am into that." I feel myself get so red my ears are hot. "I'm verse. I… I just didn't expect that from you. You scream 'top energy'. Ya know."

His voice is laced with heat. "Well, make me scream your name instead."

I crawl up his body and reach past his head into the nightstand. My goal was to get the bottle of lube, but the movement has positioned my stomach at his mouth. I feel his lips tickle my skin before large hands grab my hips and move me like a rag doll. The tip of my cock is poking out of my pajama pants. His mouth sucks at me through the fabric.

"Take these off now."

His voice is rough and forceful. But I welcome the possessiveness in his eyes. It has been far too long since someone has looked at me with that much fire. I would let him brand me with his name if he talked to me like that again.

Owen's expression is a countdown warning declaring I have ten seconds before he just rips the pants off my body. I drop the bottle of lube on the bed and roll off him. Quickly removing my pants and throwing them across the room. I move one inch towards him, and he lifts me back into the same position. I grip my thin wood headboard. A simple queen bed from a build-it-yourself kind of place. Thankfully, I don't have Owen's strength, or the wood might snap.

He grabs my cock and angles it towards his mouth. He takes me in and my legs shutter with pleasure. He sucks and moves me with a tight grasp on my hips. I whimper on instinct when he releases me from his mouth but moan in pleasure when it is replaced by his tongue dipping in my hole. He laps at me like an oasis in the desert.

"Fuck." I scream on a breath.

After a few more delicious licks me gives his attention back to my dick. Before he takes me in his mouth, a wicked grin appears. "Gabriel?"

"Uh huh." I answer out of breath.

"Fuck my face."

"What?" His filthy words catch me off guard. I don't answer. He takes all of me into his mouth. I moan his name when I feel the back of his throat and the press of his tongue. He pulls me out with a wet pop.

"Don't make me tell you twice."

Oh, God. No one has ever spoken to me like this. I melt onto him. Beginning slow thrusts into his mouth. I hear the bed creak under our movements. It's not used to so much weight. So much muscle. So much thrusting.

Owen directs my hips to move faster, and I oblige. Picking up my pace. It becomes too much. I remember the plug still inside him. I lift off and slide down his body. My dick dripping from his saliva. He widens his legs and lets me kneel between them. I slide my hand down his hard length and stop when I am met with the polished metal. With a gentle tug I pull it out. I try to set it on the bed next to me, but it rolls onto the floor. I notice the dip in the bed and catch the lube before it follows the plug out of my reach.

The bottle is slick. It must have been partially opened and was just leaking this whole time. That's a future problem. It would wash out. I only buy water-based lube anyway. I pour some in my hand and rub it along my cock in slow strokes. I am still sensitive from Owen's mouth and desperately trying to draw this out. With my fingers glistening from the lube, I press two fingers into him. He is ready from the plug, but I want to make sure he is slick enough to take me.

I pump my finger a few times then position myself at his entrance. He lets his head flop back. My eyes trail down his hard body to my waiting cock. "Fuck." I exclaim. "I forgot to put on a condom."

His head whips up. "I haven't been with anyone in three years. I know it's pathetic, but you understand why."

I nod. I know I am clean. I went to the clinic with Jackie and got tested two months ago. Even though I knew damn well I was in the middle of a dry spell. I have never been one for emotionless hook-ups. Owen is the closest thing I have had to a relationship in a long time.

"I was tested two months ago. I haven't been with anyone since." I leave out the part about not being with anyone for much longer than two months.

The look he gives is an open invitation to continue. He bends his knees to give me better access. His thick thighs could crush me, and it would be a great way to die. I press into him an inch. He feels so good that I curse at the ceiling. This causes him to chuckle which

I cut off by thrusting deeper. I grab his dick and stroke him until he is hard again. I find my rhythm fast. Thrusting and stroking. I am not going to last long and oh crap, there goes the bottle of lube rolling on the floor.

I am buried as far as I can go. He does, in fact, shout my name, and I shout his in return. My movements are frantic. "I'm going to come." He moans.

"Me too."

I stoke him with my slick hand and thrust deep. His hands grip my thigh as ribbons spill from him. Coating my hand and his stomach. I follow him over the edge and remain inside. He clenches around me, and it draws out my orgasm. Milking everything I got.

I collapse on top of him. My dick slips out and we stay together sharing exhausted breaths. The rise and fall of his chest lifts me. I could fall asleep right now. Completely sated and spent. However, we are practically glued together and should probably clean up. I am most likely dripping out of him at this exact moment.

"We should get cleaned up." I finally say.

He rolls me off of him with a lazy smile. "You wait here. I'll get the shower going." Owen sits up and presses a kiss to my forehead before stepping off the bed. I watch the curves of his body flex as he tries to stand. He is shaky on his feet, and I am proud to have caused it. He steps once and did not notice the lube now spilled on the floor. His feet fly out from under him like a cartoon. In slow motion I roll out of the way as he slams down on the bed. The action causes a loud crack followed by the entire bed collapsing to the floor.

We lay there. Sticky. Panting. On my broken bed. And laugh. We laugh harder than I have laughed in years.

My room looked like it was hit by a hurricane. Towels here piled on the floor from cleaning up lube that leaked from a bottle. My nightstand was on its side. Knocked over when my bed frame broke. The splintered wood is stacked against my closet door. After cleaning up from the disaster that followed the best sex of my life, we slept with the mattress on my floor.

Owen is still sleeping on his stomach. His arms are tucked under his pillow exaggerating his muscled shoulders. The urge to bite them is strong.

I scoot a bit closer. Considering all the fun ways I can wake him up. I don't get to do any of them though. A loud door slamming causes Owen to stir. Followed by my roommate Jackie who just returned home.

"What the fuck happened here?"

Owen turns to look at me with groggy eyes. We did

not get much sleep. Two hours after we broke the bed—yes, broke the bed—Owen initiated round two. Leaving me wonderfully sore in the best way.

I jump up from the mattress on the floor and grab my green robe hanging on the back of my door. Wincing as I stretch. A satisfying ache blooms, but it's the kind I wear like a badge. When I step out into the living room. At first, I wonder if I hallucinated Jackie. Then I hear a series of curse words from the kitchen.

"God damn it! What the hell? Fuck!"

I round the corner and stop short. She is standing with her hands on her hips and shaking her head. She looks like a disappointed parent who came home early from vacation only to discover their teenager threw a rager while they were gone. A look that I am far too familiar with from my high school days.

"Um, hi." I move past her and grab a broom and dustpan from the pantry. "Sorry about the mess. It was an accident, and we were caught up in…well we were trying to-"

She slides a scrunchie off her wrist and ties her wild curls into a puff atop her head. "You and Owen fucked in the kitchen?" She picks up the pan and puts it in the sink. I sweep while she starts washing dishes.

"No, we were just kissing in the kitchen."

Jackie glanced at me with one skeptical brow raised.

"So, you fucked in the living room?" Her sharp smirk send a wave of relief through me. She's not mad. No, Jackie is proud. My actions last night were closer to her typical behavior. Owen has me dropping inhibitions faster than any other relationship prior.

"No, that was just kissing too." I dump the dustpan in the trash and stand at her side.

Jackie stops the water and looks at me like she is trying to read something in the reflection of my eyes. She hums once. Ready to cast her final judgment based on my response to one last question. "But you did fuck. Right?"

I face palm. "If I answer you, will you not ask me you details?" She nods. "Yes. We slept together."

She pulled me into a hug, pinning my arms at my sides. Her soapy hands pressed onto the back of my shirt.

"I know what his means to you, Gabriel." She sighs. After a hard squeeze, she releases me. "Have you had the talk yet?"

"What talk?" I glance down at my feet and immediately regret not grabbing my slippers. The kitchen tile is tacky from soy sauce.

"The 'Are we boyfriends' talk." Jackie wiggles her eyebrows. "Are you going to take the job in Oxford and move in with him? Adopt babies and live happily ever after on a fairy tale pumpkin patch."

I want to shout…yes. To tell her that I've completely fallen for Owen. That I can't imagine a future without him in it. This past month has flown by at the rate of a rom-com, but somehow it feels like everything in my life is leading to this moment. To him. It's as if the universe aligned, conspired, pulled invisible strings to guide me to his doorstep. Deep down, I truly believe a higher power brought me to him. I cannot explain, but I feel it with complete certainty.

A frown forms slowly on my face. She touches my shoulder, and I am overcome with emotions. I shut my eyes to hold back tears because I hear heavy footsteps approaching from the living room.

Owen walks in, fully dressed. He rubs the back of his neck and grins at me. I resist the urge to plant a passionate kiss on him. Somehow he is just as handsome in jeans and a henley as he is a suit. But I prefer him with nothing on. The memories of last night have my cheeks go pink.

"Good morning." Jackie waves a spatula covered in soap suds.

"Sorry about the mess."

"No worries. I owe Gabriel for having to deal with my brother crashing on our couch for weeks." She gives him a secretive smile. "Plus, it sounds like it was worth it."

"Definitely worth the cost of a new bed. Maybe one hundred new beds." He winks at me.

I press my palm on his chest and nudge him to walk backwards into the living room. "Let's go out to breakfast."

"What's that about a new bed?" Jackie asks over my shoulder to Owen.

"Nothing." I answer for him. Then speak quieter for only him to hear. "I didn't give her details."

He chuckles then playfully kisses me. We put on our shoes and head out to my favorite local diner.

It is Friday, and I've practically floated into the office every day this week. Still riding the high after a from a weekend that felt like something ripped out of my dreams. Two nights with Owen wasn't nearly enough.

We promised each other to carve out time during the week to see each other, despite the two-hour distance. It's not that far. Just a matter of an early morning and a strong cup of coffee to make it back to work on time Monday morning. Totally worth it. The exhaustion is worth it also. Adrienne will want my help most Saturday and Sunday afternoon. And I expect to get very little sleep. Because let's be honest, when Owen and I are together, the last thing we want to do is sleep.

My phone dings and it's a picture of the garden beds at the Oxford Community Arts Center. Adrienne sends another photo of a pile of dowels and chicken wire.

> The garden beds were installed according to your plan. What am I supposed to do with the other stuff?

No one is at their desks when I look around the office. Jeremy peeks out of the conference room and waves me to come inside. He looks anxious and mouths the word "hurry".

I drop my messenger bag onto my desk and flip open my sketchbook. Snapping a quick photo and texting it to Adrienne. It's a drawing of a garden tunnel. Sized perfectly for children to duck through. The arch is designed to cradle climbing roses. Hardy and perennial, they'll bloom year after year. Creating a whimsical gateway through the garden straight out of a storybook.

She responds quickly.

> I don't know how to do that.

"Gabe, what is taking so long? Get in here." Jeremy whisper screams across the office.

I text back to Adrienne as I walk.

> Leave it for me. I will handle it this weekend.

> Thank you. You're a life saver. What would I do without you?

Jeremy holds the door open for me, and I see every employee sitting at a table. Which is only about six, sense we are a small firm. At the head, where Carlton usually sits, is a man in his forties wearing sunglasses the size of goggles and a hoodie. Everything he is wearing could be seen on a spoiled teenager except his opulent gold watch. That screams "money money money".

"There he is." Carlton declares. "Gabriel will be leading the design on the Turatello Resort Project." He points at me with an open hand then motions to the seat across from him. This is it. My big break. I am taking the lead on a project with the biggest budget the firm has ever had.

"It's nice to meet you." I shake the man's hand.

"Oren." His name and clicks in my brain. Oren Kako is one of the richest men in the world. He has been buying companies and taking credit for their inventions for decades. All with money he inherited from his families' ruby mines in Africa. He is known for posting sexist, racist, and homophobic things online. And I just shook his hand.

I suddenly feel sick to my stomach.

"I didn't know you were related to the Turatello family, Mr. Kako."

He pulls an energy drink out of the front pocket of his hoodie. When he pops the tab it fizzles onto the polished wood conference room. Carlton got this table through a friend that works in the FBI office. It's a mid-century conference table that hosted many meetings during the cold war. I see Carlton's eyes narrow on the spill. Jeremy pulls a paper towel roll out of a small cabinet and cleans it up quickly. Oren guzzles the drink before answering me, oblivious to the commotion happening around him.

"I'm not related to them. I was in Monaco when the news broke about two houses burning down." He finished his energy drink and handed the can to Jeremy to discard. "The biggest lot on Lake Como becoming available was just what I wanted. And bonus, I don't have to demolish anything. It's gonna be the perfect place to chill when I need a break."

I hold back physically cringing from his words. I open my notebook to a new page. "What did you have in mind?"

"I want a boat dock. A pool. A theater. And I have to have a waterslide from the second floor to the pool. Better yet, do you think they would let us build a water slide straight into the lake? Maybe outdoor showers that look like a waterfall with a grotto like the playboy mansion?" He pulls out his phone and taps on the screen as he talks. Listing off more extravagant items for the property without making eye contact with anyone in the room.

"All of those requests sound possible." Carlton looks at me. "Don't you think Gabriel?"

I mentally bite my tongue.

"Yes, Mr. Kako. All of those requests are easy to accommodate. I will check with the city about water slide restrictions. And meet with the resort architect to begin the concept plans."

"Whatever." He stands and the rest of the table moves like lemmings. "It's less of a resort and more of a private residence that I will get to choose who can visit. You know. A vacation spot where me and my friends don't have to mingle with the public."

Oren walks out while answering a call. He does not say goodbye and he does not acknowledge Carlton who held the door for him. After the elevator door closes behind him the office sits in a stagnant silence. No one wants to say what they are all thinking, but we are all thinking the same thing. Oren Kako is a douchebag, and this project is going to suck.

With my head down, I drag myself back to my desk. I should be elated. Lead designer on a luxury resort in Italy. That's the kind of opportunity people in my career kill for. But instead of pride, all I feel is dread curling tight in my stomach. My chest is too tight; my thoughts are too loud. Somehow I have more excitement about building a rose tunnel for a community garden than a multimillion-dollar resort in Italy. My anxiety is rising like bile in my throat. I need Owen. My pulse is thundering. I don't want this desk. I don't want Italy. I want my keys, my car, and a straight shot to where he is. Where everything still feels right.

The only thing Owen has in common with the ostentatious billionaire is the letter their names start with. Oren has never built anything with his hands. He probably doesn't know the difference from a hammer and a wrench. I can hear all his unrealistic requests now. Torture. Complete torture. Do I really want to work with him on a project that could last eighteen months? I wonder how Carlton would feel if I turned it down.

I push my keyboard out of the way and plop my forehead on my desk.

"Don't look so glum, Gabe." Rolling onto my cheek I see Jeremy peeking over the top of the half wall that divides our workspace. Carlton swears they are not cubicles. Instead, he calls them 'open concept offices'. "Yes, Oren will be terrible to work with. The man is practically a bond villain. But you will be around so many rich people. One of them will have a gay son with a big trust fund."

I groan. "I am not looking for a rich guy with a trust fund."

"Suit yourself." Jeremy sunk back to his office chair leaving me to wallow. Perhaps I used to dream about meeting a well-off man in D.C. from a prominent family. I envisioned spending summers in the Hamptons and ski trips to Aspen. I don't even ski. All of that feels superficial and lacking now.

My phone dings. There is no text from Adrienne. Just a photo taken through a small square window. It must be inside her house because I don't recognize it. It takes me a moment to realize why she sent it to me, then I zoom in on the person outside. The photo is taken from above, most likely a second-floor window. I can barely make out Owen in his side yard. The pumpkin patch area is huge. He has built a lot since I was there last. The bushes, rows, and brick path form a distinct shape. I know that shape. I drew that shape. I matched the lines of Owen's house. Placing benches where the large front windows are and in the center I drew a fountain. I had the idea for a pumpkin shape fountain and searched the internet to see if it existed. I scribbled the name of a concrete sculptor in New Jersey on the side of my sketch; after seeing he had made similar fountains in the past. I would recognize his work anywhere.

At the time I was just playing around. I never expected to see my vision come to life. I wonder how Owen got my design. He has added his own flare to the layout, and it is even more perfect than I imagined.

My chest is warm. Full. Soothing the mental spiral after the meeting with Oren.

Sliding my keyboard back wakens my computer screen. My inbox is filled with emails. More appear as I watch. Jeremy is sending me the estimated budget for Lake Como. Carlton sent me the contact information for the General contractor followed by another email that is just a picture of the empty corner office. The subject is "Waiting for our next Partner in the Firm… will it be you?"

I wanted it to be me, but that goal feels obsolete now. I would trade that office and the clients it comes with to teach a drawing to kids and manage a community garden.

Who am I?

What am I thinking?

Am I really doing this?

I stuff my stack of notebooks into my messenger bag. Take my supplies from the drawer and rise from my desk. I must be having an out of body experience because it feels like I am watching someone else walk.

Someone else make a life changing decision. But if I don't do this now I will find myself working for people like Oren Kako my whole life.

"Carlton." I knock with the back of my hand on his open door.

"Yes. Come in." He sets down a partially eaten Poke bowl and waved me over. I hover beside the empty chair, afraid if I sit my legs won't have the strength to stand back up. The words tumble out of my mouth before I can properly shape them. Raw, with no finesse.

"I quit."

It bounces of him like I asked for the time.

"Stuck on something? I could get Candice to help. She is finishing up a campus redesign. I could assign her to be your assistant. The project is big enough and you deserve it." He begin to type out an email, probably to Candice.

"No." I swallowed but it got stuck in my throat burying my words. After clearing my throat, I continued. "I quit. I am leaving the firm. I have another job offer and I intend to take it."

"A job offer." Carlton shrieked. "What did they offer? I'll beat it."

"Respectfully, sir, you cannot offer me what they can."

Carlton is the kind of man that solves most problems by throwing money at them or a strict NDA. He gives me a challenging look. "And what is that."

My gaze trails out over the trees in the direction of a small town nestled against the sea.

"Friends, a community, and a fulfilling purpose." I smile. And possibly love.

47
Owen

I should be waiting patiently at my house for Gabriel to arrive. The plan was for him to drive down tonight, Friday, and stay through the weekend. But my stomach has been turning. If I don't tell him how I feel I fear I will burst into flames. It's too much of me to expect him to drive to Oxford every weekend. I need to show him what he means to me. We can talk in my truck if I pick him up. That gives me four extra hours alone with him.

Unless I show up thinking it's a cute surprise and he shoos me away because I look like a desperate puppy. Not a very sexy quality.

The address stared back at me from my phone screen like a dare. Gabriel's apartment. Saved in my contacts, untouched since last weekend. Since I had him in my arms, laughing, cheeks flushed pink from champagne and desire. Since we kissed under the warm buzz of cheap kitchen lights and made a beautiful mess of his entire apartment.

But this week? Silence.

Not complete silence, not cruel, just distant. A handful of short texts. No calls. The kind of quiet that coils itself around your ribs until you can't tell if it's heartbreak or paranoia. I'm sure it's just fear. I lost someone before—twice. I can't sleep until I lay everything before him. On the phone wont due. I felt the start of another panic attack. There was only one place I could be. At Gabriel's side. If only he knew the power he had on me. If only he knew how much I care for him. My only solution was to tell him. The quiet was killing me.

Maybe Gabriel's just busy. Maybe he's second-guessing everything we shared. Maybe he's moving on.

But I can't survive with a "maybe". Not anymore.

So, I got in my truck.

And now here I am, rolling down this tree-lined street of red brick fourplexes with white porches and cookie-cutter charm. I spot the rainbow flag flapping gently in the breeze, planted in the most manicured yard on the block, and my heart jackhammers against my ribs.

This is it.

One chance to say what I feel. Don't screw it up.

I throw the truck in park and sit for a second, hands gripping the wheel, trying to steady my breathing. I'm about to run this play with no defense lined up. All my walls laying in rubble at his feet. Getting out of the truck feels like walking naked on stage. Bare to the world. Only terrifying because I am alone. I feel like I could take on the world with Gabriel at my side. Without him I feel... well I decided I don't want to know what that feels like.

The spring air fills my lungs with anxious gulps.

I knock.

Footsteps shuffle. A guy answers, shirtless, gym shorts slung low on his hip bones. My heart drops into my stomach. His hair is damp, and I hate how easy it is to imagine what he and Gabriel were just doing. Or just finished doing.

"Uh... hey. I- Is Gabriel here?"

Before the asshole-looking shirtless dude-bro can respond, I hear it. The sexiest voice and exact person I want to see.

"Owen?"

I spin around.

There he is. Standing behind me on the sidewalk, holding a file box filled with tchotchkes and loose papers, keys dangling from his fingers. His curls are a little messy. His blue eyes wide, cautious. God, he's so fucking beautiful my heart is going to burst.

"What are you doing here?" he asks.

"I needed to see you." My voice comes out thick, raw. The front door shuts behind me. Rushing down the steps I thumb behind me with a confused expression.

"My roommates brother." Gabriel rolled his eyes.

I stand exposed before him. Ready to make a fool of myself.

"I needed to talk to you. It couldn't wait. When I left last weekend, I should have told you what I was thinking. I should have been honest with how I feel.."

Gabriel just stares. His knuckles whiten on the box. "And how do you feel?"

"I'm not sure yet," I say.

His brow arches, and he laughs, but there's no humor in it. "You drove all the way here to tell me you don't know how you feel about me?"

"No." I take a step closer. "I care about you. I want to know everything about you. I want to see if this—us—is something real. Because it feels like real."

He breathes in. His expression changes from confusion to relief, the warmth flooding in behind his eyes like sunrise breaking over water.

"I think so too," he says softly.

I don't wait. I kiss him. It is quick because I am aggravated by the barrier between us. I grab the box and lightly drop it on the grass. Our bodies come together like magnets. I hold him to me with my hand tangled in his hair, grasping onto the back of his head like a lifeline. His mouth opens for me, and it's as if the past days of stress never happened, like we're rewinding the tape to that perfect moment in his kitchen, and the living room, and the bedroom where everything felt right. Playing back the walks through Oxford hand in hand. Rellving that moment I opened my door and found him standing on my front porch like a gift. Fulfilling a wish from someone who wanted me to be happy. Little did Lucas know Gabriel would be the one to heal me. Put me back together and make me whole again.

He planted a seed in my heart at that first meeting, and it grew into something amazing. Love.

"I could drive up here," I say between kisses, cupping the back of his neck. "Weekends. Holidays. Whenever you need me."

Gabriel shakes his head. "Well, that won't be necessary. I quit my job today."

I blink. "What?! That feels spontaneous. Did you have a plan?"

"Yeah," he says with a smirk. "My plan was to get in my car and drive to you. But I guess you beat me to the speech."

Say it Owen. Tell him what you want. What you need.

I look around for Lucas's voice, but I don't see him. Only pink blossoms on the trees falling like snow.

The air shifts. That push-pull of fear and possibility fizzles out into something undeniable.

"Is it too smothering if I tell you I need you near me?" I ask, voice low.

"Not at all." He slides his hand into mine. "Please smother me."

My chest cracks open, full to the brim with everything I've been afraid to say. "I want you to live with me. I know it's early to live together, but I won't accept anything else. I hope you take that job for the Community Arts Center. And don't worry about the pay cut. I got you. My mortgage is tiny, and I get income from a commercial property back in Chicago. I have given this a lot of thought. I see no other way forward without you by my side."

He doesn't flinch. Doesn't even blink. He just kisses me deep and wraps his arms around my neck. A breeze kicks up littering the air around us with pink petals.

Gabriel smiles, that slow-burning, knee-weakening kind of smile. "Owen, I don't think I'm letting you go either."

He leans in, lips brushing over mine. "I'm glad you understand, you're mine."

His breath hitches. "I'm yours."

My hands move to hold his hips. I begin to walk backwards and pull him along with me. "Yes. And I'm yours. If you want me."

He looks at me—really looks—and the world falls into place. Every fear, every late-night ache, every moment I thought I'd never love again... it all led me to this.

To him.

He playfully slips out of my grasp but keeps hold of one hand leading me inside. "Oh, I want you, Owen."

I give him a villainous grin. "Then show me how much."

We manage to wait long enough to get into his room and shut the door before the kiss turns feverish, needy, sloppy. Clothes half on, laughter echoing through the apartment, the box he dropped still tipped over in the grass. None of it matters.

What matters is this:

We found our way to each other.

Through grief. Through fear. Through all the noise of the city. Through the loneliness of a small town.

We found this.

And I'm not letting it go.

48
Owen

Six Months Later

The October air is crisp, curling with the scent of damp leaves and warm chocolate as it winds through the Hammond Historic Pumpkin Patch. I stand at the edge of it all, taking it all in. The laughter, the warmth, the life. It's hard to believe how far we've come. The place is more than restored— it's thriving. Grander than it was in its so-called glory days. Nestled beside it is the proud Victorian house, fully revived and waiting to welcome its first official guests. And not just any guests, Gabriel's parents. They're scheduled to arrive next week, and I know they've been waiting patiently to see in person what he and I have been building together. Not just the pumpkin patch or house renovations, but our life. Our rich and deeply rooted life together.

Today is the grand opening, and the entire town

has shown up in full force. Kids dart between rows of pumpkins, squealing with delight while their parents sip steaming cups of cocoa and snap photos. Laughter and conversation are filling the area, a soundtrack for a day that feels like a perfect snapshot of autumn.

This—this is how it was always meant to be. A cornerstone in the community. A place where traditions root themselves every year. The house, the land, it's been waking up for months now. But today it feels truly alive. Complete.

At the recently finished cocoa shack, I stir a big pot of thick, velvety cocoa. The scent is rich and sweet as steam rises and disappears into the crisp air. I've rolled up the sleeves of my orange flannel, and I'm sweating a little from the heat in the shack, but I wouldn't trade this moment for anything. Beside me, Gabriel greets customers with that magnetic smile of his. He's wearing a tan button up and burnt orange bow tie, a gift from me, and he pulls it off in a way that makes my heart jump every time I look at him. With his copper hair catching the light like fire on maple leaves, he looks like an autumn prince.

I may have made the house livable, brought the bones back to life, but Gabriel made it a home. He filled it with joy, late night cooking, cozy mornings, and purpose. He gave me a reason to buy a grill and now I cook for Adrienne and her family every Friday night. And despite me living next to them for four years, Gabriel has become their favorite fake uncle. He wears the title with pride, sneaking them candy when their mother is not looking.

Every wall of the house has been blessed with art we gathered on our many antique store trips. He even let me pick a few myself. Although, I have no issue letting him take the lead when it comes to design. The mantle above the fireplace has been ordained with photographs from weekend getaways, including one that required taking his Jeep on a very dusty off-road trail. It ended with a picnic near a waterfall and a selfie. Me grinning like a lovesick fool and Gabriel nuzzling into my chest to avoid the spray from the water.

I hand over three cups of cocoa, each topped with pumpkin shaped marshmallows, then I lean in and press a kiss to Gabriel's temple. Just a brief touch, a simple thing. Temporarily fulfilling my craving to touch him. He smiles up at me like I just gave him the moon.

I would—if he asked—give him the moon.

When the last customer in line is served, we each take a cup for ourselves and step out into the crowd. Our hands brush as we walk, linking pinkies.

We stop near the center of the patch, at the fountain. Sculpted like a giant pumpkin. The townspeople gather, forming a loose semicircle. I decide to use the bench as a stage so the people in the back can see me. After I climb up, I pull Gabriel up with me, my arm slipping around his waist. He blushes immediately and hides behind his cocoa like a shield.

I chuckle and clear my throat. "Three and a half years ago," I begin, my voice steady thanks to the man keeping me up at my side. "I wasn't sure I'd ever find my way back to anything that resembles happiness."

A hush falls over the crowd.

"But this town stood by me," I continue. "It gave me something to believe in when I needed it most. And then I met Gabriel." I turn, catching the way he looks at me. The sparkle in his blue eyes. The glow that radiates from him. "He's been the ray of sunlight breaking through the storm."

A few people murmur in agreement, and somewhere in the back, Adrienne lets out a loud "whoop". Gabriel ducks his head again, red now creeping all the way to his ears. "That's so cheesy." He gushes.

I squeeze him into my side before continuing. "Today, we open the Hammond House Historic pumpkin Patch. Not just a place to find the perfect pumpkin, but a space for memories, for traditions, for laughter and for—love." I lift my cocoa in a toast. "So go pick your pumpkins, and don't forget to grab a ticket for next week's Community Arts Center showcase. Gabriel and I will see you there."

The crowd bursts into applause and cheers. Their support wrapping around us like a soft sweater. I turn towards Gabriel and lower my forehead to his, breathing in the moment before whispering the words I've told him every day for the past two months. "I love you so much.

He gives me that big smile, the one that makes my knees go weak. Our kiss is quick and gentle. "I love you like crazy." He responds.

Right then the fountain sputters to life, water spouting from the top and cascading down its sculped ridges, catching the sunlight like something out of a fairytale. More cheers erupt through the crowd. Louder now, and kids rush forward to dip their hands in the water.

We step down from the bench. I notice Gabriel's eyes lingering on the edge of the fountain, where a bronze plaque catches the light.

In loving memory of Lucas Roth

Sending me love from beyond.

Some mornings, I catch Gabriel watching me from the window as I stand before the plaque. Reading his name over and over. Eyes closed, lips moving in a conversation meant for no one but the wind. It's not grief anymore. It's something gentler now. A visit to a friend. A flush of warm memories. A declaration of thanks.

For the first time in years, I feel complete.

I'm confident—

Everyone is exactly where they belong.

The End

Acknowledgements

Ever since I jumped into this wild author journey, I've been blessed with the best support squad I could ask for. My husband deserves an award (or at least a cookie) for not only keeping the kids out of my office so I can focus on writing but also for creating all my book covers and artwork. I think he might secretly be my biggest fan… or maybe he just really wants to avoid seeing the laundry pile up!

Then there's my superstar friend, Toni Reeves, who has bravely read everything I've written, including the plot twists I almost regret. Her feedback and encouragement is absolute gold. She's like my personal cheerleader, only with less pom-poms and more constructive criticism. Tell your husband that you deserve that margarita machine.

And, of course, my amazing community on Discord—shoutout to the *Textual Tension* server! Whether we're swapping story ideas, talking about what we're reading, or just sharing way too many memes, you all make this journey feel like a party. Our weekly chats feel like my second home, and it's honestly my favorite "place" to be.

My Author Alliance on TikTok – we have become codependent on each other. Our giant group chat is my lifeline on rough days. I would not be able to continue on this Journey without you.

A super special thanks and warm hug for Tyler. The redhead whose personality melted into my character Gabriel. May this story put the vibes into the universe that manifests a strong everlasting love for you. If only they knew what a catch you are.

To everyone who's read, shared, or posted about my book on social media—thank you. Seriously, you may not realize it, but each post, each comment, each share can change an author's life. You are truly amazing and so, so essential in the indie world. Cheers to all of you for making this ride so incredible

About the Author

R.R. Mangold grew up in a tiny Oregon town, where she fell head over heels for theater, fashion, and writing—basically anything that would let her play dress-up and write about it. She eventually made her way to a fashion school in Los Angeles, where she filled journals with scribbles of movie plots, play ideas, and novel outlines. Finally, she decided her dreams couldn't hide in the shadows anymore, and *To Touch A Reaper* became her debut published work!

When she's not writing, Rena's likely hanging out with her husband, two kids, and her loyal hound dog in Utah. You'll find them either gaming like pros or hunting for the coolest rocks around!

More Books by R.R. Mangold

To Touch a Reaper: A hauntingly beautiful paranormal love story

To Train a Demon: A dark workplace comedy

To Divorce a Ghost: Do you believe in love after loss?

No Shade in the Desert: A Sapphic urban fantasy

Visit www.MangoldBooks.com and subscribe to the newsletter for book announcements and ARC/PR opportunities.